DEATH OF A BEAN COUNTER

DEATH OF
A BEAN COUNTER

Sandra Balzo

This first world edition published 2019
in Great Britain and 2020 in the USA by
SEVERN HOUSE PUBLISHERS LTD of
Eardley House, 4 Uxbridge Street, London W8 7SY.
Trade paperback edition first published
in Great Britain and the USA 2020 by
SEVERN HOUSE PUBLISHERS LTD.

British Library Cataloguing in Publication Data
A CIP catalogue record for this title is available from the British Library.

ISBN-13: 978-0-7278-8946-1 (cased)
ISBN-13: 978-1-78029-670-8 (trade paper)
ISBN-13: 978-1-4483-0369-4 (e-book)

All Severn House titles are printed on acid-free paper.

Severn House Publishers support the Forest Stewardship Council™ [FSC™],
the leading international forest certification organisation.
All our titles that are printed on FSC certified paper carry the FSC logo.

MIX
Paper from
responsible sources
FSC
www.fsc.org   FSC® C013056

Typeset by Palimpsest Book Production Ltd.,
Falkirk, Stirlingshire, Scotland.
Printed and bound in Great Britain by
TJ International, Padstow, Cornwall.

ONE

'You're not serious.'

'Deadly,' my partner Sarah Kingston said. 'Don't you think you're overreacting? The thing can't bite you.'

'But it's just not our kind.' I eyed the two-foot-high, shiny, black espresso machine on the counter of our coffeehouse, Uncommon Grounds. 'It's . . . *automatic.*'

'You're such a snob.' Sarah doesn't hold much back. In fact, I can't think of anything she's ever held back.

Ignoring her, I glanced lovingly toward our shop-worn, not-so-shiny espresso machine. The twin, black-handled porta-filters, the knobs you twist to control the amount of steam coming from the jutting wands, the grinder to pulverize the beans to just the right consistency, the tamping tool to – you guessed it – tamp the ground espresso in the porta-filter. Not to mention our beloved and battered stainless steel milk pitchers.

I turned to our barista Amy Caprese for support. 'You can't possibly want your job to be reduced to pushing a button. A kindergartner could do it.'

Amy, she of the striped hair, multiple piercings and henna tattoos, was our cross between a punk rocker and an earth mother. She was not only a champion barista, but a wizard of latte art, personalizing the espresso drinks with hearts or unicorns or whatever a customer requested. The thought of her being satisfied sitting behind a counter and pushing buttons was unfathomable to me.

But now our wildchild barista said, 'I think Sarah might be onto something.'

Sarah gave me a superior look, which scarcely registered since it was pretty much the natural order of things around here.

But this . . . this machine was not natural. And I couldn't

believe neither my partner nor our star barista agreed with me. 'The reason people come to Uncommon Grounds is the care that we take with their drinks. The ritual. We grind each shot of espresso and tamp it just before we twist the porta-filter onto the machine and push the button to pull the shot. We froth ice-cold milk to just the right consistency and texture for their particular espresso drink. We layer the components in a cup or mug and top the drink with an exquisite bit of art before presenting it to the customer.

'And now you want to just . . . just . . . push a button?'

'You make it sound dirty, Maggy,' Sarah said. 'Personally, I—'

'Wait, Sarah,' Amy said, holding up her hand. 'I think we have a misunderstanding here. Maggy thinks we want to replace our espresso machine with the JavaDo.'

Too cutesy for words. JavaDo. 'And you don't?'

'I do,' Sarah said. 'Personally, I've ground and pulled and tamped and frothed enough in the last year for two full lifetimes. Time to punch buttons, like everybody else does.'

'In gas stations and fast food joints,' I protested.

'You're a snob, Maggy Thorsen,' Sarah said. 'I didn't know that about you.'

'Maybe I am about coffee,' I admitted. 'But so are the people who come here.'

'The JavaDo espresso machine wouldn't be for us to use here in the shop, Maggy,' Amy said. 'We would sell them.'

Oh. Although that didn't make a whole lot more sense to me. 'Why would we sell espresso machines?'

'Profits,' Sarah said, eyebrows elevated. 'I hear they're all the rage.'

'Profit, *singular*,' I told her. 'If we sell a customer his or her very own Java*Don't*, we'll never see that customer again. They'll make their espresso drinks at home.'

'Of course they'll come back,' Amy said. 'For exactly the reason you've been talking about. The ritual of the individual hand-pulled shot, the latte art, the human interaction.'

I hate having my own argument used against me. Especially when it's a damn good one. 'But Java*Don't*—'

'Stop being juvenile,' Sarah snapped. 'It's JavaDo.'

I might not always be the adult in the room, but I usually had a few grade levels on Sarah, at least. 'Don't you think the company is asking for it?' I pointed to the logotype on the box. 'When you call something Java*Do* and suddenly it d—'

'Don't!'

'Exactly.' I folded my arms. 'When JavaDo suddenly *Don't* you have to answer for it.'

'I meant *don't* be so small-minded. You haven't even tried the machine out.'

'Fine.' My arms were still folded. 'Show me.'

'You wanted fresh, Maggy?' Amy had gone into Vanna White spokesmodel mode. She waved her hand in front of the touch screen and it lighted. Then she tapped a picture of a latte and grinding commenced. 'Each shot is ground fresh to order just before brewing.'

I had to admit that was kind of cool. I stepped back and watched as the soulless thing kicked out a shot of espresso with a gorgeous crema. 'Nice. But what about the frothing? It—'

The gurgle of the machine as it sucked milk from the carton next to it interrupted me.

'Commences automatically.' Amy smiled at me. 'Don't worry, Maggy. This isn't like the machines you find in lunchrooms.'

'Untrue.' Sarah reached past Amy to reposition the cup as the steamed milk poured out. 'This espresso machine is perfect for offices, big or small. You can change the number or strength of shots, how much steamed milk and froth you'd like. JavaDo gives the discriminating coffee consumer exactly what he or she wants, when he or she wants it. And it's a boon for productivity because nobody has to run out for their espresso drinks.'

'Espresso drinks they'd presumably buy from us,' I pointed out, even though I could see where this was going. My partner was in sales mode, gearing up to sell coffeemakers rather than lattes or real estate. 'Your idea is that we'd stock these machines in the store?'

'Not only that,' Amy said, 'but we'd be an exclusive JavaDo dealer. The only one in Brookhills.'

Not exactly the feat she made it out to be. 'Brookhills is a tiny market area.'

'Small, but affluent,' Sarah said. 'There are more espresso drinkers per capita in Brookhills than Milwaukee or Chicago.'

Somehow, I doubted the espresso question had been asked on the last census. And if it was, our large neighbor fifteen minutes to the east and even larger neighbor ninety minutes to the south would probably beg to differ.

But then Sarah had years of experience presenting Brookhills – and the Brookhills homes she had sold – in the best light possible in comparison to the surrounding areas. Brookhills had better schools or lower taxes or higher average incomes, swifter trash collection, whatever.

But now my formerly part-time partner was full-time, having just sold her company, Kingston Realty, in order to devote her full attention to Uncommon Grounds.

And here we were a month later, the targets of Sarah's full attention, which was kind of like getting a foghorn in the ear. Hard to ignore, as much as you pray you could. JavaDo was the fourth new idea my partner had hatched in the month, the last being turning Uncommon Grounds into an after-hours wine bar.

Not that there was anything wrong with new ideas. If they were mine. Or even Amy's, since our young barista had a better – or at least more current – marketing mind than I did these days.

Amy blessedly had pointed out to Sarah that the depot neighborhood was relatively deserted at night after the last commuter train from Milwaukee came through. And that even if the place started hopping, getting a liquor license would mean a long, drawn-out battle with the city.

But now even Amy seemed to be buying into this new brainstorm of Sarah's.

'I don't get it,' I said. 'We would be competing with ourselves. We need to draw people into Uncommon Grounds, not encourage them to stay at home.'

'And that's exactly what we'd be doing,' Sarah said. 'Amy and I have been researching this, and we already have the top two things that bring people into a coffeehouse.' Sarah held up two fingers and ticked them off. 'Loyalty cards and free Wi-Fi.'

'Magazines and newspapers are third on the list,' Amy said. 'We should beef up our selection.'

'And where is selling do-it-yourself espresso makers on this list?' I asked.

'It isn't,' Amy said. 'But studies show that people want to own home machines, regardless. It doesn't mean they'll stop coming here. They do that for the experience, the socialization—'

'And the pecan rolls.' Our baker Tien Romano had emerged from the kitchen, a resealable plastic tray of said rolls in her hand. 'I'm taking these last ones to Dad, unless anybody else wants to take them home.'

Tien and her father Luc had owned the food market in the same strip mall that housed Uncommon Grounds for the first two years. When the mall had collapsed, literally, Luc retired, and Tien had come onboard with us to do our baking. In exchange, we gave her the use of our kitchen at night to prepare food for her catering business.

'Get thee behind me, Satan.' Amy was holding her index fingers in the sign of the cross to ward off the calories of Tien's buns. 'I've just lost the five pounds I put on because of those buggers.'

Personally, I was fine with maintaining and even nurturing my five-pound pecan roll around the middle. But: 'We still have some from yesterday, Tien. Though I'd love to have you stay for a minute.'

'Oh,' Tien said, setting down the tray. 'Do you need help?'

'Only talking some sense into these two. They want to stock home espresso machines.'

She reclaimed the rolls and flashed me a pained smile. 'I'm afraid I would only tip the scales further against you. I don't think it's such a bad idea. Try to keep an open mind.'

'Expand Maggy's mind?' Sarah groused. 'Got a pry bar on you?'

'Afraid I don't have one of those,' Tien said. 'But if there's anything else you need, let me know.' Flashing Amy the peace sign, she ducked out the side door to the parking lot.

'She is so damned nice.' Only Sarah could make 'nice' a fault.

For my part, I was feeling ganged up on, and for good

reason. I'd been ganged up on. 'I can't believe you are all so enthusiastic. This is full-on retail sales we're talking about.'

'What do you call this crap?' Sarah swept her arm toward the shelves of gifts and cups of various sizes, shapes and slogans.

'Coffee paraphernalia,' I said. 'To go along with what we do, not take its place.'

'Speaking of that, Maggy,' Amy said. 'Now that we're up and running in our new location, I think it's time to do some more branded items using the line-drawing of the depot. Maybe an Uncommon Grounds coffee mug and T-shirt – long-sleeved, of course, since this is Wisconsin.'

'Wearables?' Sarah said. 'Sizes mean inventory.'

'You're worried about a few T-shirts and you want to stock those?' I pointed at the giant espresso maker. 'Think of the space and cost of inventory. I'd bet just one of these JavaDos costs more than the total of all this "crap", as you put it.'

'But that's the beauty of JavaDo,' Amy said. 'We'd have the demonstrator here, but when we sell a machine it's shipped directly to the customer's home. No inventory. No investment.'

'And no risk,' Sarah said.

'There's always risk,' I grumbled. 'What happens if something goes wrong with a machine we sell? We hire a computer programmer and go into the JavaDo repair business? Bet there's money in that, too.'

'JavaDo picks them up from the customer and leaves them a loaner.' Amy had her arms folded across her chest like a mom tired of dealing with a whiny child.

'Seems a little too good to be true,' I muttered.

Amy glared at me.

Change was not my thing, necessarily. And right now, I had enough change going on in my home life, thank you very much, what with Sheriff Jake Pavlik moving in and our getting engaged. Not to mention adding a new dog to the family and—

'Twenty percent on each machine we sell,' Sarah was saying. 'But the real benefit to us is increased bean sales.'

I came out of my reverie. 'You mean the little pods? The ones that cost so much?' And maybe had a huge mark-up/ profit margin?

'Uh-uh,' Sarah said, taking the stainless-steel cover off one of two bowl-shaped bins on top of the machine to reveal whole beans. 'Not that we couldn't get into the pod machines if we wanted to. But this particular model of espresso machine holds two different kinds of whole beans. So, say regular for mornings, decaf for late afternoon and evening, when you don't want caffeine.'

'Or flavored beans.' Amy lifted the other bin lid, and I got a whiff of hazelnut cinnamon. 'And we all know that the most profitable thing we sell in this store are whole beans.'

It was true there was a good profit margin on beans and almost no labor involved in dumping the whole beans into a bag and handing it to a customer.

I still felt like I was being maneuvered. And, therefore, whiny. 'So, what did you do? Meet with the rep behind my back?'

'Yup.' Sarah put the bin lid back on and picked up the clear latte cup. 'Have you ever seen such great crema?'

'And the layering,' Amy took it from her and held it up to the sunlight coming in through the front window. 'Isn't it beautiful?'

Yes, again. And also again: 'But you met with a rep without telling me?'

'It's my fault.' Amy's pink cheeks matched the second stripe from the left in her multi-hued do. 'Kip made the suggestion and Catherine was available that very night. You've been so busy, I—'

'*We*,' Sarah interrupted, '*we* went ahead because we knew you'd lift your leg on the idea and ruin a perfectly good dinner.'

Now I really was ticked. 'JavaDo sprang for dinner and you two didn't invite me? Nice.' By which I mean it wasn't. 'Where is this all coming from? Are you planning to set me adrift and take over the ship?'

'Let me guess: *Mutiny on the Bounty*,' Sarah said dryly. 'Last night's classic movie?'

I nodded. 'Trevor Howard and Marlon Brando. 1962.'

'Fascinating,' Sarah said. 'Now back to your question, Captain Bligh. Where this is coming from is an effort to be profitable. Doesn't that sound like a good thing?'

'We are profitable,' I said stubbornly.

'There are some months that you and I don't even take a paycheck, Maggy.'

It was true. Late summers could be tough, but here we were in October, so all was good. Or at least I could pay my mortgage. 'I don't know what you're complaining about. Your house is paid for and you must have gotten a gazillion dollars for Kingston Realty.'

'I received a fair price for Kingston Realty, which I've invested,' Sarah said primly. 'Kip says—'

Kip again? First Amy and now Sarah. 'Are you both talking about Kip Fargo?'

'Just how many Kips could there be in Brookhills?' Sarah asked.

Kip was chief counsel at First Financial, where I'd managed public relations before opening Uncommon Grounds nearly four years ago. A couple years after that, the corporate attorney had left First Financial also, going out on his own to form Fargo Financial. 'Not only are you meeting with reps without me, but you've hired a corporate attorney? We're not even a corporation.'

'Not for Uncommon Grounds, you ninny. Kip is doing tax law and investments now and handled the sale of my company.'

Oh.

'He did a damn good job,' Sarah continued. 'I cleared a good sum and with his investment advice I'm on my way to doubling it. He advises Mary Callahan, you know, and has made her a ton.'

Mary was my CPA and also Brookhills head librarian.

'I've never been much into the stock market,' Amy said, 'but when Kip explains financial strategy it just makes sense.'

'You invest with him, too?' Apparently, everybody had money to invest but me.

'Not yet, but who knows? I may.'

'He has you hooked in more ways than one – huh, Amy?' Sarah asked.

The color of Amy's flush moved one stripe to the right. 'We'll see.'

I thought I understood now. Except . . . I didn't. 'What about Jacque?'

Jacque Oui owned the local market and considered himself fishmonger to the stars and an expert on all things culinary. I'd never been fond of him, but Amy was. Or at least had been, the last time we'd talked about him.

Which must have been a while back.

'If you weren't totally self-absorbed,' Sarah said, 'you'd know Amy and Jacque broke up nearly three months ago.'

'I'm not—' OK, I was. 'Three months?'

'Yup,' Sarah confirmed. 'Long enough for Jacque to go oui, oui, oui all the way home.'

Our rainbow barista was usually more tolerant of my partner than I was, but now she rolled her eyes. 'For the last time, Sarah. Jacque flew to France on family business. It had nothing to do with our break-up and, besides, he's back now. I'd appreciate it if you'd drop the stupid joke.'

'Well.' Sarah sniffled. 'That's kind of hurtful.'

'*You're* kind of hurtful,' I told her and turned to Amy. 'Are you doing all right?'

She waved her hand. 'Oh, sure. It's probably for the best.'

'There was the age difference,' I said.

Nearly twenty years between her and Jacque.

'Honestly, that was never a problem,' Amy said. 'In fact, Jacque and I used to laugh about the fact that when he finished college, I was barely potty-trained.'

Amy's tone must have been too nostalgic for Sarah, because she snorted. 'Wouldn't have been so funny when he was the one in diapers.'

'What do you mean?' Amy asked.

'You know. Incontinence?'

'I think that what Sarah means' – if only I had a dollar for every time I'd said that – 'is that the age difference didn't mean much now, but it might have when you were both a few years older. Think about it: when you are just turning sixty, Jacque will be eighty.'

'And incontinent?' Amy's voice had gone up a half octave.

'Not necessarily,' Sarah said. 'Though with male plumbing, it's kind of a crap—'

'Stop!'

My partner grinned. 'Anyway, you're with Kip now.'

'Who is my age,' I couldn't help but point out. 'His son went to school with Eric and his daughter is just a little younger.'

'So, what does that make Kip?' Sarah said. 'Eighteen years older than Amy, instead of twenty? That's progress. Besides, changing *Kip*'s nappies down the road might be worth it. The guy's got dough.'

'That's very sensitive of you,' Amy said, 'but I'm not interested in Kip's money. In fact—'

'You're welcome.' Sarah turned to me. 'You both should be thanking me, in fact.'

'I'm supposed to thank you?' I asked. 'For what?'

'My matchmaking. I introduced Kip to Amy, just like I did you to Pavlik.'

Sheriff Jake Pavlik, now my fiancé. 'You didn't introduce us. I met Pavlik when Patricia was killed. I was the prime suspect in her murder, if you'll recall. He was the investigating officer.'

'Meet-cute.'

Only in books. 'How can you say that? The victim was your best friend.'

'Are you talking about Patricia Harper?' Amy asked. 'Your former partner in Uncommon Grounds?'

'Yes,' I said. 'Before Patricia died, I'd never met Sarah *or* Pavlik.'

'Then you have Patricia to thank as well,' Sarah said.

For being murdered, apparently. I would have asked Sarah if she was off her meds, but we'd beaten that bi-polar horse to death.

So instead I picked up the brochure on the counter. 'Back to Java . . . wait.' I looked up. 'Two *thousand* dollars?'

'And we get twenty percent of each sale,' Sarah said. 'Four hundred bucks.'

'Just for demonstrating a really top-drawer coffee machine and making it available to our customers,' Amy said. 'And it will expose us to new markets, Maggy. We'd be the only JavaDo dealer in southeastern Wisconsin.'

I glanced over at Sarah, who shrugged. 'We need to consider

this, Maggy. Change is not always bad.' She cocked her head. 'And I'm not always wrong.'

Now I felt ashamed. Which is probably what she intended. 'I don't think you're always wrong. I just—'

I was saved from finishing the sentence by the door chime tinkling.

I looked up to see Pavlik push in. 'This is a nice surprise.'

County Sheriff Jake Pavlik was medium height, with dark hair that curls as it touches the collar of his leather jacket. His eyes are blue-gray and tend to shift from the light to the dark end of that spectrum along with his mood.

'Is something wrong?' The eyes were dark, muddy gray and, even more telling, Pavlik was accompanied by a young sheriff's deputy, who didn't look like he was just stopping in for a cup of joe.

'What did you do now?' Sarah whispered into my ear.

I moved toward Pavlik, as the deputy turned to close the door behind him. 'Eric?' My voice came out in a croak.

I'd talked to my son Eric just the night before. He was exploring his ancestry as part of a DNA project at college in Minneapolis and regularly peppering me with questions about my side of the family tree. Most of which I couldn't answer, because . . . well, my folks were Norwegian, and nobody talked much. A hug meant somebody was dying. 'Is he OK?'

'Eric?' Pavlik repeated, and then his eyes changed yet again as he realized what I was asking. 'God, yes. Eric's fine.'

'Then what—?'

The deputy interrupted, looking up from the notepad in his hand to scan the room like it was a lecture hall rather than a coffeehouse with three, count them, three people in it. 'Amy Caprese?'

Eyes wide, Amy raised her hand.

Pavlik shook his head. 'You don't have to scare the wits out of the woman, Fergussen. I told you that I know her.'

'But if she's a—'

Pavlik waved him quiet and moved toward the counter where Amy still stood. I followed.

'Amy,' Pavlik said. 'I understand you're acquainted with Kip Fargo?'

'Well . . .' She glanced at me before she answered. 'Yes. Yes, I am.'

'Did you happen to see him last night?'

Her eyes got even bigger. 'We went out to dinner.'

The deputy interrupted again. 'Where?'

'Alfonso's.'

'When?'

'Seven o'clock reservation?' Amy's voice squeaked a bit when she said it.

'And after dinner?' Pavlik asked. 'Did you go back to his place?'

Amy colored up again. 'Well, yes. But we . . . I didn't stay over.'

'I'm sure the sheriff wasn't asking that,' I told her. 'Were you?'

Apparently, he was. 'What time did the two of you get to the house?'

'Arrived about nine, maybe? And I left maybe a half hour later.'

'Early evening,' Pavlik observed, echoing my thoughts.

'We had an argument and—'

'Shoosh.' Uneasy about where this might be going, I put my hand on her arm. 'I don't think you should say more, Amy.'

'Ma'am,' the deputy said tightly. 'You need to stay out of this.'

'Then *you* should have stayed out of our coffeehouse.' Sarah was more a mother lion type than she appeared on first glance.

Holding up the same hand now to stop Sarah before she got *her*self into trouble, I turned to Pavlik. 'What happened?'

He hesitated and swiveled to face Amy. 'I'm sorry, Amy. Mr Fargo is dead.'

'Dead?' Amy's face had gone ashen.

'When? How?' Worst fears confirmed, I was all about time of death. And cause.

But Pavlik didn't quite answer either question. 'Mr Fargo missed a meeting at his office this morning. When he didn't answer his phone either, somebody went by the house and found him.'

Amy was standing stock-still, a slash of red across her

cheeks like she'd been slapped. 'Did he . . . I mean, oh God, he wouldn't have. Just because I . . .'

'Just because you what, ma'am?' The deputy and his notebook again.

'I told Kip I wouldn't marry him,' Amy said, and turned to me, tears in her eyes. 'It was just too soon, Maggy.'

'Of course, it was.' Three months of dating and the guy – the much older guy – pops the question. Maybe I should have put Kip in touch with my ex, Ted, about the wisdom of that. 'I'm sure Kip understood that.'

Unless he'd offed himself as a result.

'You didn't tell me Kip proposed.' Sarah sniffed. 'But even so, I don't see the guy committing suicide.'

Everything I knew about Kip made it seem unlikely, too. But isn't that what everyone says in this kind of situation?

'How did he die?' I tried again.

'Mr Fargo was shot,' Pavlik said.

'Was shot.' Not 'gunshot wound', which might still have been self-inflicted. 'Was shot' indicated to me, at least, that another person had pulled the trigger. 'Were there signs of a break-in?'

'There was . . . disarray,' Pavlik said. 'Indicating a possible attempted robbery.'

The deputy couldn't seem to help himself. 'Or a quarrel. Lovers' maybe.'

And with that, Amy hit the floor.

TWO

Amy was already trying to get up when I reached her. 'Best to stay flat,' Pavlik said, a hand on her shoulder. 'Did you hit your head?'

'No, no,' Amy said, sitting despite his best efforts. 'I'm fine. It was just . . . such a shock.'

'That he was killed or that we knew you'd argued?' Deputy Fergussen asked.

'She *told* you they had an argument, Sherlock,' Sarah snapped at the deputy. 'The man asked her to marry him and she said no—'

'I said I wasn't sure,' Amy interjected. 'Or at least that's what I meant.'

'I bet it was,' Fergussen said, looming over her. 'But Fargo wouldn't take it like that, would he? A man with all that money was probably used to getting what he wanted.'

I glanced toward Pavlik, hoping he was going to shut down his employee. But for now, he seemed to be willing to let the line of questioning play out.

Sarah elbowed the guy back, as I put out a hand to help Amy onto her feet.

'Kip obviously loved her,' I told Fergussen, as Amy stood. 'I'm sure he was more sad than mad,' I said.

Amy shifted her head uncomfortably. 'Not exactly.'

'Shoosh' was apparently a concept she wasn't familiar with.

Happily, the deputy seemed to have missed what Amy had said. 'What?'

All the barista had to say was 'nothing', like Eric did every time he mumbled something he didn't want me to actually hear. But instead Amy cleared her throat. 'I said he was angry at me. Very angry.'

'Amy, you don't have to say anything,' I said. 'In fact, you shouldn't.'

'Well, I'm not going to lie,' Amy said, getting defensive.

'It's not a lie if there's nobody alive to say otherwise,' Sarah piped in. 'It's like the tree falling in the forest.'

The barista thought for a second and then shook her head. 'I have no idea what you just said.'

The deputy seemed to, though, and he took a step closer to Sarah. 'I hope you're not suborning perjury, ma'am.'

'She's not under oath, so it can't be perjury, Deputy Dog.' My partner was in his face.

'Sarah,' I warned. 'You shouldn't—'

'Stand down, Fergussen,' Pavlik ordered. 'Now.'

The deputy took a half step back. Reluctantly. Sarah, who hadn't given ground, snickered.

A look from Pavlik quelled it.

'Does Amy need a lawyer?' I asked him.

'Depends.' It was the deputy who answered, pointing his pad at Amy. 'Does she think she needs one?'

Pavlik seemed to have had enough. 'How about you write on that thing, instead of waving it in people's faces, Fergussen? In fact, consider yourself my note-taker.' And nothing else, his tone said.

Fergussen apparently didn't know that tone as well as I did. 'I'm just questioning the suspect.'

'Suspect?' Amy gasped.

'Fergussen.' Pavlik shot the deputy a look that would have shriveled my guy parts, if I had any. 'I talk. You don't.'

'But—'

'And yet, he speaks,' Sarah said to the wind.

The hand not holding the notebook clenched into a fist at the deputy's side. 'Why don't you just shut your—'

'Fergussen.' Pavlik said it in a low tone. 'Wait outside.'

The deputy hesitated, still bristling, then turned on his heel.

Pavlik turned to us as the door closed behind him. 'I'm sorry. He's new on the job.'

'He wanted to slug me,' Sarah said.

'We've all wanted to slug you at times,' I told her. 'But the guy does seem to have anger issues.' I was watching Fergussen pace back and forth past our porch window, mouth moving like he was muttering to himself. Or talking on Bluetooth.

'I'll take care of him,' Pavlik said. 'But, Sarah, keep in

mind that we're here officially, not socially. Witty banter can get you into trouble.'

'Or even unwitty banter.' I was trying to soften Pavlik's point, appropriate though it might be. Sometimes Sarah just didn't know when enough was enough.

'I'm calling a lawyer.' Sarah snagged her cell phone from the counter.

'Because you're not witty?' I doubted she was registering a complaint of police misconduct.

'You don't *think* I'm witty,' Sarah said. 'But no, I'm calling a lawyer to represent Amy.'

The barista glanced uncertainly out the window like she was the prey the uniformed man was stalking and then back at us. 'Am I being arrested?'

'Of course not,' I said.

The official Pavlik was more measured. 'I'm afraid we're going to need to get a statement from you. You were one of the last people to see Mr Fargo.'

'One of the last?' I asked. 'Not *the* last.'

'Of course, not "the last",' Sarah said with her phone to her ear. 'The killer was the last. Or "zee last", as Amy's former squeeze would say.'

'Now why would you bring Jacque up?' Amy snapped.

'Honestly not sure. He just popped into my head,' Sarah said, taking the phone away from her ear to punch a number. Most likely she was caught up in a 'punch one for . . .' maze.

'Well, pop him right out of your head. Jacque has nothing to do with this.'

'Of course not,' I said, exchanging glances with Sarah as she went to speak into her phone.

Pavlik didn't respond to Amy's outburst, but he wouldn't have missed it. Instead he said, 'Do you have time now to come down to the station, Amy?'

'Can't you just talk to her here?' I asked.

'We need to follow protocol, especially since the witness is a friend.' He smiled to reassure her.

'The witness' didn't look reassured.

Sarah slid her phone into her apron pocket and turned back to us. 'Your attorney will meet you at the station.'

'One quick phone call and you've retained somebody?' I asked.

'Speed dial,' Sarah said. 'I'm usually your "one phone call from the slammer", so I keep a stable of lawyers at the ready.'

Oh.

'Thank you,' Amy said in a small voice, as Pavlik touched her elbow.

'Not to worry,' I said, following them to the door. 'You'll be back in time for closing.'

Amy didn't look so sure.

'Don't say a word to the coppers until the lawyer gets there,' Sarah called.

I stopped Pavlik at the door, as Amy continued out onto the porch where Fergussen was waiting. 'You can't possibly believe Amy shot this man because he asked her to marry him. It's absurd.'

Pavlik put up his hand. 'I'd stay and explain how many things we *don't* know at this point, but I don't want Fergussen taking Amy in by himself.'

I got that point, at least. Fergussen was already taking Amy down the steps to the squad, his hand gripping her upper arm. Happily, no handcuffs. Yet.

'We're coming with you,' I said, undoing my apron.

'The store is still open,' Pavlik said.

'Not anymore.' I flipped the sign to *Closed*.

Sarah was standing waiting with my coat and followed me out.

'They hook these together so they can't be stolen, don't you think?' Sarah asked as we took seats in a bank of four chairs like in an airport. Except we were in the waiting area of the sheriff's department.

I chin-gestured toward the deputies coming and going, not to mention the desk officer facing us. 'There are probably easier places to steal chairs, I would think.'

'And nicer chairs.' She thought about it. 'I'm thinking they don't want them broken over somebody's head then.'

That seemed more likely, if a little theatrical. 'You've been here before?'

'The sheriff's department? Sure. But usually just passing by to get to the county assessor or somebody like that. Not actually sitting here with the perps.'

First 'coppers' and now 'perps'? And Pavlik thought I was the one who sounded like a bad TV movie.

'I don't think they keep axe-killers out here in the waiting room.' I watched a dad and two daughters enter and sit down. 'Are you OK?'

'It's just kind of creepy.' She glanced around uncomfortably.

'Your cousin is in state prison,' I reminded her. 'That's not creepy?'

'Yes, but so is Ronny. He belongs there.'

'And Amy doesn't. I agree.' I put my hand on her shoulder. 'She'll be out of there in no time. They don't put people in prison for turning down a marriage proposal.'

'Case in point,' she said, brightening, 'you said no to Pavlik at first, when he asked you to marry him.'

Actually, I'd done more bobbing and weaving than outright answering, but no need to go into that here in the sheriff's department waiting room surrounded by his subordinates. 'Yes, and I'm out here in my civvies instead of in there wearing orange.' I frowned. 'Or whatever color they wear here at County jail.'

'My point is that Amy wouldn't kill Kip any more than you would have killed Pavlik after you turned him down. That's the way we reason with Pavlik.'

'Amy didn't help matters when she volunteered that Kip was really angry.'

'See? You think she should have lied, too.'

'I *think* she should have just kept her mouth shut. Once she'd said Kip was angry – which is a subjective thing in the first place – telling her to stuff the genie back in the bottle wasn't helpful.'

'Maybe she'll think twice next time.'

'Next time she's questioned in a murder?'

Sarah sniffed. 'You make it sound unlikely, when we both know it's happened to you more than once.'

True. But I was special. 'Amy went back to the house with

Kip, so maybe they didn't get into the argument right there at the restaurant.'

'Meaning that their argument was private and could have remained that way.'

'Yes, yes, yes. I get it. You don't think Amy should have told Pavlik they argued or that Kip was angry.'

'She shouldn't have even said she rejected him,' Sarah said. 'If it hadn't been Pavlik, maybe she would have been more careful.'

'Fergussen was there, too,' I reminded her. 'Now there's a "copper" that would put me on my guard.'

'But not our honesty-is-the-best-policy barista.'

'The thing is, the fact Amy turned Kip down is a reason for Kip to kill Amy, not the other way around.'

'That's true,' Sarah said. 'I suppose Amy thought their argument would explain her leaving her new fiancé at nine thirty p.m. Though there's always premature ej—'

'Not here.'

Sarah looked at me.

I felt my face get red. 'I mean, don't talk about it here. But to your point, Amy opened with me this morning, so I guess she could have used that as an excuse for going home early.'

'She's twenty-seven, Grandma.' Sarah was chewing on the inside of her cheek. 'I wonder how the restaurant scene all went down.'

'I'm sure that's exactly what they're asking Amy this second. I just hope she doesn't say any more until her attorney gets here.'

'Gilbert? He's already here.'

'Gilbert Mundy? Please don't tell me you called your cousin to represent her.'

'Step-cousin. And what's your problem with Gilbert?'

'Other than he's a raging alcoholic?'

'Recovering raging alcoholic, Maggy.' Sarah repositioned her butt in her chair. 'Have a little compassion.'

'I did have compassion when he went into rehab. Even when he had the DUI on his way home from rehab and you left work early to bail him out.'

'He doesn't have anybody else. His big brother's in jail.'

That would be Cousin Ronny. 'How long has little Gilbert been "recovering" this time?'

'Six months, which is a new record. And I'll have you know he attends two meetings a day. In fact, he was at his AA meeting at the church across the street' – she gestured toward the window – 'when I got hold of him. Left the meeting straight away to be here before they brought Amy in.'

Which might say more about how seriously he took his recovery than it did how good a lawyer he was. 'I should have called Bernie.' Bernie Egan is the husband of my other former partner – the living one – in Uncommon Grounds, Caron Egan.

'Bernie's a tax attorney.'

'But he knows people,' I hissed. 'Other lawyers. Presumably some of whom aren't alcoholics.'

'Recovering alcoholics.'

Even that. 'Recovering or not, alcoholic or not, Gilbert Mundy is not a criminal defense attorney.'

'Ah, but there's my genius. Gilbert's new partner is Rhonda Higgins and *she's* a criminal defense attorney.'

'Rhonda Higgins? Really?' The woman was a defense attorney, and a good one. She'd left Brookhills a few years ago for Chicago where higher crime rates meant more opportunity. 'I didn't know Rhonda was back. Why didn't you just call her?'

'She's not back-back. She just opened a satellite practice in Gilbert's office, because she eventually wants to retire here. But she's not taking new clients unless something big pops. You know, like another Jeffrey Dahmer.'

'Flesh-eating serial killer. That's a lot to hope for,' I said. 'For a defense attorney, I mean.'

'You're telling me. That's why we're going in the back door.'

'Gilbert is our back door?'

'Exactly.'

'Let me get this straight. You think Rhonda will back-stop Gilbert, so you honestly don't care if Gilbert stays on the wagon or not.'

'I prefer not, for Amy's sake. Rhonda's a much better lawyer.'

'So, in the Sarah Kingston Code of Ethics it's perfectly fine to hope that an alcoholic – your step-cousin, in fact – will slip up and go back to drinking?'

'Where is all this righteous indignation coming from? A minute ago, you were discounting Gilbert as a drunk.'

Gilbert *was* a drunk. And might be again. Though hopefully not. God willing. 'I'm only concerned about Amy's representation.'

'As am I. Which is why I've hedged our bets.'

Fine. 'Hopefully we won't need Rhonda. She's big-time and this whole thing is ridiculous.'

'Tell that to your sheriff fiancé, who is in there grilling our employee and friend as we speak.'

'Let's be fair,' I said. 'They have to find out what Amy and Kip talked about. She was the last to see him.'

'No.'

'No, she's not the last one to see him?'

'No, I don't want to be fair. I just want her out of here.'

Somebody was crabby. 'This kind of stuff takes time. I'm sure they want to know what kind of mindset Kip was in when she went home.' Other than 'angry', as Amy had put it.

'And whether he was expecting somebody else to stop by and shoot him.'

That would be helpful, as well. 'I'd love to know where things stood between them when Amy left.'

'Probably not amicable, since she did leave.'

'But like I said, she was opening this morning. She might have intended to sleep at home all along, instead of staying over and getting up at five. In fact, do we even know if the two of them were sleeping together?'

'The man asked her to marry him.'

'So?'

Sarah rolled her eyes. 'This isn't a Jane Austen novel. We usually try these things out before we get married. Make sure all the parts are working.'

I loved Jane Austen. But I got Sarah's point. 'I suppose. Especially since she was buying used.'

'Or not buying, in this case.'

'When did you introduce them?'

'Oh, now you believe I introduced them.'

'I always did. It's Pavlik and me you can't lay claim to.'

She ignored that. 'Let's see, it's the first of October today? I guess it must have been early July. That's when I seriously started thinking about selling the business.'

'And hired Kip?'

'Yeah, valuing and selling a business isn't easy, and I had no idea where to start. Mary Callahan recommended Kip and he came by the shop here to discuss it.'

'That's when he met Amy? Was that before or after she and Jacque broke up?'

'They were already having trouble.' Sarah shrugged. 'You had a choice between an uppity French fishmonger and a smart, Ivy-League bean counter, which would you take?'

'Neither, but then I'm not a gold-digger. You're saying Amy is?'

'No, sadly. I'm the one who appreciated the fact that Kip had money.'

'So you're the gold-digger.'

Sarah snorted. 'Only when I'm hiring somebody to handle my finances or investments. If a person can't make their own fortune, why would I believe they can do it for me?'

Good point. 'Just how rich is Kip? Or was he?'

Sarah cocked her head, studying my face. 'Your tone just changed. You're thinking.'

'Thinking?' Beyond the desk sergeant a door opened and then closed. Still no sign of Amy. 'You say that like it doesn't happen often.'

'I mean you're reflecting, pondering, contemplating Kip's murder. Which means you're thinking motive.'

'Maybe so.' I shrugged. 'Money is always top on the list, of course, and it sounds like Kip has it. That doesn't help us get Amy out of here any faster, though.'

'She turned down that money when she said she wouldn't marry him.'

'At this point we only have Amy's word she said no.'

Sarah sat back abruptly, the cheap plastic seat protesting.

'You just ripped the chair.'

'And you just accused Amy of lying.'

Which is what Sarah herself had wanted Amy to do earlier. 'I would trust Amy with my life, but I'm trying to see the situation through the investigator's eyes.'

'Who you're living with. But in this case your loyalty should be with Amy.'

'I told you it is. But the best way I can help her is by being aware of what they' – I nodded toward the door from the lobby to the County Sheriff's offices – 'are thinking.'

'And then what? Wish it away?'

I shrugged. 'Find alternatives, though we need to know a whole lot more than we do. For example, Kip has a successful business and accumulated wealth. Not to mention kids.'

'I think we've established all that.' Sarah stood up and rolled her shoulders to stretch.

'Wouldn't he want a prenup? I mean he's an attorney and financial advisor – wouldn't that be *Getting Remarried 101*?'

'I suppose so.' Sarah was craning her neck, trying to see past the desk. 'What the hell is taking so long?'

Since she hadn't answered my question and I couldn't answer hers, I said, 'I wonder if they talked about it. A prenup, I mean.'

'We can ask her when she gets out of there.' Sarah checked her watch. 'It's nearly seven.'

Uncommon Grounds' closing time. We'd been in the sheriff's department lobby for nearly four hours, meaning we'd lost four hours of business.

Sarah must have been thinking the same. 'We should have asked Tien to come back. Keep the store open.'

'Should have,' I admitted. 'Or even called from here and had her re-open. But I kept thinking they'd be done any time. Who knew this would take so—?'

As I said it, the door opened, and Amy emerged. Behind her was a burly young man, toting a lawyer's briefcase. A document was half-sticking out of it.

'You're losing something,' I told the young man – one Gilbert Mundy. Gilbert did seem to have cleaned up his act, which meant that he didn't wreak of bourbon, even at seven p.m. That had been his usual M.O. at 7 a.m. He was still disheveled, though.

'Oh, yeah, sorry.'

I wasn't sure if he was apologizing to me or the crushed legal document left dangling.

I turned to Amy, as he hurried away without another word. 'You OK?'

She nodded, blinking back tears and opened her mouth to talk. Nothing came out.

'Let's go to Maggy's place,' Sarah said, putting her arm on Amy's shoulder. 'We'll order pizza.'

'I'd like that,' Amy said shakily. 'Maybe have some wine, too?'

'Oh, you betcha,' Sarah said. 'Why do you think we're going to Maggy's?'

THREE

'm not sure where I got the reputation of having a wine stash.

But the fact was, I did have a fairly good selection in the kitchen cupboard next to the sink. 'For red, we have Cabernet or Merlot. And a Cab/Merlot blend. Oh, and a Syrah. White, we have Sauvignon Blanc or Chardonnay.'

'With or without oak on the Chardonnay?' Sarah asked.

'With.'

She groaned.

'I like oaky Chardonnay, so sue me.' Or go to somebody else's house.

'Is red all right, Amy?' Sarah asked, kindly deferring to the one of us who was currently under investigation. 'It goes best with peperoni and sausage.'

'Sure,' Amy said.

I didn't know why we went through this. We always drank red. And certainly we always drank red with pizza. White wine, though, stood a fighting chance with either Chinese or Thai takeout. Can't say we're not flexible.

I made the executive decision to open the Cab rather than the Merlot and poured three glasses, handing two to Sarah. She led the way into the living room and waited for Amy to sit down before handing her one.

Sarah settled on the couch next to her. 'What did they ask you?'

Amy, who had just taken a sip, choked and started coughing.

'Think you can give her a second to swallow?' I handed Amy a napkin just in case she started spewing. New rug.

'It's OK,' Amy said, taking the napkin and blowing her nose on it. 'They wanted to know things like what Kip and I did yesterday. What we talked about. When I left.'

'And? Gilbert told you not to say anything, right?'

Amy was the bone. Sarah, the dog. And speaking of dogs, where were mine?

'I told them the truth.' Amy took a second sip of her wine and managed to swallow this one.

'For God's sake,' Sarah exploded. 'I'll kill that good-for-nothing, drunk excuse for a lawyer.'

'Sarah, Sarah,' I admonished. 'A little compassion, please?'

'It's not Gilbert's fault,' Amy said, holding up her hand in an amended stop sign which looked more like a toast given she still had her glass in it. 'I told him I have nothing to hide.'

'Where was he going in such a hurry?' Sarah continued her rant. 'Probably off to a bar in search of a drink.'

That seemed unfair. 'Give your cousin a break. He's trying, at least.'

'For God's sake, Maggy.' Sarah threw her hands wide, almost knocking her wine glass off the coffee table. 'I'm not saying anything you didn't say yourself four hours ago.'

I grimaced. 'I know. Sounds worse coming from you.'

'Anyway,' our barista/peacemaker said, 'I told the sheriff everything I know. As I will tell you. Just ask away.'

'You don't have to talk,' I said, taking the chair across from her.

She smiled. 'I knew what I was letting myself in for when I came here.'

'I ordered the pizza.' At the word 'pizza', a furry head popped up from the corner behind the couch. Frank sniffed the air twice and, finding no tantalizing aromas, went back to sleep. 'It won't be here for a half hour, but there's no reason we have to talk about Kip until it gets here. Or anytime, in fact.'

'Yes, there is,' Sarah said, frowning. 'How else are we going to find out anything?'

'She means in order for us to help,' I said. 'But the fact is, Amy, if you'd rather just eat or just have the wine and go home, that's fine.'

'Yeah, Maggy hasn't had any of her wine yet,' Sarah said, her eyes squinty. 'She can drive you.'

My partner was punishing me. But I wouldn't let her know it hurt. 'I'd be happy to do that. Or call you an Uber.'

'That's right,' Amy said. 'My car is still at Uncommon Grounds.'

'Thanks to the Brookhills Sheriff's Department courtesy car,' Sarah said. 'But you shouldn't drive home after the wine anyway.'

'Not to mention the trauma of the day,' I added. 'Are you sure you want to go home at all? You're welcome to stay here.'

'I might take you up on that. I can't imagine getting to sleep, though, knowing Kip was lying there dead in his own bed last night.' She shivered.

'They found him in bed?' Sensitive Sarah wasn't to be deterred.

I tossed her an annoyed look but picked up my wine glass. If Amy didn't stay over, we'd send her home later by Uber.

Amy was nodding. 'Yes, which is not where I left him, before you ask. Kip walked me to my car and, last I saw him, he was going back up the circle drive toward the house.'

'Where is the house?' I asked.

'Piccolo Lane in Poplar Gardens.' Amy wrinkled her nose. 'You know, that old neighborhood off Lower Poplar Creek Road?'

'Do I *know* it?' Sarah's tongue was practically hanging out. 'That's the most desirable area not only in Brookhills, but in southeastern Wisconsin. I'd kill to get one of those houses.'

'Maybe somebody felt the same way.' I was less enthralled by Poplar Gardens because my ex-husband Ted's mother-in-law – Eve Whitaker Slattery – had a family home there. And Eve was a bitch.

The original part of Brookhills runs north and south along Poplar Creek. Lower Poplar Creek is where the rich folk settled in the day. Upper Poplar Creek was for the rest of us and my house was about as Upper as you could get.

But on the bright side, there should be plenty of well-heeled neighbors and security cameras on Piccolo Lane to collaborate Amy's story. 'Did you see anybody as you left?'

'Or better yet, did they see you?' Sarah added.

Amy shrugged. 'The sheriff asked that, too. There were a couple of cars parked on the street. A darker-colored one a ways farther down and another light-colored one that we passed on the way to my car.'

'You parked on the street instead of in the driveway?' That would make it more likely she and Kip had been seen.

'Yes. I didn't want to block in the GT2, so—'

'Kip has a GT2?' Sarah interrupted.

'GT2 RS.' Amy frowned. 'Not the most comfortable car in the world.'

'That's because it's a race car,' Sarah said.

'Why are we talking about cars?' I asked. Except that Sarah was obsessed by them. Of course she probably thought the same about me and murders.

'Because it's a Porsche,' Sarah said. 'A Porsche 911 GT2. Do you have any idea what one goes for?'

'Unfortunately, yes.' Amy said. 'Kip told me.'

'Well, tell me,' Sarah said. 'I don't run in those circles.'

'Oh, sorry,' Amy said. 'I thought it was a rhetorical question. This one was three-sixty.'

I frowned. 'Three-sixty—'

'Three-hundred-sixty-thousand dollars,' Sarah clarified.

'For a *car*?' I'd thought my now three-year-old Ford Escape had been an extravagance when I passed my battered mini-van with the faux wood side panels on to Eric for school. I told him not to thank me. He did, anyway, but then Eric's a good boy.

'Not just a car, Maggy,' Sarah said, eyes shining. 'The GT2 is a genuine race car. Zero to sixty in 2.7 seconds. Can you believe that?'

'No.' But it might come in handy if somebody was trying to kill you.

'You can take this right onto the track.'

Which is why every attorney needed one, apparently. 'Does Kip race?'

'No,' Amy said. 'He just likes nice cars.'

'Nice' seemed an understatement, given the car cost more than my house did. But back to my obsession. 'You said you and Kip passed a parked car as he walked you to yours. Was there anybody in that car?'

Amy frowned. 'I had an impression there was, but I

purposely didn't make eye contact, so I have no idea if it was a man, woman or child.'

'Why didn't you want to make eye contact?' I asked.

Amy cocked her head. 'He asked that, too.'

'Pavlik?'

'Yes. No wonder you two get along so well.' She said it with an edge, which wasn't Amy's way at all.

Sarah heard it, too. 'Maggy and I have talked about this. It's helpful for us to know what Pavlik is thinking and Maggy can bring us that perspective, as irritating as it might sometimes be.'

Thanks, friend.

'I guess.' Amy's arms were folded like she wanted to protect herself from me and any bad sheriff juju.

'Think of it this way,' Sarah continued. 'Maggy isn't so much sleeping with the enemy as informing on him.'

'I'd like to think I'm doing neither,' I said.

Amy picked up my now forgotten wine glass and held it out to me. 'I was being snarky, Maggy. I'm sorry.'

I took the wine peace offering. 'You don't have to be sorry. I said we shouldn't interrogate you and here I'm doing it.'

'For my benefit.' Amy lifted her own glass and clinked it against mine. 'Cheers.'

She set the glass right down again. 'Kip was walking me to my car and we weren't talking. I just wanted to disappear. I didn't look in the car because if there was someone in there, I'd have to pretend everything was all right.'

'Do you think it was a neighbor's car?' I asked

'I don't know. I told you I didn't look.' She was getting irritated with me again. 'Not that I know any of the neighbors anyway. The houses are far apart.'

By Upper Brookhills standards that was true. 'I just wondered if Kip seemed to recognize whoever it was.'

'Oh.' Amy wrinkled her nose. 'I think . . . yes, I think maybe he did.'

'Why? Did he wave or say hello?' Sarah asked.

'No, just the opposite. He hesitated as we got close to the car, and then kept going, but quickly. Like he didn't want to talk to them either.'

Which meant maybe there was somebody in the car after all. But why, at nine thirty at night on a darkened street? 'Was the car parked in front of Kip's house or farther down at a neighbor's maybe?'

'The people on either side are probably too far away and there would have been plenty of places to stop in front of their houses. It could have been someone visiting the people across the street, I suppose.'

'Did you notice anything about the car?' Sarah asked.

'Not really. I mean, it wasn't flashy like Kip's. Just little and kind of non-descript. I don't even remember the color.'

We had 'little' at least. 'And you didn't hear it running as you passed?'

'No, but I wouldn't have. It was one of those . . .' She sat up straighter. 'I guess I do know something, after all. It was one of those Toyota electric ones.'

'The Prius hybrid?'

'Yes! That's it.' She started to get up. 'Should I call the sheriff? He said if I remembered anything—'

Sarah waved her back down. 'Maggy will tell him in bed tonight. Another perk of being a double agent.'

'I am not a double agent.' But Sarah had just reminded me of something. 'Amy, you said Kip died in bed. If you left at nine thirty, it must have been considerably after that. Was he in the habit of going to bed early?'

'Not really. Though he'd felt a little "under the weather" lately.'

'Please. Is that what he said?' Sarah demanded. 'That's the guy's version of, "I've got a headache tonight, dear".'

Amy flushed.

Time to move on. 'Amy, did anybody at the sheriff's office tell you the time of death?'

'No. Only that they think he was shot in his sleep.' Amy took a deep uneven breath. 'I hope he was shot in his sleep.'

'It's the way I want to go,' Sarah said.

Personally, I'd skip the bullet part. 'Tell us about that night at the restaurant. You said Kip asked you to marry him?'

'With the ring box and on bended knee, right there.'

'You said it was Alfonso's?' It probably didn't matter, but I liked to be thorough.

A nod. 'Seven o'clock reservation. Kip's usual table, which was the best table in the house, of course.'

'Nice,' Sarah said. 'He had the whole thing planned?'

'Orchestrated, in that I'm surprised he didn't hire one.' Again, that edge was in Amy's voice. 'He settled for a single violinist.'

'He was trying to impress you,' I said.

'Impress me?' Amy seemed more baffled now than irritated. 'It was like he had never met me.'

It was true that the bells and whistles of an old-school proposal didn't seem like Amy's thing. Amy was a free spirit. We all knew that, but had Kip? They'd only dated three months. Had he been paying attention? 'Maybe Kip thought you were a romantic under the rainbow-striped hair and piercings?'

'I am a romantic. But making a show of getting down on one knee at a fancy restaurant isn't romantic. It's . . . pretentious.'

'How did you handle it?' I asked. 'It must have been terribly awkward.'

'It was,' Amy said. 'I didn't want to embarrass him in the restaurant in front of the diners. And the owners. And the wait staff. Even the violinist.'

'What was he playing?' Sarah asked curiously.

'"When a Man Loves a Woman".'

'Huh,' Sarah said. 'Great when Percy Sledge sang it. Not sure about the violin.'

'It wasn't bad, but . . . it was all about him. Like the whole thing. Everybody was watching.'

'What did you do?' I asked.

'I was so shocked and . . . well . . . embarrassed that I just kind of played along. It was agony. Everybody was congratulating us. Kip bought champagne for the whole place.'

'That does sound awkward,' Sarah said. 'What kind of champagne?'

'Dom Pérignon, what else?'

Sarah shrugged. 'I'd have gone Cristal. But that's just me.'

I thought we should move on. 'Then you said "yes" at the restaurant, Amy?'

'I just kind of hugged him and cried. He took it as a yes.'

Not surprisingly.

But I felt for Amy. On the spot, she would have had to decide whether to turn Kip down in front of a crowd of people or let him save face there, only to dash his hopes later.

Neither was good. But neither was the situation Kip had put her in, despite what sounded like his best intentions. 'When *did* you tell him you couldn't marry him?'

'When we got to his house.'

'I assume he was shocked after putting on the big show at the restaurant?' Sarah asked.

'It wasn't *my* show,' Amy snapped, then sucked in a lungful of air and let it out slowly before she continued. 'As we left, the maître d' came running after us because Kip had forgotten to pay the bill. I was quiet on the way home after that and he thought it was because of the bill or that he didn't tip enough again.'

'Kip Fargo stiffs waiters?' I was surprised.

'He tips ten percent, at most,' Amy said. 'I told him he doesn't know how it feels to make minimum wage as a server. I always tip twenty percent and I make peanuts.'

Because we pay peanuts. 'But you did tell him? That you didn't want to get married, I mean.'

'Yes.' She had been staring into her wine glass, and now looked up. 'I'd just split from Jacque three months ago, and I was going to get engaged? I couldn't do that. It would be such a slap in the face.'

To Jacque. Interesting. 'Did you break up with Jacque or was it the other way around?'

'I broke it off,' she said. 'But it doesn't mean I don't care about him.'

No, it didn't, but—

'And to make matters worse, Becky was there, smiling.'

'Becky?'

'The cashier at Schultz's?' Amy looked miserable. 'She was two tables away at the restaurant while this was all going on. She had her phone out; I'm sure she was taking photos and video. I think she was texting Jacque.'

Schultz's was the oldest market in Brookhills and was owned by Jacque. Becky was Schultz's long-time cashier, dating back to the original owners. And no, those people weren't Schultzes either. I had no idea where the name had come from.

'Doubly awkward,' I said.

'It was awful,' Amy said. 'Here Kip is on one knee giving me this big honkin' ring and toasting with champagne, and all the time I can see Becky's cell phone—'

'Where is it?' The question came from Sarah.

Amy stopped. 'Becky's cell phone? How should I know?'

'No, the "big honkin" ring.' Sarah was looking at Amy's left hand. 'You're not wearing it.'

'Of course not,' Amy said. 'I took it off and gave it back to Kip at the house. Like I told the deputy, I told Kip I couldn't accept it. At least not now. Not that Fergussen seemed to believe it. That man is horrible.'

'He puts the bad in bad cop,' I said. 'So how did Kip take it when you told him?'

'Probably went over like a lead balloon,' Sarah muttered.

'He got really mad,' Amy said, eyes wide. 'It was as if he was a kid having a temper tantrum. He said he'd gone to a lot of trouble and I'd ruined everything.'

'You'd spoiled his big plans,' I said. 'I assume you explained things were just moving too fast for you?'

'I tried. But it was as if I – and what I wanted – wasn't even part of his consideration. It was all the money he'd spent, the trouble he'd gone to, what people would think.'

'Apparently the guy is used to getting what he wants,' Sarah said, picking up her wine. 'You're better off without him.'

'She'd be better off without him if he weren't *dead*,' I told the woman who had been so proud of the fact that she'd introduced the two of them. 'The current situation is awfully messy.'

'Ya think?' Amy said it like Eric would have. Just one step away from a 'duh'.

'And to make matters worse, I'm out one attorney-slash-financial adviser,' Sarah said, getting up. 'Pizza's here.'

The doorbell rang.

'How did you know the pizza was here?' I called after Sarah as she opened the door.

'I can smell peperoni a block away.' Returning with the

pizza box, she looked around. 'Speaking of olfactory acuity, where's Frank?'

'Right there.' I pointed to the corner, where Frank was still splayed out. Our new chihuahua Mocha's head was now resting on his back like a pillow. A pretty high pillow, given their respective sizes. 'Did you pay the guy?'

'Nah, I put it on your tab,' she said, sitting down with the box.

I didn't know I had a tab.

'Is Frank sick?' Amy asked. 'I wondered where he was when he didn't come barreling in to greet us. I thought he must be out for a walk with Pavlik.'

I stood to distribute the plates. 'Fat chance. Since Mocha joined the family Frank has become a couch potato.'

'More like he's becoming the couch,' Sarah said, sliding the pizza onto the coffee table and flipping open the box.

Frank's head went up at the sound. Mocha growled and Frank's head went right back down.

'*Some*body's Chihuahua-whipped.' Sarah pulled out a slice of pizza and waved it in Frank's direction. 'You really want to choose Mexican over Italian, puppy?'

Mocha issued a low throaty warning. Frank didn't move.

Amy was watching them. 'Is it love or fear?'

'A little of each, I think,' I said, offering a plate to Sarah.

'Nah, I'm good.' She sat back with the slice on the palm of her hand. 'Who's to say they're not one and the same?'

'Truly?' Being a good hostess, I put a piece of pizza on a plate and passed it to Amy before I sat down to devour mine. 'You believe love and fear are synonymous? What kind of sick relationships have you been in?'

'None. My life is an open, boring book,' Sarah said. 'I just mean that it doesn't have to be fear of the other person' – she gestured to the giant puppy puddle in the corner – 'or canine, in this case. It can be fear of displeasing them. Which I'm very happy to see Amy doesn't suffer from.'

'Me?' Amy seemed astonished.

'Sure,' Sarah said. 'The easy thing would have been for you to take the ring. Say yes.'

'I did, though. At least in public.'

'And then told him the truth in private, so you wouldn't humiliate him. My point is you could have just taken the ring, married him and gotten divorced like everybody else.'

'That's the easy thing?'

'Sure. Though, who knows? With a little time, you might have changed your mind and married him anyway.'

Amy crossed her arms. 'If I were ready.'

Sarah nodded at me. 'Notice she used the subjunctive instead of the normal past tense?'

I had, in fact.

Amy swung her head toward me. 'What?'

I sighed. 'You said, "If I *were* ready" instead of "If I *was* ready".'

'So?'

'So "were" is the subjunctive form, used for an imaginary hypothesis,' Sarah told her. 'Not something actually in the realm of possibility.'

'The man is dead,' I said. 'If Amy *was* ready to take the ring from him now, it would be a little creepy.'

'True.' Sarah seemed disappointed.

'It was hypothetical because I would never have taken a ring from him ever,' Amy burst out. 'Kip was old. And smelled like garlic.'

'Jacque is older and smells like fish,' I pointed out.

'But he seems younger. Kip is losing his hair and he has my father's fingers.'

'In his freezer?' Sarah asked.

'In his . . .' Amy looked bewildered.

'Ignore her,' I told Amy. 'I know what you mean. I looked down at my own hands the other day and thought, "Oh, my God. I have my mother's hands".'

'Exactly,' Amy said, nodding.

Sarah rolled her eyes. 'Anyway, Amy, I'm glad you were honest with Kip rather than just not giving him an answer for months.'

I know a shot across the bow when I hear one. 'Meaning me? I'm not sure how my relationship got pulled into the middle of this all of a sudden, but you can just lay off Pavlik and me. I've gone ahead and committed to marrying Pavlik.'

'So how big is it?' Sarah asked, snagging another slice.

I was confused. 'How big . . .'

But Sarah wasn't talking to me.

'No idea,' Amy said. 'It had a big square stone and then a bunch of smaller diamonds around it.'

'Not my style,' Sarah said. 'Give me one perfect diamond without all the glitter. Yellow or white gold? Or maybe platinum?'

'Yellow gold.'

Sarah wrinkled her nose. 'Jewelry equivalent of oaked Chardonnay.'

Another shot at me. Though they were kind of the same color.

'Old timey,' Amy said, agreeing with Sarah. 'It wasn't at all what I'd consider modern.'

'Maybe the ring was an heirloom,' I suggested. 'From Kip's mother or grandmother.'

'No, he bought it for me.' Amy frowned. 'He said it had – and would – cost him a lot, like he'd be paying off the debt for a while.'

'Probably trying to make you feel guilty,' Sarah said.

'Maybe it can be returned,' I said, though it didn't seem to matter much now. 'The kids can try. I assume they're his heirs.'

'What about their mother?' Sarah asked. 'Did you know her?'

'I think she died years ago, when Jason and Jayden were little. That was before I knew him.'

'How long *have* you known him, Maggy?' Amy asked, as her phone buzzed. 'I didn't realize you two had even met.'

'We were colleagues at First Financial,' I said as she dug the mobile out of her pocket. 'I didn't know him socially – just through work and the kids' school, of course, Jason and Eric being in the same year.'

Amy looked up from her phone. 'It's Jacque,' she hissed like he was standing on the other side of the door. 'What'll I do?'

'What do you want to do?' I asked.

She hesitated for a second. Then: 'Hello, Jacque?'

FOUR

'She's still in love with him, you know.' Sarah closed the door as the Uber bearing Amy – who'd decided to go home after all – backed out of the driveway.

'In love with Jacque, you mean?' I shoved the empty pizza box into the recycling bin and shook my head. 'I never understood what she saw in him in the first place.'

Sarah plopped down in an overstuffed chair. 'You only say that because he hates you.'

It did make it hard to warm up to the man. 'Jacque is just such a phony. You said it yourself earlier. "Zee this" and "zee that". Who talks like that?'

'Pepé Le Pew?'

'I don't think he's even really French.'

'Pepe's not "really" anything, being a cartoon skunk and all.'

'You know damn well I meant Jacque.' I bent to pick up two licked-clean plates. Mocha and Frank had deigned to join us in time to snag the last two pieces of pizza. 'And what was that phone call all about? If Amy is right, Becky was practically live streaming the proposal last night. What's he doing, calling to beg her to reconsider?'

'More likely he knows Fargo is dead and is reclaiming his territory.'

'I wouldn't put it past the man. The last thing Amy needs is more complications in her love life.'

'Or in Kip's case "don't love" life. Garlic breath, huh?'

'The young,' I said. 'They expect perfection. I remember trying not to fart or burp in front of Ted.'

'I've always just let it all hang out in my relationships,' Sarah said. 'Probably why none of them went anywhere.'

'Farting on the first date probably comes off as a lack of real effort,' I said.

'Yet burping can usually be forgiven. Weird.'

Other than one ill-fated relationship three years ago, I knew almost nothing about Sarah's past relationships. 'Have you ever—'

I was interrupted by the dogs – Frank nearly bowling me over and Mocha tripping me – as the front door opened.

'Daddy's home,' Sarah said, standing. 'Shall I stay to help you grill Pavlik or would you prefer to do that alone?'

'Help me like you just helped me clean up?' I asked.

'A box and a few dishes? I got the pizza, as you'll recall.'

Yet didn't pay for it. 'I think I can handle this alone.'

'Gotcha.' She grabbed her purse. 'See ya,' she told Pavlik as she sailed out the still-open door.

'Something I said?' Pavlik closed the door behind her.

'No, she just wanted to give me a chance to ask you about Amy.'

'Thinks you can get more out of me that way, huh? Which might be entirely possible if that's pizza I smell.'

I looked down at the two plates still in my hands. 'Sorry.'

'You fed my pizza to the dogs?' Pavlik collapsed onto the couch and both dogs stretched out on the floor in front of him.

'They were here, you weren't.'

'I was working.'

'You're absolutely right.' I went to the kitchen and put the plates in the sink. Returning with a clean glass, I picked up the wine bottle. It was empty. I set it back down. 'I can whip you up something.'

'Like what?'

I thought about it. 'Toast and peanut butter?'

'I'll make it.'

Pavlik liked his toast unburned and his peanut butter spread to all four edges. And don't even get me started on how he felt about the errant butter knife contaminating his peanut butter jar. Blending lives is hard.

'No, you sit,' I told him. 'I'll get it.'

'No butter,' he called after me. 'And slather on the peanut butter right after the toast comes out of the toaster, so it melts?'

'Of course,' I said over my shoulder. 'Want some wine?'

'With peanut butter? Who does that?'

Depended on the day. 'Orange juice?'

'Sure.'

As Pavlik munched on his perfectly made toast and sipped his OJ, I settled on the couch next to him. The two dogs still sat in front of him, waiting.

'Huh,' I said. 'They didn't beg when we had the pizza. Just kind of wandered up like they were the next in line at the buffet.'

'And yet you felt obliged to give them my pizza.'

Well, yes. 'I'm starting to worry about Frank. He only eats when Mocha gives him permission.'

Pavlik squinted at the giant fur ball at his feet. 'You starving, Frankie Boy?'

With a 'whump' Frank landed between us, practically launching me off over the arm of the couch.

'Doesn't seem skinny to me,' Pavlik said, wedging his thigh out from under the sheepdog. 'Besides, you have to admit he was putting on a little tonnage.'

I'm sure Frank's eyes, if I could have seen them under his fringe of mussy bangs, narrowed. 'Pavlik's not being judgmental, Frank.'

'I am, a little. But only for his own good.' Pavlik had finished his first piece of toast and moved onto the next. I apparently passed muster.

'Sure.' Lifting the sheepdog's bangs to make eye contact, I found said eyes closed. 'He's sleeping. How is that possible? He just jumped up here.'

'Mocha must have worn him out. Though all I see the two of them do most days is sleep and eat.'

'Maybe they play while we're gone and that's why they're sleeping when we get home. They're exhausted from a full day.'

'A full day of sleeping.'

Maybe, but I had to admit having two dogs was almost less trouble than having one. I hadn't had to throw Frank's slimy tennis ball for weeks. Of course, having Pavlik here helped with that, too. He didn't seem to have an aversion to the slime.

'Anyway,' I said over the top of Frank's furry head. 'What can you tell me about Kip Fargo?'

'The man was shot to death in his own bed.'

That I knew. 'Anybody hear the shot?'

'The neighbor next door said she woke, startled, around one thirty a.m.'

'Did she know by what? Or where it came from?'

'No,' Pavlik said, setting aside his empty plate. 'There was just the single gunshot, so it would have awakened her, but not necessarily enough to identify the sound or locate the source.'

Mocha got on her tippy toes to belly up to the coffee table in order to clean the crumbs from Pavlik's plate. I let her finish and then pushed it to the center of the table. 'Does the coroner have a time of death?'

Pavlik nodded. 'Eleven p.m. to two a.m., so it fits.'

Well after Amy left at nine thirty p.m.

'You said somebody from the office came to check on him and found the body.' The person who finds the body is a logical suspect, as I knew too well. 'Who?'

'Jayden Fargo. And before you ask, the gardener was unloading his truck out front and saw her go into the house.'

I grimaced. 'Jayden found her father.'

'I'm afraid so. You know the family?'

'I worked with Kip at First Financial and Eric went to school with Jason – that's Jayden's older brother.' I was shaking my head. 'Jayden's a couple years younger.'

'I'm sorry,' Pavlik said, giving me a one-armed hug over the top of Mount Sheepdog. 'Sometimes I forget how small Brookhills is.'

'Not even six degrees of separation here,' I said. 'You said earlier that the office sent somebody to the house when they couldn't get hold of him. How could that be Jayden? I thought she'd have gone off to Madison to school with her brother. This should be her freshman year.' The University of Wisconsin's flagship campus about an hour west of us was where Kip had gone as well.

'According to Jayden, she's working at her father's firm while she decides what she wants to major in.'

'You don't believe her?'

Pavlik swallowed a grin. 'I think it's more that her brother is quite a partier and Dad didn't want to bankroll more of the same until Jayden had a plan.'

It didn't seem fair to punish Jayden because her brother was a goof-off. But then I had been an only child and Ted and I had just Eric, so what did I know about siblings? 'If Jayden is living at home, she must have seen her dad after Amy left last night.'

'Sorry, but no. Jayden has an apartment with a couple of friends in Wauwatosa.' A suburb between Brookhills and Milwaukee.

I rolled my shoulders to try to loosen the knot forming between the shoulder blades. 'That's too bad. When was the last time she saw her dad then?'

'At the office yesterday. When Kip didn't show up for a nine o'clock meeting with a client or answer his cell this morning, Jayden went to the house.'

'What time was that?'

'Quarter to ten. Well after the coroner's window for the time of death obviously.'

At least that meant Jayden was in the clear, though it did nothing to help Amy. 'How is Jayden doing?'

'She's upset, as you'd expect. Her brother drove in from Madison this afternoon and is staying with her.'

'Was it . . . awful?'

'The scene, you mean?'

I nodded. The idea of the girl finding her father dead by natural causes was bad enough. But dead by a gunshot wound was . . . yeah, awful. 'Where was he . . .?'

'Head. Entry wound, no exit.'

As terrible as that sounded, it meant the scene in the bedroom might not have been as horrific as it could have been. The inside of Kip's head would have been an entirely different thing. 'Hollow point?'

Hollow point bullets expand once they hit, meaning that after entering the skull, the bullet wouldn't have had the power to exit it like a through-and-through. I'd heard one officer equate what it did inside to a food processor.

'According to ballistics, yes. A hollow point round.'

'There can't be much of the bullet left for matching, assuming you have a gun to match it to.' It was a statement with a question inside of it, namely: do you have the gun?

'Occasionally, you get lucky with hollow points.'

Now that didn't answer my unspoken question, did it? 'Have you found the gun?'

'Why didn't you just ask that?'

'Makes me feel stealthier when I eek it out of you without you realizing.'

'But I always do realize.'

'That does take the fun out of it, I have to admit. Is there a reason you don't want to tell me about the gun?'

'Just to mess with you. Truth is, the killer took the gun with him or her.'

Killers had an annoying habit of doing that. And the 'him or her' didn't go unmarked.

'Amy is not the "her".' I twisted my head to study his face. 'She left at nine thirty – hours before Kip was shot or even went to bed. He walked her to her car.'

'Apparently.'

We were getting to the non-committal portion of the program. 'She said there were two cars out front and she thought there might be somebody in one of them.'

'She told me that, too, but couldn't expand on it.'

'As we talked, she realized the car she passed was a Prius.'

Pavlik's brow furrowed. 'Well, that's convenient. She suddenly just happened to remember?'

'Yes, she did,' I said, sitting up straighter and jostling Frank in the process. He groaned. 'She told me she didn't glance toward the car because she didn't want to engage with anybody in it.'

'You're thinking she subconsciously registered there was somebody in the car?'

'Exactly. No need to avoid eye contact with a parked car. So, I asked if she'd heard the car running, maybe, and she said, no, but she wouldn't have heard anything anyways because . . .' I waved for him to finish my sentence.

'Because it was a Prius. Well done,' Pavlik said, leaning over to give me a kiss. 'Anything else? Color maybe?'

'No, so maybe it was nondescript gray like your Toyota.'

'Silver.' Pavlik had corrected me before on this.

'Right,' I said. 'Still boring.'

'Still unassuming. Which is a good thing in my line of work.'

'When you're not riding in one of those flashy cars with the light on top and siren screaming.'

'Exactly. There's a time and place for all things. The Toyota is for when I don't want to be noticed.'

'Like the Prius wasn't noticed. Is there a gate guard or security cameras?'

'No guard, no gate,' Pavlik said. 'This is old money Brookhills, remember? Apparently, they can't imagine the riff-raff would dare breach their invisible walls.'

Where was Big Brother when you needed him? 'Staff? You mentioned a gardener.'

'Nobody who would be working at one a.m. Are you looking for witnesses or suspects?'

'I'd be happy with either, honestly.'

'I thought so,' Pavlik said. 'As for the gardener, he flew in on a red-eye this morning, which is why he was just getting to Fargo's at ten. Other than that, there's just an older woman who comes by to clean and cook, but she goes home at six.'

'No live-in help?'

'I'm afraid not, duchess.'

Funny. Though I did love me some *Downton Abbey* re-runs. 'Time of death alone should exonerate Amy. She was gone by the time the neighbor heard the shots.'

'Assuming one thirty a.m. was indeed the approximate time of death. And also assuming we can find some corroboration that Amy left at nine thirty.'

'Too bad she didn't take a cab or a ride-share home like she did tonight,' I said, leaning down to give Mocha a scratch.

'Amy was here tonight?'

'Yes, I thought you knew that. Amy, Sarah and me. That's how I found out about the Prius.' I was studying his face. 'Why?'

'I just thought you talked as she left the station or back at the shop. I didn't realize she'd come back here.'

I slid back a smidge. 'Is that a problem?'

He grimaced. 'I'm not sure. It's just a little . . . unorthodox for a murder suspect to be having pizza in the sheriff's living room.'

I opened my mouth and he held up a hand, obviously conflicted. 'I know, it's not really my living room. It's your living room and your house and of course you should invite anybody you want. But . . .'

'It just feels off to you,' I finished for him. 'First of all, it's our house now. We're not married yet, but we've pretty much pledged our troth. What's mine is yours, yada, yada, yada.'

'Romantic.'

'No, Seinfeld,' I said, laying my head against his shoulder – no small feat with the sheepdog still in place between us. 'Though I guess the expression dates back to the 1940s. Seinfeld just populari—'

'So, what's second?' Pavlik interrupted.

'What?'

'You said, "First of all, it's our house now", which I appreciate. Was there a second?'

I wrinkled my nose. 'Can't remember. It was probably something along the lines of, "I can't just not invite people over because they're involved in your murder investigations".'

'You'd have no friends,' he concurred. 'At least the way you're going.'

'My point.' I thought about it. 'Probably.'

'Good enough,' he said. 'I was thinking we were heading toward a major conflagration.'

'Heck, no. Can't fight in front of the kids.' I nodded toward Frank and Mocha.

The fact that Pavlik felt so conflicted was kind of endearing. But he was also right that these types of things were going to lead to conflict. For now, though, I was happy to have my guy and my dogs and be trying to figure out a way to save my barista.

Pavlik must have been thinking of Amy, too, and wasn't about to let our little detour deter him from the pursuit of information. We were made for each other. 'Amy didn't say anything about returning to the Fargo house?'

'Last night? No. Why would she have gone back?'

'To apologize maybe?'

'For what? Bruising his ego?'

'Maybe. I'm sure that with the big deal proposal at the restaurant, her turning him down just minutes later was a blow. Maybe she felt badly.'

'I don't think she would go back. If anything, she'd have sent a text.'

'To apologize for dumping him. That's kind of cold, don't you think?'

'Beats going back to see him and raising his hopes again.'

'I guess,' Pavlik said. 'Besides, this guy moved in the best circles, had a successful business, lots of prestigious clients, friends. I'm sure he'd have moved on.'

If he hadn't died. 'As easy as that?'

'They'd known each other all of three months,' Pavlik said, sitting back. 'Amy felt rushed and that's understandable. On Fargo's side, he was a good deal older than her and starting to feel it, by all accounts. He probably just wanted to seal the deal. It's natural.'

Natural that the 'old' guy – pretty much Pavlik's age as well as my own – was out trying to bag the younger woman.

Time to steer the subject toward another possible subject: Jacque. 'Have you considered Jacque Oui?'

'Amy's former boyfriend?'

I agreed with Sarah that Amy still loved Jacque. And, presumably, Jacque loved Amy. However, I didn't love Jacque. 'Yes. He called her.'

'When?' I had Pavlik's attention. 'Where?'

'Here. Tonight.'

'Why?'

'I don't know.' Which was killing me. 'She took the call outside and then stuck her head in to say she'd called for a ride home.'

'What do you know about their break-up?'

I shrugged. 'Not as much as I'd like to. Apparently it happened three months ago.'

'About the time Amy started seeing Fargo.'

'Yes, but that was the effect of the break-up, not the cause. Sarah says Amy and Jacque were already "having trouble" when she introduced her to Kip in early July.'

'It was Sarah who introduced them?'

'Yes. She and Kip had a meeting at the shop to discuss selling Kingston Realty and Amy was there.' And the rest was history. Or at least was now.

'Who broke up with whom?'

'I asked that. Amy says she broke up with Jacque.'

'Oui couldn't be happy about that. He's even older than Fargo.'

'Meaning more middle-aged angst, which apparently sent him to France.'

Pavlik sank back, disappointed. 'Oui is in France then.'

I kept the theory alive. 'Not to worry. He's back now.'

Pavlik grinned. 'You act like I'm trying to pin it on him.'

'No, I act like *I'm* trying to pin it on him. I never really liked Jacque.'

'Because he criticizes your cooking?'

'That's putting it mildly. He refuses to sell me fish, claiming – loudly, I might add, and in the middle of the store – that I'll incinerate it.'

'You did set the bread on fire that time we had him and Amy over.'

'I was going for crusty crostini. I had no idea that bread could actually burst into flames like that.'

'Nor I,' Pavlik said, his tone as dry as my crostini before it combusted.

'Anyway, count your blessings,' I continued with a grin. 'My family is Norwegian. I could be soaking fish in lye and feeding it to you instead of incinerating it.'

Pavlik held up his hands in innocence. 'Hey, my mom's side is from the land of gefilte fish. I don't judge.'

'Jacque does.'

Pavlik seemed to stifle a grin. 'Your working theory is that Oui killed Fargo?'

'Kip was a threat. He'd proposed and Jacque had no way of knowing last night that Amy had turned him down.'

'If she did.'

'She did. She told you that.'

'Yet that's not what the people we interviewed at the restaurant said. According to their waiter, they hugged and ordered champagne.'

'Kip apparently made it a very public proposal. Amy didn't have the heart to turn him down on the spot in front of everyone. She told him later in private.'

'So she said.'

If she did. So she said. 'You're prevaricating.'

'You think so?'

I rest my case. 'I know so. That's three words, too.'

He had the grace to grin. 'You know that I can't take one person's word for anything. Even Amy's. Or especially Amy's, given she's a friend.'

'I know.'

'The problem is that there are lots of people who swear they were every bit the happy, newly engaged couple when they left the restaurant. We even have video.'

I pursed my lips. 'From Becky somebody?'

'Rebecca Ronstadt. How did you know?'

'She's a long-time cashier at Schultz's Market. Amy saw her at the restaurant.'

'Which is why you think Jacque knew about the proposal and reacted badly?'

'You said it yourself. It was very public. Very celebrative. Can you imagine how Jacque must have felt when he saw the video?'

'But do we know he saw it?'

'No, but Amy assumes he did, which is good enough for me. For all we know Becky was streaming it live.'

Pavlik shook his head. 'It sounds kind of cruel. Does your boss thank you for sending live video of another guy proposing to his girlfriend?'

'I said Becky worked for Jacque for a long time. He isn't a picnic to be around short-term – I can't imagine what he's like over years. Maybe that's why Amy said the woman was smiling as she texted.'

'You're saying Ronstadt didn't like her boss. Or, alternatively, she doesn't like Amy.'

'Or just enjoys being a busybody and causing trouble. But my point is that the proposal – assuming he knew about it, as we think – gives Jacque a motive to go to Kip's house last night.'

'I suppose he might have assumed Amy was there, as well.'

I hadn't thought of that. 'I can't imagine Jacque intending Amy any harm, but I guess he might have gone to confront them.'

'And instead of finding them both there in bed at one a.m. he found Fargo sleeping alone and still goes ahead and shoots him?'

'Wouldn't you be tempted? I mean, empty house, guy's asleep. One pull of the trigger. Nobody's the wiser and Jacque gets the girl.'

But Pavlik seemed hung up on my first sentence. 'Did you honestly just ask me if I'd be tempted? Of course, I wouldn't be tempted.'

Apparently Pavlik's love did know its bounds. I tried not to be hurt. 'But you're not Jacque.'

'No. I'm not.'

'But think of it, Pavlik; all very dramatic, all very French. The rival to Amy's affections is dead, so what's left but for Jacque to call Amy and offer a shoulder to cry on and his cravat to wipe her tears.'

'Oui wears a cravat?'

'No. But a cravat is French.'

'Actually, I think it's Croat.' Pavlik's phone signaled a text message and he picked it up. 'If Amy turned down Fargo, like you say, Oui doesn't have a motive.'

'But he didn't know that,' I told him as he punched up his messages. 'And if you truly don't believe she turned him down – if she and Kip were the happy, newly engaged couple – why would she have left right after getting back from dinner?'

'If she did.'

Yeah, yeah, yeah. 'Nine thirty is early enough that somebody must have seen her leave. Or it was on security camera.'

'I told you – no security cameras.'

'Truly? Where can you go today where there aren't security cameras?'

'Poplar Gardens. They value their privacy.'

'Privacy isn't the only thing valuable there, I hear. Sarah probably would have killed for the Fargo listing. Not literally, of course.'

'For once, neither you nor she is a suspect. Unless you know something I don't.'

'What I know,' I said, getting up to put his licked-clean plate in the dishwasher, 'is that Amy didn't have anything to do with Kip's death. And I think you know it, too.'

'We will see.'

'Please,' I said. 'Enough of that.'

'No, I really mean we will see.' He held up his phone. 'We've located the Prius and its driver.'

FIVE

A my called me at the shop as I prepared to open the
next morning. 'I'm sorry, Maggy – could you do
without me today? I'm not sure I can get out of bed,
much less face people.'

The inquiring minds of Brookhills were sometimes insa-
tiable. 'Don't worry about it, Amy.' I heard a crash and what
sounded like a voice in the background on the other end
of the line. 'Did you go home to your folks?'

I knew the Capreses lived in a northern suburb of
Milwaukee.

'No, no. That was just television.'

Hmm. 'Well, you go back to bed, there's no reason for you
to be here. Sarah and I can handle it.'

Or we could, if Sarah were there. 'You're sleeping?' I
demanded when she finally called some four hours later in
response to half a dozen voicemail and text messages I'd left.
'It's ten o'clock. I've been here all by myself since opening.
And I'm afraid we're going to hear from some ticked customers
who couldn't get their orders before their trains boarded.'

There were advantages and disadvantages to being housed
in a commuter train depot. The advantage was the charm and
built-in clientele each morning and evening. The disadvantage
was they all arrived at once and were in a hurry. When there
were two of us, we could set up a separate brewed coffee line.
Today somebody who just wanted a simple 'cuppa joe' had
to wait behind the person who wanted a 'large three-shot
nonfat no foam extra hot latte'.

'How should I know you were alone? Amy is scheduled to
work from when we open to noon.'

'I know,' I said, picking up my own large three-shot nonfat
no foam extra hot latte. Which was cold, like most of the
drinks we made for ourselves throughout the day. 'I guess
we should have realized she wouldn't be up to it. She said

she called and left a message at both our houses early this morning before she called here. Didn't you get it?'

'I was sleeping. Obviously.'

Obviously. 'Well, will you get up now, please, and come help me? For the afternoon rush, if nothing else.'

'I suppose.'

'You don't have to sound so grudging about it. Have a little sympathy – our barista is suspected of murder.'

'If I got out of bed early every time one of us was accused of murder – or accused somebody else of it – I'd never get any sleep.'

Blah, blah, blah. 'Get up!'

'OK, fine. I'll be in, but I have to stop at the bank on the way.'

'Gotcha.'

As I went to hang up, Eric's picture flashed onto the phone. I clicked. 'Hi, sweetie.'

'Hi, Mom.' I like to think of Eric as my best work. My son even let me call him sweetie at the age of twenty. Good thing, since I'd probably still be doing it when he was sixty. 'Are you at the shop?'

'Yup, but it's the morning lull. How's the work on your paper going?'

'On ancestry? I already turned that in.'

'I'm sorry I couldn't be more help on my side. My folks just never talked about that stuff. I had "aunts" and "uncles", but I'm not even sure they're related.'

'You did the same thing to me, you know,' my son told me. 'All your and Dad's friends were "aunt" this and "uncle" that.'

'Well, you couldn't call them by their first names and it seemed easier than Mr or Mrs Whatever. You must have thought you had a huge family, when it's really quite small – at least on my side.'

'You'd be surprised. I'm on this genealogy site now, and they notify me when I have a new DNA match.'

'Really?' I took a sip of the cold latte and made a face nobody could see. 'Then what do you do?'

'You can contact them.'

Contact strangers? To talk about family? My very Norwegian-ness quaked at the idea. 'Isn't that a little intrusive?'

'Not really. I mean, people are on the site in the first place so they can find out more about where they came from. You indicate whether you're willing to be contacted and decide how much information you'll share.'

'How much did you share?'

'How much did I have?' he asked. 'I mean, "I think my maternal grandparents came from Norway sometime" isn't exactly a jackpot of info.'

'I suppose not.'

'You should do the DNA testing, Mom. We'll show up as parent/child.'

'Not a surprise, since I saw you emerge.'

'Mommmmmm,' as only a disgusted child can say it. 'That's gross.'

'You have no idea.'

Eric shifted the subject, much as I did when Sarah was annoying. 'Do you know if you're a hundred percent Norwegian?'

'I always heard both my mom and dad's sides came from Norway, but . . .' I shrugged, like he should be able to hear me.

'You'd know if you did your DNA. It's not like we can ask Grandma and Grandpa.'

'I know,' I said. 'You always think you'll have time to ask these things, and then you don't.'

'I get it. So before you kick off, I have a couple of questions for you.'

I grinned. 'Mr Sensitivity. Go ahead.'

'I'm showing up as like thirty percent western European, like Germany, France, Switzerland. Would that be from your side or Dad's?'

'I honestly don't know. Your dad's name, Thorsen, is of Norwegian derivation.' I hadn't changed back to my maiden name after the divorce, mostly because I wanted my name to remain the same as Eric's. 'I don't know about your grand-mother on your dad's side. Have you asked him?'

'Yeah, and he was going to go through some boxes of old stuff, but I don't think he's had a chance. Mia is keeping him busy.'

Mia was Eric's half-sister, an adorable one-year-old, with Ted's subsequent wife Rachel. Who was in jail. The wife, not the baby. 'I'm sure Dad has his hands full. As for my side, you probably know more than I do.'

'We'll get on the computer, and I'll show you it all next time I see you. I get emails practically daily saying this person is like my second cousin or third or fourth. And I've never even heard of them. It's awesome.'

'Can't wait to see it.' I was lying. Sarah had cousins and they were nothing but trouble.

'I'm going to send you a DNA kit for your birthday.' Eric wasn't going to give up. 'It gives you a sense of self, you know? Plus, wouldn't you like to know if you're genetically prone to certain diseases and stuff? And maybe find new relatives?'

I wasn't sure how much information was too much. The 'self', family and diseases I was already aware of seemed plenty to keep me busy for the next forty years. 'I'll think about it.'

The door chimes jangled as Eric let me off the hook and we hung up. A blonde woman with what looked like a lawyer's briefcase sailed in.

'Morning!' I said. 'What can I get you?'

'Are you Maggy?'

'I am.' Until DNA told me otherwise.

The woman made her way to the counter quickly, her hand out. 'I'm Catherine Barry. The JavaDo rep?'

She said it like I should know. 'Pleased to meet you, Catherine. Are you here to see Amy or Sarah? I'm afraid neither of them is here right now.'

'Actually, Sarah set up an appointment for me to sit down with you. She didn't tell you?'

No, of course she didn't. And scheduled it for a morning she wouldn't be here. That explained why she hadn't been answering her phone.

'She must have forgotten,' I told Catherine. 'I'm afraid I'm here alone holding down the fort. We've had a death—'

'I heard about Kip Fargo and I'm quite honestly devasted.' She collapsed into a chair at the nearest table, setting her case on the floor. 'What a terrible waste.'

'You know Kip, too?' I seemed to be the odd person out these days.

'Kip is the one who recommended Uncommon Grounds as a possible exclusive dealership for JavaDo in the area.'

She made it sound like we should be honored she'd allow us to sell her espresso machines in our store. 'And introduced you to Sarah?'

'And Amy,' Catherine said, unlatching her case and thumbing through before pulling out a file. 'That was . . . let's see, two months ago? I think Sarah said you were out of the country.'

And I think Sarah was lying. She'd likely planned the meeting for a day I was off, just as she'd planned this one for when she was.

'Kip and I go way back,' Catherine was saying. 'How do you – did you – know him?'

'We both worked at First Financial.'

'Really? That's where I met him, too.' She was smiling, happy to have found something we had in common to build upon.

'Did you work there, as well?' I asked.

'No, but First Financial's Private Banking division handled my family's accounts and Kip's as well. We met at one of the events.'

Private banking was what we called the area that dealt with only the bank's wealthiest clients. Apparently, the run-of-the-mill bank customer has no need for privacy.

I studied Catherine. She was a gorgeous woman of indeterminate age – the kind of 'indeterminate' that money can buy.

I would have thought she was far more Kip's type than Amy was, but then what did I really know?

Not enough. And chances were Catherine could tell me more. I circled from behind the service counter to sit across from her. 'And Kip still advises you on partnerships, investments and such?' Or did.

She flushed. 'I handle my own investments, but Kip was a genius when it came to relationships.'

Interesting. 'How so?'

She must have read something on my face and smiled. 'Not that kind of relationship, though Kip and I did have a go at one point. I prefer younger men these days.'

'Good for you,' was all I could think of to say.

'It is,' she said, with a grin. 'Very good for me. But my business relationship with Kip has been good, too. He helped me acquire JavaDo and find retail outlets like yours to act as dealers. It was a very symbiotic relationship – a win/win.'

Segue accomplished, Catherine reached down and slid out a brochure. 'Have you had an opportunity to try out the C42?' She tapped her glossy fingernail on the equally glossy photo on the front of the brochure.

'Amy demonstrated it for me,' I said, nodding at the real thing on the counter. 'But we haven't had time to discuss the idea further given Kip's death—'

'Amy must be totally devastated. I understand they'd just gotten engaged.'

Unlike Pavlik, I took Amy at her word that she'd rejected Kip's proposal. Catherine apparently didn't know that. 'Where did you hear that?'

The question must have come off as accusatory, because she shifted in her chair before answering. 'I . . . uh, well, to be honest, Kip told me he was proposing at dinner on Wednesday night. I just assumed he'd done it.'

'He did.' I didn't see any reason to tell Catherine how Amy had answered.

'Damn.' Catherine twisted the diamond stud in her ear. 'Maybe it would have been better if he'd never gotten the chance. To have all the joy and excitement of the engagement and then to come crashing down like that the very next morning.'

'It was a terrible shock.'

'At least she knows how he felt about her, I guess. It—'

The sound of feet came pounding up the side stairs and the door from the train platform swung open, hitting the wall hard.

Before I could get up to see who was causing the ruckus, the troublemaker rounded the corner. 'That bastard!'

'Which bastard?' I asked mildly. Sarah's tantrums weren't an everyday occurrence, but they did happen often enough for me to take them in my stride. 'We do have a customer, you know.' I gestured toward Catherine.

'The dead bastard.' Sarah stomped over to the table. 'And Catherine isn't a customer.'

'No, she's the meeting you set up without telling me.'

'Wah, wah, wah. I gave you an opportunity to meet a nice woman and learn something. Maybe make some money. Sue me.'

It was difficult to contest any of those points, at least with the 'nice woman' sitting right there. 'I just don't like to be ambushed. No offence,' I assured Catherine.

'None taken.'

Sarah was looking back and forth, back and forth between us. 'If you two are done making nice-nice, can we get back to me?'

I swept my hand in a well, go ahead gesture and she did. 'I just came from First Financial and there's something going on with the investment account Kip set up there for me. I can't access it online and even First Financial can't – or won't – give me a balance.'

'You were able to get into it before?' I asked. 'Online I mean?'

'Yes, of course. I'd sign in and it popped right up along with my checking and savings accounts. It's not showing up anymore.'

'I'm sure it's just a bank computer glitch.' The JavaDo rep stood, shoving her file folder hurriedly back in her case and slid a card across the table to me. 'I should be going and let you two talk. I'll be in touch.'

'Some glitch,' Sarah said, as the door closed behind Catherine.

'Did she seem uncomfortable all of a sudden?' I asked, craning my neck to see the woman getting into her car out front.

'Would you mind focusing on me for just one second? Every dollar from the sale of Kingston Realty is in that account, and I can't get into it. Hell, I can't even see it.'

She plopped down in the chair next to me. 'One point five million dollars. Gone.'

SIX

'**Y**ou made a million and a half on Kingston Realty.'
I'd said it before I'd called Pavlik to ask about
Fargo's business accounts, and now I was repeating
it. It seemed like a lot of money.

The lunch and early afternoon crowd had come and gone
and now we were waiting for the after-work commuter trains
to chug into the station. We were back at our table.

'Kingston Realty represents twenty years of my life, Maggy.
It's really not that much.'

It was to me, especially when you considered that Sarah
also had made a very nice living off sales commissions over
those twenty years. What would the purchaser of Kingston
Realty be buying exactly? The name, of course, and the reputation of the firm. Those had value. What else? Probably a
mailing list. Yard signs.

No matter how you cut it, it seemed like Kip had brokered
a good deal for Sarah. If only she could find the money.

'Catherine didn't seem to think it was a big deal,' I said.
'But then she was a Private Banking client, so I assume she
comes from money.'

'Private Banking?'

'For "special"' – finger quotes – 'clients. Meaning the ones
with the most money. Personalized services, investments,
trusts. In the old days there was even a Women's Department,
that just dealt with the spouses.'

'Who were all women at the time? What did the bank do
for them? Schedule facials? Massages?'

'Got me. That was before my time.'

'The bad ol' days,' Sarah said. 'So, what did Pavlik say again?'

'I told you. He said that Kip's accounts are frozen and that
may be why you couldn't get to the one he set up for you.'

'Maybe,' Sarah said. 'But frozen and invisible seem two
entirely different things. What else did he tell you, Maggy?'

'Pretty much nothing.' I shrugged. 'I think he's clamming up on me.'

'Because of Amy being a suspect?'

'And you, now.'

'I'm a suspect? If I could kill him now, I would, but I didn't even know my money was missing until this morning.'

'If it *is* missing. Let's not jump to conclusions,' I said. 'It's probably not surprising that Kip's accounts are frozen. That can happen even with a natural death until an executor is appointed and all. But in the case of a murder, if they're looking into his financials that . . .'

Sarah waited for a moment, before letting out an exasperated, 'That *what*?'

'That may mean they've found some improprieties. Which would open up a whole new area of investigation. And suspects.'

'Like me?'

'Like anybody he might have cheated who knows about it.'

'Which I didn't,' Sarah said.

So she says, I could hear Pavlik saying. I shook my head.

'What?' Sarah demanded again.

'Just hearing voices.'

'Kip stole Sarah's money?' Amy asked. After closing, we'd stopped at our barista's apartment to see how she was doing.

'We don't know that,' I said.

'Well, I know that I don't have it.' Sarah was looking around. 'And you don't have furniture.'

'I don't sit much,' Amy said, apologetically. 'And I prefer the floor to a chair.'

'Bean bags are fine,' I said, before Sarah could tell her what she preferred. 'There's a yoga mat there, Sarah.'

'Have you called the police?' Amy asked, settling into lotus position. 'About your money, I mean.'

Sarah sank down onto a blue yoga mat and tried to cross her legs. 'Maggy called Pavlik.'

'What did he say?'

'Only that the accounts were frozen, pending investigation,' I told her as I took a yellow bean bag. 'Sarah is getting ahead of herself.'

'I'm getting ahead of myself?' Sarah asked incredulously. 'You're the one who already has me down as a suspect.'

'You and anybody else he bilked. If he did bilk anybody. I'm just trying to help Amy. The more suspects the better.'

'Even if they include me?' She gave up on the leg-crossing.

'But why would Kip cheat his clients?' Amy asked. 'He's rich in his own right.'

'Doesn't mean he's not a crook.' Sarah's opinion of Kip had changed dramatically over the last day. 'Them that's got gets. Or takes.'

'Maybe.' Amy was staring out the window.

'What?' I asked, following her gaze. 'Is somebody here?'

'I thought I heard a car door.'

That reminded me of something. 'Was Jacque here this morning?'

Amy started. 'I'm sorry, what?'

'Jacque called last night and this morning I could swear I heard somebody who was also swearing. Maybe he stubbed his toe?'

'Geez,' Amy said, glancing around uncomfortably. 'Do you have a camera in here?'

'No, just good ears. And there's only one person I can imagine who would say, "*Sacrebleu*".'

'My God,' Sarah said, 'what a little idiot you are.'

'I'm not an idiot.' Now her legs *and* arms were crossed.

'That's right,' I told Sarah. 'After all, Amy was hurting and Jacque offered comfort. The only stupid thing that Amy did was to take it.'

'But I—'

'Kip proposed two nights ago,' I said.

'And I turned him down.' The arms stayed folded.

'Even if you felt absolutely nothing for him,' I said, 'it doesn't change the fact that the man was murdered.'

'And you may have slept with the murderer last night,' Sarah told her.

'Jacque?'

Bingo. No wonder Amy hadn't been able to get out of bed. 'Yes, Jacque. If you're right and Becky was sending him videos from the restaurant, Jacque knew that Kip proposed, and he thought that you accepted. Maybe he went to the house in order to confront him. When he found him asleep, Jacque—'

'*Shot* him? That's ridiculous.'

'No more ridiculous than your doing it,' Sarah reminded her. 'Or me. Sleeping with Jacque right now is a terrible idea.'

I was glancing around. 'He's not here now is he?'

'I . . . no, I told him to go home when you called to say you were coming over.'

'Great,' Sarah said. 'We're your staunchest allies, your first line of defense—'

'Not to mention your employers,' I added for no particular reason.

'And you're lying to us?' Sarah asked.

'I didn't lie,' Amy said defensively. 'I . . . I just didn't tell you.'

There was a tentative tap at the door.

I rolled my eyes. 'Better let him in.'

Chastened, she went to the door and turned the knob to swing open the door. 'Jacque, I—'

She stopped. 'Please. Come in.'

As Amy swung the door wide, a girl walked in.

SEVEN

'Jayden,' I exclaimed, struggling to my feet to take the girl's hands in mine. 'I'm so sorry.'

Jayden Fargo was a few inches taller and a few years older than the last time I'd seen her, but there was no mistaking the thick, copper-blonde hair and blue eyes, now filled with tears. 'Maggy, I'm so glad you're here – I've been so upset.'

I didn't know why she was happy to see me in particular. But if my being there helped in some way, I was glad, too.

'Come in and sit down,' Amy said, pulling up a bright-blue bean bag. 'Would you like something to drink?'

'No, I'm fine,' Jayden said, folding her long legs under her neatly as she collapsed onto the bean bag. 'Actually, I'm not fine, but I'm also not thirsty. Are *you* OK?'

Amy's own eyes teared. 'It's so sweet of you to worry about me at a time like this.'

'You lost him, too.'

Amy's face reddened, and her mouth opened, but blessedly Jayden was still talking. 'Daddy told me and Jason at lunch on Wednesday that he was going to propose. And now . . . I can't believe they actually think you might have killed him.'

The color in Amy's face drained away and she knelt next to the girl to take her hand. 'I'm so sorry, Jayden. It was just so soon and I—'

'It did seem fast,' Jayden said. 'But like I told Jason, the important thing is you made Daddy happy. I just didn't know what you'd say, given the age difference and all. In fact, when I saw him lying there . . . It's stupid, but I couldn't help but wonder if maybe you'd said no, and—' She broke off, fighting sobs.

'But I did say no, Jayden.' Amy said, looking stricken. 'I told your father I wouldn't marry him.'

'I know. The police told me.' The girl squeezed her hand. 'It's OK.'

'It doesn't feel OK,' Amy said in a whisper, looking down at their entwined hands.

Sarah cleared her throat. 'You sure nobody wants a drink?'

'I have Aperol,' Amy said, getting up hastily. 'How about I make us all spritzes?'

I had no idea what that was, but since Jayden was nodding, I joined in.

'Got any vodka?' Sarah asked.

'You finished it the last time you were here,' Amy said. 'I'm afraid it's spritzes or beer.'

'What kind?' Sarah asked, following her. 'If you've got . . .'

I turned to Jayden as the other two disappeared into the kitchen to check out the supply of brewskies. 'It's not stupid to have wondered if your dad had killed himself when you found him, Jayden. It's the more likely bet in a gun death.' I felt awful the moment I said it, but Jayden seemed a little buoyed.

'Really?' The girl swiped at her nose. 'I felt guilty even thinking it, but Daddy has been feeling his age lately – complaining about losing his hair and all. Amy . . . well, I think she made him feel young again. Like I started to say, I was afraid that she turned him down and he did something stupid.' She laughed, though there was no humor in it. 'Kind of dumb to feel better that somebody killed my father, I guess, than that he killed himself.'

'Not dumb at all,' I said, lowering myself onto my own bean bag. 'This way, your dad is still the person who you thought he was. And it's all right to be angry at the person who took him away from you.'

'Rather than angry at him?'

'At him, or Amy, or whoever else might have done some-thing to upset him. Even yourself for not realizing he was troubled.'

'Sure, suicide leaves questions, but so does homicide.' Beer bottle in hand, Sarah held the door into the kitchen open for Amy, who was balancing a tray of drinks. 'Namely who could have killed him? There's Amy, of course, and who else?'

'Ouch,' Amy said, setting down the tray to hand me a short

glass filled with ice and something reddish brown. 'Is there a knife sticking out of my back?'

Jayden giggled and then slapped her hand over her mouth. 'I can't believe I laughed.'

Sarah handed her a glass from the tray. 'You're hysterical. Drink this.'

'What is it?' I took a sip.

'Aperol, Prosecco and a splash of soda,' Amy said. 'Oh, and I put a slice of orange in it.'

'You don't have chairs,' Sarah said, taking a swig from her bottle, 'yet you stock Aperol, whatever the hell that is, with all that other crap?'

'Aperol is an Italian aperitif like Campari.' Jayden took a sip.

'Oh, shit!' I said, reaching over to stop her. 'You're what? Nineteen? You're not supposed to be drinking.'

'And yet she is,' Sarah said. 'We'll send her home in a taxi.'

'I Ubered over,' Jayden said. 'Besides, I just turned twenty-one.'

I wasn't sure I believed her, but it was good to see the girl relaxed enough to lie about her age. 'Is Jason home?'

'He drove back yesterday.'

'Are you staying at the house or your apartment tonight?' I asked.

'The guest house. Jason, too. The police won't let us into the main house, but I . . . just want to be close.'

'How long will they keep the house off limits, Maggy?' Amy turned to Jayden. 'She's marrying the sheriff, you know.'

'I do,' Jayden said. 'That's why I was glad to see her here. I figured she was helping you.'

'I'm afraid I can't influence an investigation,' I told Jayden.

'But she can inform on it,' Sarah said.

'*No*, I can't,' I said firmly. 'Pavlik doesn't tell me more than he tells the public.' Mostly.

Jayden looked crestfallen.

'I do think your house will be off limits until the crime scene technicians are done,' I told her. 'Maybe another day or so?'

'Well, that will be good. Jason and his girlfriend were doing it when I left and the wall between his bedroom and mine isn't all that soundproof.'

Ugh. I didn't want to be a prude, but 'doing it' a few hundred yards from where your father was killed seemed messed up.

'A two-bedroom guest house?' Sarah always asking the pertinent question. 'Yours is one of the few houses I haven't been inside in Poplar Gardens. To my knowledge it's never been on the market.'

Sarah was probably kicking herself for selling the realty business just when the Fargo gem might be coming onto the market. Not that she couldn't represent them personally, of course. She just couldn't use one of her Kingston Realty signs.

'It's stayed in the family since my grandfather built it,' Jayden told her.

'If you and Jason decide to sell it, I'd be happy to give you a market estimate.'

'Geez, Sarah,' I said.

'What? You want them taken by some unscrupulous agent?'

'Kip hasn't been dead forty-eight hours.'

'It's OK,' Jayden said. 'You're welcome to come by the house and look, Sarah. My dad and brother are all about the financial stuff – what things are worth and all. I never really cared much, but I guess I'll need to harden up.'

'No, you needn't,' Amy said, leaning over to touch her arm. 'You need to stay you.'

'Thanks.' Jayden sniffled and then cleared her throat. 'So Maggy, how can we help Amy? I hate that this is happening to her.'

I cocked my head. 'Amy left your dad at nine thirty and I'm certain that will be proved very shortly, with or without me.'

Pavlik had told me only that the Prius owner was a woman last night, and I'd forgotten to ask for an update when I'd called him about Sarah's frozen account. Still, even if the woman hadn't been in the car and there were no witnesses to Amy's leaving, there was no reason to raise the fear level in the room any higher than it already was.

'That would be wonderful,' Jayden said. 'It's been so awful thinking that an innocent person can be accused like that.'

'The sheriff just has to eliminate all the suspects, one by one,' I said. 'It's nothing personal.'

'Yeah,' Sarah said. 'You and Jason will probably be next.'

Jayden's eyes flew open. 'Us?'

I held up my hand. 'It's just routine. They always look at the family, but Jason was in Madison and we know there's a witness who saw you arrive at the house long after your dad died.'

'Who?'

'Your gardener.'

'Oh, yes. Rafael, of course.' The girl looked relieved. 'He even called nine-one-one for me because I was shaking so badly.'

'See, you don't have anything to worry about,' Amy assured her. 'You have one more witness than I have.'

I didn't mention the Prius driver had been found, not wanting to give Amy false hope until I knew she was truly off the hook.

'I just don't understand why somebody would want to kill my dad,' Jayden said.

'Was anything stolen?' I asked. 'Pavlik said there was "disarray", but that could mean anything.'

'I remember the lamp on the end table in the living room was on the floor,' Jayden said. 'I picked it up when I was calling out for my dad. Then when I went into the bedroom, I saw the mirror on the dresser across the room was broken and a drawer left open. That's when I turned toward the bed and . . .' She took a deep, shaky breath. 'The sheriff did ask if I could tell whether anything was taken, but I told them to talk to Jason when he got home. I didn't want to go back in.' She shivered.

'Your dad might have had an inventory,' Sarah said. 'For insurance purposes.'

'Maybe,' Jayden said. 'Jason would probably know that, too.'

I was thinking about the mirror and the lamp. Pavlik had said there was just the single shot. Since there was no exit wound, the bullet that killed Kip hadn't continued on to break the mirror. And what about the lamp? Toppled in a rush to leave? 'Did you notice any open doors or windows?'

'I had to unlock the front door to get in,' Jayden said, thinking back. 'I can't say about the rest of the doors, though, because I didn't try them. The bedroom windows were closed. I remember the sheer curtains were . . .' She trailed off.

'Were what?' Amy asked gently.

The girl was looking out Amy's front window into the gathering dark. 'White. I just remember how very white they were.'

Most likely in contrast to the red stain on the sheet or pillow under her father's head. Just because there was no exit wound, didn't mean there wouldn't be blood.

'Is there anybody outside of the family who stands to gain from your father's death?'

'Outside the family?' Jayden repeated, her cheeks flaming a bit. 'You mean besides Jason and me?'

'Well, yes.' I was embarrassed, but it had to be asked. 'A business partner maybe?'

'Of course,' Jayden said.

She said it in a puzzled tone, like it was something we should know. Or at the very least Amy, who she now turned to, should know. 'Daddy didn't tell you?'

Amy went to sit back on her bean bag and nearly toppled. 'Tell me what?' she asked, righting herself.

'That he'd changed his will.' Jayden seemed to be trying to reason it out. 'I'm surprised he didn't tell you when he proposed, but I suppose he wanted it to be a surprise.'

I was almost afraid to ask, but I did anyway. 'Changed his will how?'

'Adding Amy, of course,' she said. 'She's his main beneficiary.'

EIGHT

'I swear that Amy was as astonished as we were,' I said to Pavlik in bed later that night. We were spooning. Frank and Mocha were not with us. 'She had no idea.'

'That's entirely possible.' He pulled me closer.

Pavlik's willingness to believe me on face value led me to believe he, once again, knew more than I did. 'You talked to the woman in the Prius, didn't you?' I snuggled my butt closer. 'Tell me about her.'

'No.' He was nuzzling the back of my neck.

'No, not this second because you want to do something else, or no period.'

'No period. For now.'

I squiggled away and turned to face him. 'Seriously?'

'Seriously. But I still want to do something else.' He reached out and hooked me around the waist, drawing me toward him.

'I'm not sure I can do that,' I said. 'You're withholding information.'

'So you're going to withhold sex?'

I was thinking about it. 'Why won't you tell me? This Prius driver could exonerate Amy. She might even be a suspect herself, right? I mean, what was she doing out there, just sitting in her car.'

'Right.' He was nuzzling again.

'Can you at least tell me her name?'

'Nope.'

'Because I would know her?'

Now he pulled back. 'Don't you know everybody in town?'

'Then it's a local,' I said, sitting up. 'Age?'

'Old enough to drive a car, and I'm not going to play twenty questions.'

I wouldn't need twenty. Female and maybe young, given the 'old enough to drive' comment. 'Jayden?'

'You're saying Fargo didn't stop to talk to his own daughter? Or Amy didn't recognize her?'

Maybe not Jayden. Then who? There were only so many females in the script. 'The housekeeper, what's-her-name?'

'You don't know her name? You disappoint me.'

'It's early days,' I said. 'It *was* her?'

'The housekeeper is seventy-nine years old, widowed, loves mystery novels and has cataracts so she can't drive at night. She was long gone before they got back from the restaurant Wednesday night and Thursdays are her days off. Happy?'

'Absolutely not.'

He sighed. 'I should have told you she was a hot blonde who had a thing for Fargo, just to get you to lay off.'

'And then you could lay on?'

'Crass, but kind of cute.' He moved an errant strand of hair off my forehead and kissed me.

'Are you going to tell me?'

'Nope.'

'Fine, you win.' I kissed him back and then we both won. Twice.

'You sure you didn't recognize her?' I asked Amy the next day as we were cleaning up from the Saturday morning rush.

'I told you, I purposely didn't look at her.' She sniffed the air. 'Black Opium – nice.'

I shoved a chair in. 'Not if you take a bath in it. Anyway, I inferred from what Pavlik said that the Prius driver is somebody we would know, or at least a local. I don't know why he won't tell me.'

'Maybe because one of your friends is already a suspect and he doesn't want to pile on.'

'Actually, two, if you include Sarah.' I swung open the front door to air out the place and turned. 'Assuming her money really is gone.'

'You truly believe that Kip stole it? Why? He has money of his own.'

'You can never have enough.'

The voice had come from behind me and I jumped to see Mary Callahan, Brookhills librarian, CPA and tax-preparer.

Maybe because of the triple role, she seemed to know everything that went on in Brookhills.

'Where in the world did you come from?' I asked, as she brushed past me and into Uncommon Grounds.

'The sheriff's department?' Mary's speech pattern turned almost every sentence into a question. I've wondered whether that's how she gets her information? People just answer her? Even when she doesn't ask a question?

Now, though, she seemed at a loss. 'You have to help me, Maggy.'

I swiveled to take in the Prius parked on the street. No wonder I hadn't heard her drive up.

Amy had followed my gaze. 'You were in the Prius?'

'Of course,' Mary said, sitting down at the nearest table. 'You walked right past me.'

'But I didn't really see you,' Amy said, pulling out the chair I'd just shoved in and sitting across from her. 'I was preoccupied.'

'That's putting it mildly.' Mary leaned forward, her blonde bob swinging to cover her face. 'You honestly didn't see me?' she repeated, incredulously. 'That means I didn't have to go to the police.'

'You turned yourself in?' I went to close the door and then, getting a whiff of residual Black Opium, decided to leave it open instead.

Her brown eyes opened wide. 'It's not like I'm a suspect. Or I hope I'm not a suspect?'

'But you were sitting in front of the house,' Amy said.

Sarah had said Kip made 'a ton' of money for Mary. 'You were a client of Kip's, weren't you? What were you doing at his home?'

'I'd been trying to reach him all day, so when I drove by the house and saw the lights on, I stopped.'

And waited.

Amy frowned. 'Kip's house is on a dead-end street in Poplar Gardens. How could you have been driving by?'

Mary rubbed the back of her neck.

'And at nine thirty at night?'

'You might as well spill it, Mary,' I said. 'You just came

here straight from the sheriff's office. I assume you're not here because I make good coffee.'

'Um, no.' Her chin lifted. 'I was hoping you could help me? With the sheriff and all.'

'"And all" being what?'

'That creepy Deputy Fergussen, for one.' An unexpected tear popped over her lower eyelid and trailed down her cheek. She brushed at it. 'I think you're right. I am a suspect in Kip's murder.'

'Not to worry,' Amy said. 'You have plenty of company.'

'I've heard,' Mary said, reaching out to pat her arm. 'And I'm sorry.'

'Why do you think you're a suspect?' I asked. 'Other than the fact you staked out his house.'

'I told you,' Mary said. 'I had to. I couldn't get hold of him on the phone.'

'Why did you need to talk to him? And why didn't he want to talk to you?'

'That's just it,' Mary said, leaning forward earnestly. 'There has to be something going on. I wanted to capture some unrealized stock gains and have been trying to sell off the shares and take a disbursement. Kip keeps putting me off. Then a few days ago, I signed into the account and the balance was down, not up. And down considerably, compared to the market. There had been a sale of shares, but no disbursement or re-investment that I could see.'

'So where is it?' I asked.

'Exactly my question. Or the question I intended to ask Wednesday night, but he walked right past my car.'

'That means you saw Amy leave.'

'Yes.'

Amy closed her eyes and took a deep breath and let it out before she opened them. 'Thank you.'

'No need to thank me. It's just the truth.'

'You never did get a chance to talk to Kip?' I asked Mary.

'No. I didn't want to interrupt the two of you and then on the way back he crossed to the other side. I know he saw me.'

'You didn't go up to the house after I left?' Amy asked.

'I did, or at least I tried to,' Mary said, looking sheepish, 'but then realized I'd left the car running.'

The problem with a car that doesn't make any noise. That and it being able to sneak up on you.

'By the time I went back and turned it off and got up the driveway to the house, Kip was already inside.'

'Did you ring the bell?' Amy asked.

'Of course. I saw the curtain twitch, but he didn't come to the door.'

'Maybe he looked out to see who it was, hoping you'd changed your mind,' I said to Amy.

'What did you change your mind about?' Mary asked. 'I couldn't quite figure out what was happening between you two that night.'

'He asked me to marry him,' Amy said.

'Really! Except, you didn't look very happy.'

'She said no.'

'Which for some reason made me a suspect, too,' Amy said.

'There was also the will,' I reminded my barista. 'Jayden and Jason would have told the investigators about that.'

'But aren't they just implicating themselves by doing that?' Amy asked. 'It would look like they killed Kip before he could change his will.'

'According to Jayden, he'd already changed his will. They'd have been better off killing you than him.'

'Well, that's horrifying.' Amy was chewing on that.

'Killing Amy?' Mary was looking back and forth between us.

'Apparently she's heir to the victim's fortune,' I said.

'I had no idea Kip had changed his will, though.' Amy held up her hands. 'So how can that be a motive?'

'I have no idea where my money is so how can *that* be a motive?' Mary echoed. 'Except I'd kill the man if he weren't already dead.'

The librarian/CPA glanced around. 'Don't repeat that?'

'If it's any comfort,' I said, 'Sarah is having trouble accessing her account. It—'

'How could that be a comfort?' Mary asked. 'I mean, other than adding another suspect to the field.'

'Kip's accounts have been frozen because of his death.

Maybe that's why Sarah isn't able to access her account and why you—'

'Were you listening to me, Maggy? I was able to access my account. There's just sixty-three thousand dollars less in it. And that happened before Kip died.'

'Sixty-three thousand?' Amy repeated. 'Are you sure?'

'Of course I'm sure. It is – or was – my money.'

'Why is that significant?' I asked.

Amy turned toward me, dazed. 'It's significant because that's exactly what Kip told me my ring cost.'

'If Kip bought Amy a ring with Mary's money, does that mean it's Mary and Amy who are engaged?'

'Very funny,' I told Sarah. 'What it means is that maybe Kip was stealing money from his clients to cover his private expenses. Could it be that he's not as wealthy as he pretends?'

'Got a nice house. Nice car.'

'But are they paid for?' I was remembering something Amy said. 'When Kip was mad because Amy gave him back the ring, he said he'd be paying for it for years.'

'A lie to make her feel guilty.'

'Or he was talking about "paying" in a different way. He'd already stolen the money. What was he supposed to do? Put it back?'

'He'd have to return the ring first,' Sarah said.

'If they even take engagement rings back.' I was warming to my idea. 'And he had other expenses. A kid in college, which is never cheap, and one about to go.'

I had a thought. 'Maybe that's why he wanted Jayden to take time off before enrolling at UW. He really didn't have the money.'

'Why not just steal that money like he did for the ring?'

'That's a lot of money over a long term?'

'You take a little here and a little there from a lot of people,' Sarah said. 'Like me.'

'Anything new on your account?' I asked. 'Weren't you going to stop by Kip's office?'

'I did. Fargo's office is dark and your sheriff's deputies aren't telling me anything.'

Whenever they were bad, they were *my* sheriff's deputies. 'Where are we going now?' I was done with my shift and sitting in the passenger seat of Sarah's 1975 lemon yellow Firebird.

'The Fargo house. Jayden talked to Jason about it and he called me. They want me to look at the house. So we're going to look. See what the place is worth.' She couldn't quite hold back a grin.

Not to rain on her parade, but: 'Do we know the place isn't still off limits as a crime scene?'

'Jason said the hall to the master bedroom is taped off, but they've been allowed back into the rest of the house.'

'I assume they know we're coming?'

Sarah looked over at me. 'Of course. You don't think I'd just burst in uninvited, do you?'

'Yes. You do it to me all the time.'

'That's different. You're my friend. This is business.'

'You don't own that business any longer. You sold the realty so you could concentrate on coffee, remember? You can't sell this house.'

'I don't own the company anymore, but I'm still a broker. And I plan to sell this house.'

Must be some house to lure her out of real estate retirement, short-lived though it was.

Which I saw it was as we pulled in.

The front yard was a thick green carpet punctuated by the occasional well-pruned tree. The circle drive framed a pond and the house beyond the pond was a rambling mid-century modern, timber with red brick elements.

'This can't be a genuine Frank Lloyd Wright, can it?' The place – and the thought – literally took my breath away.

The famous Prairie-style architect was born in Wisconsin in 1867 and had maintained a home and school in Spring Green, where his mother's family had settled about an hour northwest of Madison. Named Taliesin, the property is still the sight of the School of Architecture and Wright-style homes sprinkled the landscape down through Chicago, where Wright also had a home and office.

'Or an apprentice,' Sarah said. 'But if so, it was an awfully good one.'

'I'll say. And no wonder they need a gardener.' I climbed out of the Firebird, taking in the pond which was surrounded by a spectacular show of crimson and yellow mums befitting the fall season. I had no doubt they'd be out of there the moment a leaf drooped, replaced by poinsettias for the next season.

I preferred to let my plants fend for themselves. Made them stronger.

'Nice, huh?' Sarah said.

'Very,' I admitted, looking around. The only thing I could criticize was the disconnect between the organic feel of the house, itself, and the carefully manicured grounds. 'I'm not sure Wright would have approved of the lawn. Less mowing, more prairie was his thing.'

'Luckily for us, he's dead,' Sarah said, taking in the full scope of the house. 'Well, not luckily because I'd love to have a dozen more of these to sell.'

'I wonder why Amy parked on the street that night,' I said, measuring the distance to the street.

'She said she didn't want to block the drive,' Sarah said.

'It's a circle. She could have parked on either side of it.'

'Maybe the GT2 was already in front of the door.'

'Or she wanted to make a quick getaway.'

'I can't believe you just said that.'

'I don't mean after killing him,' I said. 'I meant that if she wasn't really feeling the relationship and got an inkling he might be planning to propose, maybe she wanted an unimpeded escape route.'

'So, she was going to have him drop her at her car after dinner?' Sarah seemed skeptical. 'Why not just meet him at the restau—'

The sound of a heavy door opening interrupted her, and a tall, redheaded young man stuck his head out from behind a brick wall at the entrance of the house. Or where I thought the entrance was. 'Sarah, good. Jayden just left.' He seemed to notice me for the first time. 'Mrs Thorsen.'

'Jason.' I stepped up the three brick steps and hugged him. 'I'm so sorry about your dad.'

'Thanks, Mrs Thorsen,' he said, waving us around the wall

and into the door hidden behind it. 'It's been a shock. And then add dealing with the business and estate and all.' He shrugged. 'I'm trying to take some of the pressure off Jayden.'

I assumed the last was to explain why he'd been happy we – or more likely Sarah, the real estate agent – had arrived after Jayden left. 'She doesn't want to sell the house?'

Jason let us pass by him into the house. 'Jayden is conflicted. The house has been in the family for years.'

'I don't blame her for not wanting to sell,' I said, pivoting to try to take in all 360 degrees. To my right was a living room, to the left what seemed like a bedroom wing. We stepped into the living room and saw that it was open to a dining room and beyond that was likely the kitchen. The back wall of the living room had floor-to-ceiling glass looking out onto the back.

'Are those the accordion doors that move completely out of the way?' Sarah asked.

'Of course,' Jason said, as he demonstrated how the panels folded back onto themselves, opening the entire width of the room to the yard beyond. 'Dad saw it on TV and had to have it.'

'Bless his heart,' Sarah said.

'But-but . . .' I knew I was stuttering. 'Isn't this a Wright?'

'Right what?' Jason asked, turning.

'A Frank Lloyd Wright,' I said. 'Isn't it protected?'

'Oh, him,' Jason said, as only a young person can about an architect who had died nearly fifty years before he was born. 'That's up for debate, I guess.'

'An apprentice, most likely,' Sarah said, surveying the backyard. 'No pool?'

'Waste of money in Wisconsin,' he said.

'They actually can lower the price of a house here,' Sarah admitted, craning her neck to see left and right. 'Plenty of room out here if somebody wants to put one in.'

'But even if it *was* a Wright apprentice, the house dates back to the forties or fifties, doesn't it?' I asked. 'Shouldn't it be on the historical preservation list?'

The idea of somebody just ripping the back wall off a Wright house – even one that was open for debate – was like ripping an arm off your firstborn. OK, maybe not. But still.

'Dad went to a lot of time and money to make sure it wasn't on the list,' Jason said. 'City meetings and all. I thought it would be kind of cool if it was a Wright house. You know about the massacre?'

'At Taliesin.' I was surprised the kid knew anything about Wright. Though this was a story that would catch anybody's attention.

'Yeah,' Jason said, turning to Sarah. 'Wright dumped his wife and kids for some bimbo and set her up in this big house in Spring Green. Then one day at lunchtime some servant locks the doors and sets fire to the house.'

'Really?' Sarah asked, looking back and forth between us.

'Really.' I couldn't believe a Wisconsin real estate agent wouldn't know the story. 'You never heard this?'

She shook her head.

'And that wasn't the coolest part,' Jason continued. 'As some people escaped, the guy was waiting for them with an axe.'

My unflappable friend seemed flapped. 'No.'

'Yup, killed the bimbo, her two kids and like five other people. Pretty impressive body count back in the day.'

'The day being 1914,' I said, dryly. The kid was giving me the creeps.

As Sarah and the ghoul continued to talk, I stepped out onto the patio for a breath of fresh air. Like the front, the back was a large expanse of carefully manicured green lawn with a young tree here and there. A man was kneeling at the base of one, planting the same mums I'd seen out front. A hammer was on the ground next to him, presumably from pounding in the support stakes on the tree.

Rafael the gardener, I deduced. 'Those plants are beautiful. Are they just regular mums?'

The man stood up, stripping off his work gloves. 'Cushion mums. They stay low and will fill in thickly, I hope, around the trees. It's a little late in the fall to be planting them.'

'You must be Rafael,' I said. 'I'm Maggy Thorsen.'

'Rafael Rojas.' We shook.

'The landscaping back here looks new,' I said.

'It is. Mr Fargo had me clear out the natural brush when he had the doors installed.'

'Don't tell me it was original prairie planting.'

A regretful grimace crossed his face. 'It was. But Mr Fargo preferred lawn – a wide open view. I only recently persuaded him to put in the trees.'

I really, really hoped this wasn't an original Wright. But I had more pressing matters to get to. 'Jayden said you were a great help Thursday morning when she found her dad.'

He leaned down to pick up the hammer. 'I did what I could. But, in truth, there was little that could be done.'

'Kip was already dead.'

'Yes.'

'Where were you when Jayden came out . . . was it the front door?'

'Yes.' He tilted his head. 'I was carrying a length of PVC pipe up the driveway when she stumbled out, crying and screaming.'

'You didn't pull up the driveway?' Like Amy.

Rafael gave me a peculiar look. 'Mr Fargo preferred nobody park on the circular drive. There's a service road around back, but since the pipe was for the frog refuge in the front pond it was just easier to walk up.' He shrugged his shoulders.

'Is the front landscaping recent, as well?'

'Not so new. Mr Fargo had plans to change the entrance.'

'Because it wasn't grand enough?' I guessed.

A small grin. 'The style of the time was a smaller, more private front door.'

'Behind the brick wall,' I said. 'Do *you* think this house was designed by Frank Lloyd Wright?'

His head dipped. 'Mr Fargo very much didn't want it to be.'

'But why? A Wright would be more valuable.'

'To some, but Mr Fargo did not intend to sell anyway. In the meantime, he could not make everything as he liked.'

And Kip apparently wanted things the way Kip wanted things. 'Did you say, "frog refuge"?'

'Yes, though that was my idea, not Mr Fargo's.'

It was like the man could read my mind.

'I have some new varieties arriving tomorrow,' he continued, 'that haven't wintered here yet. If I submerge a length of plastic pipe in the pond, it gives them someplace safe to hibernate.'

Interesting. Or not. I just wanted the man to talk. 'There are both frogs and fish in the pond then?'

'Yes. My small attempt at a natural habitat.'

Until Kip had him rip it all out and install a statue of David. 'I understand you'd just flown in Thursday morning.'

An uncertain look at the change of subject. 'Yes. And you are again?'

I smiled. 'Maggy Thorsen. I'm sorry if I seem to be grilling you. My friend Amy is—'

Now Rafael was smiling. 'Amy of the pink hair. She is a fan of the prairie architecture, as well. And you are her boss the detective.'

'Not really a detective, but this sort of thing does seem to follow me.'

Rafael cocked his head, brown eyes surveying me. 'Death is not a good thing to follow such a beautiful lady.'

I felt myself flush. 'I'm just trying to help Amy. She was the last one to see Kip apparently. Jayden said he died in bed, though, which was long after Amy left.'

'Yes, when I went inside with Jayden, her father was in bed, his eyes closed. If you didn't see the wound and stippling on the side of his forehead and blood on the pillow you would have thought he was sleeping.'

'He was on his back?' When Rafael nodded, I asked, 'And the wound was on which side?'

He raised his right hand, remembering. 'His right side, the one toward us as we approached the bed.'

'Thank you,' I said. 'I didn't want to ask Jayden this level of detail.'

'I understand. Though I'm sure she would have tried to answer, despite how difficult it was for her, if she knew it was for Amy. They are friends.'

Something in the way he said it made me ask, 'Jason is not a friend of Amy's.'

Rafael held up his hands. 'I don't want to say that.'

'But . . .' I waited.

He grinned. 'I don't believe it is personal. But Jason didn't seem happy his father was remarrying.'

Jason's glee at recounting the bloody demise of Frank Lloyd Wright's 'bimbo' seemed a little more ghoulish. And a lot more personal. 'Because of money? Or because Amy wasn't much older than he was?'

'Perhaps both?' Rafael dipped his head. 'When a man marries a woman of his own age, one is unlikely to outlive the other by too many years. When a man marries a much younger woman, it may be a very long wait before the children inherit what they believe they deserve.'

'This house, for example.' I raised my hands.

'For example.'

'Jason is talking to a real estate agent about selling right now,' I told him.

'I am not surprised.' He flipped the hammer still in his hand and caught it by the handle. 'Perhaps he wishes now his father wouldn't have succeeded in clouding the heritage of the house.'

'Perhaps,' I said. 'Or perhaps he'll sell it to somebody who has no more interest in preservation than Kip did.'

'It is possible,' Rafael admitted. 'People here sometimes pay a very high price only to tear down one house to build another one in its place.'

'True. There may be a complication selling, though. Jayden told me her father had already made a will in favor of Amy.'

'I did not know about that.' He was gazing at the house. 'But if that is true, how can he be selling the house? Wouldn't it be Amy's to do with as she pleased?'

That was a very good question.

NINE

Sarah and Jason were at the end of the hallway outside the master bedroom when I found them. Now only the door was cordoned off, crime-scene tape sealing it.

'When they're out of there,' Sarah was saying. She turned to me. 'You know some cleaning companies that specialize in crime scenes, don't you?'

From what both Rafael and Pavlik had said, clean-up would consist of disposing of the mattress, bedclothes and pillow. There also would be a mess from fingerprint powder, as I knew from experience. 'I'll get you a name.'

'Unfortunately, we'll have to disclose that there was a death on the property,' Sarah told Jason.

I noticed it was already 'we'.

'You're kidding,' the boy said. 'Is that going to mess things up?'

'Only if buyers are squeamish about living in a house where a man was murdered,' I said.

'That doesn't sound fair,' Jason said. 'What if we wait a year or so? Is there like a statue of limitations?'

'Statute,' Sarah corrected. 'And no there is not. Anything you know about the house you have a legal obligation to reveal.'

I turned to Jason. 'Speaking of complications, what about Amy? Don't you need her permission to sell the house?'

'The barista?' Jason seemed surprised and more than a little irritated at my question. 'Why should we? They weren't married.'

'I had the impression your dad told both you and Jayden recently that he'd made a new will in Amy's favor.'

'Ohhh.' He seemed relieved. 'Are you talking about what he said at lunch Wednesday?'

'Maybe.'

'Dad said he intended to, but "intention" won't hold up in court,' said the man who thought the word was 'statue' not 'statute'.

'You've checked with your father's attorneys?' Commission endangered, Sarah took up the questioning.

Jason pulled at the collar of his golf shirt. 'Dad's no idiot. He may have a new will all ready to go, but he'd never have signed it before getting married, much less proposing. And happily, the little gold-digger turned him down.' He shrugged.

I felt my eyes narrow. 'Jayden made it seem like a done deal.'

'*Jayden* has always wanted a sister.'

I never realized what a sarcastic little twit Jason was.

'Well, anyway,' Sarah said. 'Get me a copy of the deed, so we can see whose name the property is in. It's possible there's a trust and . . .'

I really didn't want to hear any more, so I wandered back down the hall.

'Hello?' I called, sticking my head into the kitchen. The room was quite small by today's standards and though it had been updated fairly recently with high-end appliances, I imagined a new owner would gut it. I walked to the door at the far end of the room. A pane of glass had been broken out of the window and covered with cardboard. The way the killer got in?

I turned the deadbolt below it to see the backyard. Somebody could have entered without being seen Wednesday night and have crept—

'May I help you?' A gray-haired woman with a round, pink face came into the room from another door, drying her hands on a dish towel. She was wearing a black dress with a white collar and could have come out of a casting call for housekeepers back in Wright's day. Or a hundred years earlier.

'I'm sorry to disturb you,' I said, closing the door. 'But might I get a glass of water?'

'Help yourself.' The woman gestured toward the water dispenser on the refrigerator.

'I'm sorry,' I said again. 'I'll go ahead and do that. I didn't want to seem nosy, going through your cabinets and all.'

'I don't think you're nosy because you're going through the cabinets.'

'You just think I'm nosy, period,' I guessed, retrieving a glass and pouring myself said water.

'Bingo.' She sat down at the table, setting aside a worn hardcover book.

'*4.50 from Paddington*,' I read from the book cover. 'One of my favorite Agatha Christies. Did you know it was originally titled *What Mrs McGillicuddy Saw*?'

'No, because it's not true. That was the American title.' She pointed to the words, 'Crime Club Choice' on the bottom of the red and black cover. 'This is the first UK edition.'

Wanting to connect with her, I tried again. 'Really? Wherever did you find it?'

'Nowhere you'll find another.'

Charmer. And obviously immune to my own charms.

'I'm Maggy Thorsen,' I said, sitting down across from her. 'And you're . . .'

'Mrs Gilroy.'

No first name, but that went along with the days of yore housekeeper outfit. I wondered if it was her or the horses that drew her carriage that couldn't see after nightfall. 'I'm so sorry about Kip. We worked together at First Financial and my son went to school with Jason.'

'You're that girl Amy's boss. And a busybody.'

'Bingo,' I said, echoing her. 'And bingo again.'

We stared at each other.

She blinked. 'I saw you talking to Rafael. What did he tell you about them?'

'I assume "them" doesn't mean plants, trees and frog refuges?'

Her features tightened, but she seemed to make an effort to at least appear civil. 'His favorite subjects, I'll admit. But I imagine you were asking about *the family*.'

She said it like the last two words should be capitalized. 'Not really, since I've probably known them longer than he has. But you've been with the Fargos for years, I understand.'

'Yes.'

She was tighter-lipped than Pavlik on a bad day. 'I did talk to him about helping Jayden when she found Kip's body. It's a horrible thing, but she seems to be holding up. I just hope that's not all for show.'

'She's cut from the same strong cloth as her father. Jason, even more so. They'll be all right.'

Says the family retainer. But at least I had started a dialogue. 'Life changes in an instant.'

'Weren't the first change around here. Even this house. That living room wall and the yard outback. Then the kitchen and master bedroom were to be next. All for that girl.'

'Kip was remodeling for Amy?' Amy was right. It didn't seem like the man actually knew her at all. 'She loves old houses.'

'But *he* wanted to give her new,' Mrs Gilroy said, arms folded. 'And what Mr Fargo wanted, he got.'

Even if it was with somebody else's money, apparently. I wondered which client was paying for the renno. 'Kip's proposal to Amy must have come as a surprise.'

'To everybody, including the girl herself apparently. No matter now.' The woman picked up her book.

Clearly our conversation had ended. I stood to put my glass in the sink. 'Thank you for the water . . . I'm sorry, I don't know your first name.'

'No. You don't.'

On this, we could agree.

'Mrs Gilroy?'

The voice came from the doorway, and the housekeeper's face softened as she turned toward it. 'Yes, dear?'

Jason came in, trailed by Sarah. 'Do you suppose we could get something to drink? Lemonade, maybe, or iced tea?'

'Of course.' She stood. 'We have both, which would you prefer?'

'I'd like iced tea,' Jason said. 'Sarah? Mrs Thorsen?'

I thought I saw Mrs Gilroy's lip curl at my name.

'Please call me Maggy, Jason,' I said.

'What would you like to drink, Maggy?' Jason asked with a smile.

'You know,' I said with a glance at Mrs Gilroy's back at the refrigerator. 'I'm fine. I think I'll just pop out and say goodbye to Rafael.'

I had to restrain myself from sticking out my tongue as Mrs Gilroy turned to glare at me.

'Mrs Gilroy doesn't like me much,' I said, handing Rafael a spade.

'She's getting cross in her old age,' Rafael said, lifting the dirt to slip the last mum in place. 'There are some days I don't think she likes me either.'

'But Jason sure lights up her life.'

Rafael got to his feet, setting down the spade. 'He always has, from what I've heard. The boy can do no wrong with her – or his sister – and, believe me, he does plenty.'

'In school? I got that impression,' I said. 'And it probably doesn't help that the University of Wisconsin in Madison always makes the list of top party schools in the country.'

'Excellent institution, all the same,' Rafael said, slipping off his gloves. 'Especially in earth sciences. My cousin is a professor of Herpetology there.'

'I'm not sure what that is, but it sounds impressive.'

'Amphibians and reptiles.' He picked up the spade. 'And on that subject, I need to move to the pond in front.'

Where he was about to work when Jayden came running out of the front door upon discovering her father's body. 'I'll come with you.'

He grinned over his shoulder. 'Do you like frogs?'

'Passionately,' I said, trailing after him.

'I think I find that hard to believe.' He stopped and waited for me to catch up.

'You think right,' I said. 'I don't know anything about frogs. I had turtles when I was a girl and even none of those lasted long.'

'Turtles need sunlight,' Rafael said, continuing on. 'A lot of pet turtles die because of that. Or they're handled too much.'

'I was probably guilty of both. What I really wanted was a dog.'

'You can't pet turtles.'

'Or take them for walks,' I said bleakly. 'And as for the sunlight, I was afraid the poor thing would cook so I specifically kept it out of the sun.'

'Yes, indeed,' he said, twisting his head to grin at me. The man had amazingly white teeth. 'I'm afraid you killed it.'

I killed them. There was more than one. Many more. But speaking of murders, 'Is there anything else you can tell me about the day before Kip died? Anything unusual?'

'Wednesday? I'm afraid I wasn't here to tell you. I went home to Cartagena for a wedding and returned Thursday morning.'

Oh, yeah – the red-eye, Pavlik had said. I hated those.

'The nursery delivered the trees Wednesday afternoon,' Rafael was saying. 'They would have been working in the back.'

I perked up. 'What nursery? Maybe they saw something as they were planting trees.'

'Valley View.' He stopped before we rounded the house and I followed the direction of his sweeping hand toward the service drive at the end of the manicured lawn. 'But they just dropped them off near the service drive for me to plant. They wouldn't have gotten close to the house.'

'All the trees?' I frowned, shading my eyes.

'There, there, there and there.' He pointed out four trees, one near the drive and the other three clustered nearer the house. Each of them had to be twenty feet high.

'They're enormous.' The last tree I'd planted had been the three-inch high twig Eric had brought home from school on Arbor Day.

'Mr Fargo preferred not to wait for them to grow,' Rafael said with a grin. 'I was hoping the nursery workers would place them in the holes I'd prepared so I didn't have to move them around myself.'

'They didn't?'

'Just the one closest to the drive, but I can't blame them. Mr Fargo paid them for truck delivery only.'

'I'm getting the impression Kip was cheap.' I was trailing after him again, now in the front of the house.

'The rich are a different breed. Perhaps that is how they stay rich.' He stopped on the driveway and pointed. 'See the refuge?'

I squinted into the pond in front of us. 'The white pipe?'

'Yes. When it gets cold, the frogs will go in there to hibernate and be safe. Today I'll put down some branches and rocks to create a habitat and shield them from predators.'

I bet Rafael never even killed one turtle. 'What's Mrs Gilroy's first name?'

He looked startled. 'Mildred. Why do you ask?

'Because she didn't want me to know.'

'And knowing now makes you feel better?'

'Knowing now makes me feel merely adequate. Mildred Gilroy is a formidable woman.'

'She is a force of nature, as they say.'

'Does that force of nature know anything about the night Mr Fargo was killed, do you think?' I'd fallen into referring to Kip as Rafael did.

'Mrs Gilroy would have gone home by five or six p.m. She does not drive at night.'

As Pavlik had said. 'But she was there earlier. Did she mention anything about that day to you? Who was here, maybe?'

Rafael opened his mouth as if he was going to answer but stopped. 'I think it's best you ask her.'

'I tried to, but—'

'I'm sorry. I don't want to tell tales.' He knelt by the pond.

'Then she did tell you something,' I said to his back.

'There – look!'

I know a diversion when I hear one, but I did 'look!' to see a small yellowy-green shape disappear into the white pipe. 'It's tiny. Is it going into hibernation?'

'Probably not yet. It is still too warm.' He reached in and plucked the creature out. 'Would you like to hold it?'

'No, I, well . . .' Suddenly, like it or not, I was holding the damn thing in the palm of my hand. It seemed as surprised as I was, its eyes wide.

'Beautiful, is it not?'

'Cute.' I held my hand out for him to take the frog and wiped off my hands on my jeans. 'And slimy, too.'

Gently replacing the frog in the pond, he fiddled with the pipe, trying to situate it more securely on the sandy bottom. Maybe I hadn't gushed enough over his frog. Or else he was just done answering questions.

'Thanks, Rafael,' I said.

He waved but didn't turn.

'Did you get anything out of the gardener?' Sarah asked as we walked down the driveway toward the car.

Faced with the option of waiting for Sarah outside in the Firebird or inside the Fargo house, I'd opted for the couch in the living room. I had to admit that the glass wall made for amazing afternoon light.

'Other than frog habitats, tree-planting and that I'm a serial turtle killer, no,' I said, stopping at the sidewalk and turning back toward the house. 'Though he did say Mrs Gilroy worships the ground Jason walks on. All two acres.'

'Until he sells it out from under her,' Sarah said.

'You got the listing?'

'No, but I will. Jason just needs to talk to Jayden.'

'And look up the deed to make sure they own it,' I pointed out.

'I can look that up with the county registrar of deeds, too,' Sarah said.

'Assuming it's in Kip's name, there's still the question of the new will. Amy may own a piece or all of the house.'

'Jason doesn't seem to think so.'

'Wishful thinking?' Or maybe he'd found the new will and destroyed it.

'You don't like the kid, do you?'

'He just doesn't seem all that sad his dad is dead.'

'Maybe they didn't get along. That's not a crime.'

'It is if you killed him.' I started walking again. 'I mean, we have to look at who stands to gain with Kip dead. If there isn't a new will in Amy's favor, then it's Jason and Jayden.'

'Presumably, but we don't even know that. Like I told Jason, he needs to talk to the lawyers, get the will and file with the court to get permission to sell any property before the estate is settled. Unless the property is in a trust.'

'Then what happens?'

'The successor trustee can sell the property at any time for the benefit of the heirs of the trust,' Sarah said, following me.

'Who's the successor trustee?' I stopped again.

'No idea. Which is why I told Jason to get hold of his father's lawyers and find out. Nothing can be done until we have either a copy of the valid trust or valid will.'

'Back to motive, the heirs have it.'

'Whether the heirs are Jayden and Jason or Amy,' Sarah

said, waving me on toward the car, 'I don't see where one has more reason to kill Kip than another. And, bigger question, why now? Jason and Jayden have probably been Kip's heirs since they were born.'

'Except now Amy entered the scene,' I said. 'You heard Jason talking about Frank Lloyd Wright's "bimbo". Practically reveling in the fact she was brutally murdered.'

'But it was Jason's father that was murdered, not the bimbo,' Sarah pointed out. 'Which in our case would be Amy. But with all this "heir" stuff you're forgetting the very real possibility that Kip was ripping people off. Besides me and Mary, I mean.'

'You think somebody took umbrage.' Love that word. 'Is there somebody in his office we could talk to? Somebody who might know what was going on?' And be willing to tell us.

'I told you I stopped by and the place was dark. I'm not sure if there's anybody working there at all, besides Kip and the kids at various times,' Sarah said. 'First Jason before he went off to school and now Jayden.'

'That's it?' I was watching a sheriff's car slow down as it approached the house.

'Occasionally there'd be somebody else to help. An office manager maybe, but they didn't seem to last long.'

'Can I help you ladies?' The car had slid to a stop and now Fergussen got out.

'Help us?' Sarah looked around. 'We're walking on a public sidewalk.'

'In front of a murder scene,' Fergussen said, snagging his thumbs in his gun belt. 'I'm just asking myself why.'

'Tell yourself it's none of your business,' Sarah snapped.

The two of them were oil and water, and I didn't know if I wanted to separate them or throw in a lighted match to see what happened.

'Sarah is listing the house,' I said, opting for the match.

'You're a real estate agent?' he asked, surveying her. 'I thought you sold coffee.'

'I sell both, though why it's any of your business I don't know.'

I tried again. 'The heirs are selling the house. Assuming Jason and Jayden Fargo are their father's heirs, of course.'

It was like I wasn't there. 'The old lady said they're fixing up the place.' Fergussen was watching Rafael rake leaves. 'I should talk to the Mexican while I'm here.'

'He's Colombian,' I snapped.

Now the deputy did look at me. 'Well, *excuse* me. But they all speak the same language, don't they? And drug and corruption-wise, Colombia's even tougher.'

'Don't you find they get dirty?' I asked pleasantly.

'What gets dirty?' He pulled his thumbs out of his belt.

'Your knuckles.'

'My what?' He looked at his hands.

'Your knuckles. From dragging on the ground.'

'You being funny?' Fergussen roared, as Sarah tugged me away.

Sarah was grinning as we crossed to the car. 'I'm impressed.'

'And I'm irate. Rafael probably has twice the education that, that, that . . .'

'I think you called him a Neanderthal.' She high-fived me over the spoiler of the Firebird. 'And you're right about Rojas being smarter than Fergussen. Mildred says he was a teacher in Colombia and is working on his credentials here.'

Mildred. They were on first name basis. 'She sure didn't want to talk to me,' I said, trying the door. It was locked. 'I wonder what she's hiding.'

'Her dislike of you, and not very successfully.'

'Me? I've never met her before.'

'She thinks you're nosy.'

'I know that. But how do you know that?'

'We chatted. She made iced tea and fed me cookies.'

'You were with Jason, the golden child.'

'No, actually, he had to take a call.' She shrugged. 'What can I say? I'm likeable.'

No. She wasn't.

'Did you ask "Mildred" about the day Kip died? Did she see Amy there?'

'No. But as all sources have reported, Mildred left at five and Amy met Kip at the house to drive to the restaurant around seven. Mildred did say Jason, Jayden and Kip had lunch together that day. She made them chicken salad. Curried, I think, with grapes.'

Lovely. 'Jason was in town then.'

'Yes, but he drove back to Madison after lunch.' Sarah climbed into the car and reached across to unlock my door.

When I didn't move to get in, she said, 'C'mon. I have to check the title and put a listing contract together.'

'You are the little optimist, aren't you?' I was staring down the street. 'Remember that other car that Amy told us about? Nobody has said who was driving it. You think Mary knows? She was sitting here for a while, from the sounds of it. She'd have noticed another car.'

'You know how we can find out?'

'How?'

'Get in the damn car and we'll go ask her.'

TEN

'Other car? What other car?'

'The one that was parked not fifteen yards behind you,' I whispered. 'Are you telling us you didn't notice it?'

We were at the Brookhills library and Mary was manning the reference desk. Yet she was giving us no information.

'I might have, but I don't want to get anybody in trouble.' She peered up at me over her reading glasses. 'You really don't know?'

'Would she ask you if she did?' Sarah asked. She was not whispering.

'Maybe.' She shrugged. 'Maggy can be kind of tricky?'

'Well, it's been a long day and she's kind of ticked. Just told off a deputy, in fact. I wouldn't mess with her.'

'Hopefully it was that Fergussen creep,' Mary said.

'It was,' I said, raising my own voice to natural levels. 'Now give.'

'It was a little green car. Foreign probably. And old. I didn't see who was inside.'

I felt my eyes narrow. 'Which is what you told the authorities. Now tell us the rest of it. A little green car? Foreign? Old? You mean like Jacque Oui's Peugeot?'

'Maybe.' In trying to avoid my eyes, she accidentally met Sarah's.

'Give,' was all my partner said.

Mary threw up her hands. 'OK, OK, OK. I admit it. Jacque was there. But that doesn't mean he killed Kip. Not that some of us didn't have reason to, the bastard.'

Sarah and I exchanged glances.

'You, because of your missing money, obviously,' I said.

'And me, because of mine,' Sarah acknowledged. 'But please note I'm not the one who called him a bastard first.'

No, the mild-mannered librarian had done that in justifying

the French fishmonger's presence outside the victim's house.
'What about Jacque? Did he have investments with Kip as
well?'

'Are you kidding? Jacque is the one who turned me on to
Kip. He told me he made him a fortune.'

'Probably, "zee" fortune,' Sarah interjected. 'And are you
saying his money is missing, too?'

'Wait, wait.' I was waving my arms and two students passing
by, their arms full of books, stopped. I waved them on. 'I
assumed Jacque was waiting for Kip in front of his house
because of Amy. That he planned to confront him for stealing
his girl, essentially.'

'It's possible, I suppose?' Mary said.

'But if Kip stole – or really embezzled – money from him,
too,' I continued, 'Jacque has twice the motive anybody else
does.' Which pleased me greatly. Not that I disliked Jacque,
it was just . . . OK, yeah, I disliked him.

Mary held up both hands. 'I'm not saying that I know why
Jacque was there. I only saw the Peugeot and, as I told the
authorities quite honestly, I never walked back there to look
in to see who was driving it. Or even if anybody was inside
the car.'

Shades of Amy. Nosiness was apparently a dying art.

'I know Peugeots aren't exactly ubiquitous in Brookhills'
– like Pavlik's non-descript Toyota Corolla, for example – 'but
you're sure it was Jacque's?'

'Baby poop green with a crunched left front fender?'

Depended on the particular baby's diet, but: 'That's the one.
He never had it repaired after he landed in the ditch during
that snowstorm last spring.'

The freak May storm had destroyed Uncommon Grounds
as well as the strip mall where we were located. Over the
intervening year and a half, we'd renovated the Brookhills
train station to house our coffeehouse and re-opened. Jacque
hadn't gotten his dent fixed.

'You got close enough to see there was a crunched left front
fender?'

Mary flushed. 'Well, yes. I could kind of see that in my
rear-view mirror.'

Sure she could. 'Come on, Mary. You knew it was Jacque all along. Did you two plan to confront Kip together?'

'No!' Her hand moved spasmodically and knocked a pencil on the floor. When she lifted her head after picking it up, her face was pale. 'We didn't plan anything. I just thought when I saw the car . . . Well, it kind of gave me comfort, you know?'

And the questions keep coming.

'Like you had backup?' Sarah guessed.

'Exactly,' Mary said, gratefully. 'Exactly that. In fact, when I went to the house and got no answer, I . . .'

'You what?'

'I . . . I went over to the car?'

I banged the heel of my hand against my forehead. 'Didn't you just tell us you didn't do that?'

'Well, yes, I guess I . . .'

'Lied?' I was reaching the end of my patience.

'Stop badgering the witness,' Sarah said, apparently playing good cop. 'Go on, Mary. Did you talk to Jacque?'

'No, I . . .'

I glared at her.

'I couldn't,' she burst out. 'I couldn't, because Jacque wasn't in the car.'

'Oh, for God's sake,' I said. 'Will you stop lyi—' A look from Sarah. 'Obfuscating. You're just making matters worse for everybody. Has it occurred to you that if Jacque wasn't in the car, he may have been inside the house?'

'Waiting to kill Kip?' Sarah asked. 'Sure. But he also might have had too much French roast and was off peeing behind a bush somewhere.'

'That's right,' Mary said, seeming to draw indignance from Sarah. 'Or in that pond.'

That woulda shown Kip, I guess. Steal my girl? I'll pee in your frog pond.

I leaned back against a bookshelf, suddenly running out of steam. It rolled and I stood back up again. 'I guess the good news is that even that clod Fergussen should be able to track the car back to Jacque. Let them figure it out. But you know what else I don't understand?'

No reply.

Mary stirred first. 'Oh, sorry. I thought it was a rhetorical question.'

'And I didn't want to waste my energy saying, "No, what?" when I already knew what was coming.' Sarah yawned.

'Fine. What?' At least *I* knew how to play the game.

'You don't understand why Amy didn't tell us Jacque was there.'

'Exactly so,' I said, turning to Mary. 'She must have seen the car when she came down the driveway, right?'

Mary bit her lip. 'I'm not sure, actually. It was dark, and her car was parked in the opposite direction, just past mine. If she didn't look the other way when she reached the street, she might have missed it.'

'Besides,' Sarah said, 'from all accounts, Amy was pretty upset.'

'Beyond upset,' Mary said, nodding. 'When she put that car in gear and stepped on the gas, I could smell the burnt rubber.'

I cocked my head. 'Amy peeled out? Like she was angry?'

'Absolutely. I assumed they had a fight.'

'I guess they had,' I said. 'I just had the impression that Amy was more sad than mad.'

'So she was both,' Sarah said. 'Sad to hurt Kip, but also mad he'd put her in this position in the first place.'

'I suppose. But it's very lucky Mary was there to see Kip alive when Amy left. Otherwise, it might have seemed like she was fleeing the scene.' Not that there seemed to be any witnesses to attest to that either.

'She was. Just not the scene of a murder.' Sometimes my partner showed more insight and sensitivity than I gave her credit for.

Mary was nodding. 'Lucky for Amy that I saw Kip alive. Not so lucky for me, since I don't have a witness that he was alive when *I* left.'

'True. And if you did, they'd have seen you actually go up to the door,' Sarah said. 'When you think about it, we only have your word for it that you didn't go inside and kill Kip.'

And sometimes Sarah showed no sensitivity at all.

'Thanks so much for your confidence in me, Sarah.'

'You're welcome.' Sarah grinned. 'Look at the bright side. You're Amy's witness; maybe Jacque really was there hiding in the bushes and saw you leave.'

'Again,' I said, 'not necessarily helpful, if it means he saw you go up to the door.'

'But he'd also have seen me turn right around and go back to my car and drive away,' Mary said. 'Wasn't Kip killed much later in the evening?'

'He was,' I said.

Mary stood. 'Maybe I should tell the police I've remembered where I saw the car before.'

'I wouldn't.' I waved her back down. 'Even Fergussen should be able to track him down from your description of the car. It'll seem funny if you backtrack now.'

Sarah's eyes were mock-wide. 'Maggy Thorsen is telling a witness to *lie*?'

'She's already lied,' I told her. 'I'm just suggesting she not own up to it. At least not yet.'

'Hedging,' Sarah said. 'You—'

'I did not lie,' Mary said indignantly. 'I just told them I saw the car but didn't . . . expand on it.'

'Or tell them you went back and saw the car was empty,' Sarah said.

'That, too.' Mary hung her head.

I was thinking about alibis. Mary alibis Amy, maybe Jacque alibies Mary. Is there someone who can alibi Jacque? Could . . . 'Is it possible Amy saw Jacque after she left Kip's house that night?'

'No,' Sarah said, looking surprised. 'At least she didn't tell us she saw him.'

'Which doesn't necessarily mean anything.' I chin-gestured toward Mary.

'I didn't lie,' the librarian muttered under her breath.

Nor did Amy, necessarily. We'd never asked her where she'd gone after leaving Kip. Or whether she was alone. But I'd be asking her both questions directly tomorrow morning. It was Sunday, and she worked eleven to close. There was no running and no hiding.

In the meantime: 'Do you do Kip's taxes, Mary?'

It was a safe bet, since Mary did mine, Sarah's and those of pretty much everyone I knew.

But Mary was startled. 'Why do you ask?'

Sarah rolled her eyes. 'Do we need to do this little confidentiality dance? The man is dead.'

'But his family isn't. And his business still exists.'

'You do both his personal and business taxes?' I asked.

'I shouldn't really say.'

Sarah's eyes narrowed.

'Fine,' Mary said hurriedly. 'I did Kip's personal taxes until this past year. He handles his own business return.'

Interesting. 'The better to hide any shenanigans.'

'Shenanigans?' Sarah repeated. 'What are you, ninety? Are you going to pick up your pocketbook and go home to watch your stories on the television?'

'Fiddlesticks,' I said, and turned to Mary. 'Why didn't he have you do his personal returns this year?'

'Oh, Kip wanted me to do them,' Mary said. 'But he never paid me for last year's filing and routinely took six months to pay for pretty much anything. I don't work for free.'

I sat back. 'What is it with this guy? Doesn't pay his bills, stiffs servers, maybe "borrows" money to pay for an engagement ring. Does he have any money that doesn't rightly belong to somebody else?'

Both Sarah and I stared Mary down.

The CPA pressed the fingertips of both hands together in a steeple but didn't answer.

'*Mary?*' Sarah's tone was less than patient.

'I can't say.'

'More like you won't,' I said. 'Which is pretty ridiculous, considering you are a suspect in the man's death.'

'I am not.'

'You are, too,' I said. 'You may not have been charged, but right now you're the last person seen at the house. You have to be a person of interest, if nothing else.'

'Did the sheriff tell you that?'

'I can't say.' In reality, Pavlik and I hadn't had much chance to talk since our conversation the night Kip's body was found.

He'd been at the department late Friday night, while I'd been up and out early this morning for work.

'Be that way,' Mary said. 'But I can be tight-lipped, too.'

'Give us *something*,' Sarah said. 'Anything.'

'Fine. All I will say is that Kip has plenty of assets. He also has liabilities.'

'Well, that's helpful,' Sarah said. 'As in, *not*.'

'Actually, I think it is,' I told her. 'I think what Mary is telling us is that Kip's finances are a house of cards. Still standing, but if one card is pulled out, one loan called, one creditor takes him to court, it will all—'

'I'm not telling you anything of the kind,' Mary exploded. 'In fact, I'm not telling you anything more, period. Balance sheets have two sides: assets and liabilities.'

Blah, blah, blah. 'And if the liabilities outweigh the assets, Kip isn't worth much. Financially speaking.'

But Mary wasn't speaking – financially or otherwise.

'Come on,' Sarah said irritably. 'He didn't pay you, and money is missing from your own investment account with him.'

'With Fargo Financial,' Mary said primly.

'You said yourself that you've never been involved with the business,' I said. 'That means you're free to speculate with us.'

'I . . .' Mary folded and unfolded her arms. 'I . . . well, I guess so.'

'This is all going to come out anyway,' Sarah said. 'And I hope Kip's assets – personally or otherwise – are enough to cover whatever is missing or we're all out of luck. You Mary, me, Jacque and who knows who else.' She snapped her fingers. 'Poof! All gone.'

The CPA was looking miserable, which didn't give me hope there was any money to be found anywhere. 'Why *did* you keep your investments with Kip and presumably pay his fees, when he wasn't paying yours?'

'I . . . I thought maybe he was just a smart businessman. You know, managing cash flow?'

'By not paying other people? You need cash to flow, too.'

'I know.' She hung her head. 'I have only myself to blame.

I knew how far out on a limb he was. I should have seen that he might get desperate and start robbing Peter to pay Paul.'

Mary's dam had broken, and I wanted to find out what I could before she clammed up again. 'Maybe he has hidden assets.'

'Offshore accounts?' Sarah suggested. 'Stuff in the kids' names? Cash in a safe deposit box?'

'Maybe.' Mary's head was hanging even lower. I thought her snub nose was going to touch the desk. 'But if he had funds somewhere, why steal from my account to buy an engagement ring?'

It was a point. And brought another to mind. 'Could he have hidden assets in Amy's name?'

'But Mary's right. If he had money to hide in Amy's name, why embezzle from us?' Sarah asked.

'Because it was fun?'

Mary's head jerked up. 'You're kidding, right?'

'Not really,' I said. 'Maybe it was kind of a game to him – hoarding and hiding his own money and embezzling and spending other people's.' I had a thought. 'He was angry that Amy said no to his proposal, but maybe it wasn't just his ego he was worried about.'

'Could he already have started moving things into her name, figuring that when they got married, he'd have control over them?' Sarah asked.

Mary frowned. 'It's not that easy. Anything Amy owned or owed before marriage would remain hers alone, unless they made an agreement otherwise. Kip likewise.'

I shrugged. 'How do we know he wasn't pressing some kind of prenup – you know, what's mine is yours and what's yours is mine.'

'So romantic,' Sarah sniffed. 'She gets all his debt. He gets all her . . . what?'

'I honestly don't know what Amy has.' I turned to Mary. 'I don't suppose you . . .?'

'You don't suppose correctly,' the CPA said. 'If you want to know about Amy's finances, ask Amy.'

So we did.

ELEVEN

And we didn't even have to wait for morning. When Sarah drove me back to Uncommon Grounds to pick up my car, the lights were still on.

'You know if we go in there, we'll have to help her close,' Sarah said as we stood on the sidewalk watching Amy vacuum through the big plate glass window.

'I hope she's already counted the register and balanced,' I said, starting up the stairs.

'Me, too. I don't know how Mary stands working with numbers all day.'

'She doesn't.' I paused at the top of the steps. 'She works with words all day at the library. Numbers are just on the side.'

'For fun.' Sarah made a face.

'One man's meat is another man's poison, I guess.' I swung open the door.

'What?' Sarah, following, raised her voice above the noise of the vacuum cleaner.

'It's a saying – Thomas Draxe, I think, or maybe—'

Amy shut off the vacuum. 'You're back! Could somebody count the till? I'd love to get out of here early.'

'Got a date?' Sarah asked.

'That's a little insensitive, even for you—' I started to say and then saw that Amy had pinked up. 'Oh, please. Don't tell me you do have a date. With Jacque, no doubt.'

Full out red now. 'We're just having dinner.'

'Do you think that being seen out with him is such a good idea?' I asked.

'Maggy has a point,' Sarah said. 'You just dumped the dead guy.'

'Do you have to call Kip "the dead guy"?' I scolded. 'He was a friend of yours.'

'*Was* being the operative word,' Sarah said. 'Besides, I'm

just asking the same question you are: how it will look – two murder suspects together having dinner?'

'Jacque is going to cook at my place,' Amy said. 'Besides, I'm not a suspect anymore and Jacque never was.'

'Wrong and wrong again, *Kemo Sabe*.' Sarah ran a finger over a table. 'Missed a spot.'

Amy plucked a wet rag from the counter and swiped at the coffee ring. 'There. And I don't have the faintest idea who this Sobby is.'

We'd go into the Lone Ranger and Tonto at a later date. Or not. 'I think Amy is right that she's no longer a suspect.' Unless, of course, she'd sneaked back into the house later. 'But Jacque?'

'Why? Just because he loves me?' Amy said. 'That's not fair.'

'It's also not fair withholding information,' Sarah said. 'Tell her, Maggy.'

Amy swiveled back to me. 'Tell me what?'

I swept my hand toward the now clean table. 'Maybe we should sit down.'

'*Maybe* you should just tell me.'

I was glad the rag in her hand wasn't a gun. Even as it was, I could tell she wanted to snap it at me. 'Mary saw Jacque there. Or at least Jacque's car. Why didn't you tell us?'

Now Amy did pull out a chair and sink into it. 'I didn't know. At least not at first.'

'He told you?'

She nodded. 'He'd followed us from the restaurant.'

'Becky?' Jacque's employee from the store.

Amy nodded. 'She texted and sent him the video, the busy-body. She had to know it would cause problems.'

In the woman's defense, she couldn't have known it would have caused anywhere near the mess Amy and Jacque found themselves in. 'Did you see him?'

'No.' Amy was shaking her head back and forth, back and forth, multiple ear-piercings tinkling. 'Not when Kip and I pulled in and not when I left. I swear.'

'Ugly little green car,' Sarah said, nose wrinkled, 'and it belongs to your then-estranged boyfriend. How could you miss it?'

'I was upset,' Amy said. 'Besides, my car was parked in the opposite direction. I only registered Mary's car because I passed it.'

'Does that mean you didn't tell Pavlik?'

'I didn't know,' she said again, and added, 'then.'

'But you know now,' I pointed out.

'My lawyer said not to volunteer information.'

'Rhonda?' I asked.

'No, Gilbert,' Amy said. 'Rhonda's in Chicago this week.'

'Good sober advice from Gilbert,' Sarah said, with a superior look toward me.

'Just hope it stays that way.'

Amy cocked her head like Mocha, when she was trying to understand something. Frank usually gave up and took a nap.

'Gilbert used to have a drinking problem,' I explained.

'Used to, being the operative words,' Sarah said to Amy's questioning glance.

'But why would you . . .' She waved off what she was going to say. 'Whatever. I guess it doesn't matter since I'm off the hook. But I wonder if Jacque needs an attorney.'

Other than Gilbert, her tone insinuated.

'Does Pavlik know that Jacque was there?' Amy's question was directed to me.

'I'm not sure honestly. Mary told Fergussen about the Peugeot, so I have to assume they've put it together. Did they ask you if you saw him Wednesday night?'

Amy seemed surprised. 'Jacque? No.'

'Are you going to ask her the other thing?' Sarah prodded.

I frowned. 'What other thing?'

'You know, about whether Kip put anything in her name?'

'I think you just asked her,' I said.

'Like what?' Amy asked.

'A bank account maybe, that he put funds in,' I said. 'Or maybe he transferred a house or car to your name?'

Amy was shaking her head. 'Not that I know of. Why?'

'We're wondering if he'd used you somehow to hide funds,' I said. 'Or intended to.'

'And that's why he was so angry when I refused to marry

him?' Amy picked up the rag and fiddled with it. 'I don't know. But then I didn't know about the will either. Would I have had to sign something?'

'I'm not sure,' I said, honestly. 'For a bank account I think he'd at least need your social security number.'

'He could forge her signature,' Sarah said. 'Did he mention a prenup or anything?'

'Actually he did, come to think of it,' Amy said. 'As we were driving back to his house. Casual-like and I didn't think too much about it, other than registering that I really needed to level with him.'

'Level with him?' Sarah asked.

'Tell him that I couldn't marry him, I mean. Before he did more than buy the ring.'

'And orchestrate a three-ring circus at the restau—' I broke off as my phone buzzed a text message.

Mom! Coolest thing! I read from Eric.

'Something important?' Amy asked as I set it down. She was probably hoping she could slip out and avoid further conversation.

'It can wait. Eric is doing an ancestry project and all these DNA relatives keep popping up. He probably has us traced back to Christopher Columbus or something.'

Another buzz. *Really! You won't believe the coincidence.*

'Anyway,' I said, sliding the phone away, 'I'd steer clear of Jacque for now. I know you—'

Another buzz. *We have a cousin like twice removed right in Brookhills. Did you know that?*

I didn't, but then I wasn't even sure what twice removed meant.

'Sorry,' I told Amy and Sarah, and texted back, *No, but I'll call you later.*

Amy was already standing and untying her apron as I finished. 'Would you two mind finishing up? I really need to talk to Jacque.'

'But I just said you shouldn't—' Before I could finish the sentence Amy was out the door.

'She doesn't listen to me,' I told Sarah, who was re-wiping the table.

'Why should she?' Sarah was now moving toward the vacuum cleaner. 'She's our employee, not our kid.'

My kid didn't listen to me either, half the time. 'Our employee just left us here to finish her job.'

'I know,' Sarah said, picking up the vacuum hose. 'I've got this.'

'Meaning I should go' – the vacuum roared to life – 'balance the register.'

Perhaps inspired by Jacque making dinner for Amy, I stopped at Schultz's for something to cook for Pavlik. Though I have to admit to an ulterior motive – a possible opportunity to talk to our cashier/videographer/stoolie, Becky.

My culinary talents lie more to pulling out the crusty bread and artisanal cheese or, in extreme circumstances, crackers and aerosol cheese, but I thought tossing a couple of steaks on the grill and a salad in a bowl might not be beyond me.

I had two steaks, a plastic box of mixed salad greens and a bottle of Lite Vinaigrette dressing when I spied Becky at one of the two open cash registers. I got in line.

The long-time cashier was about eighty and shaped like an egg. Her hair was an unnatural shade of mahogany above a pink-tinged face. 'For God's sake,' she was saying to the man two people in front of me. 'You really want a bag? Man up and save a tree.'

'But it's a bottle of bourbon,' the guy protested. 'I don't want to walk down the street carrying a bottle of booze.'

'And putting it in a brown paper bag will fool people,' she said, handing him his cash register receipt and nothing but the cash register receipt. 'Next.'

A tap on my shoulder. 'The fifteen-item or less lane is open,' the woman behind me said.

'I'm fine,' I said.

'But there's nobody there. The cashier is waving for you to come over.'

'I want this cashier.'

'Any time.' Now Becky was chiding the next customer hurriedly unloading her cart onto the belt. 'We got all night.'

'So you're just a masochist?'

I turned to look back – and up – at a tall redhead, Laurel Birmingham. 'Geez, Laurel, I'm sorry. I didn't realize it was you.'

Our town clerk shrugged. 'I figured you must be on a mission. Who's getting grilled tonight?' She nodded to the steaks. 'Besides the rib-eyes.'

I grinned. 'Becky. Do you want to go in front of me?'

'And miss it? Not on your life. Is this about Kip Fargo?'

'How did you know?'

'Come on. Brookhills is a small town and our murders usually come one at a time. It's easy to keep up.'

Very true. 'I'm glad I ran into you. I was over at the Fargo house.'

'Isn't it a gem?' Laurel said. 'I can't believe what Kip Fargo was doing to it. Hopefully his kids – or whoever he left it to – will have some architectural integrity.'

'Then it is a Frank Lloyd Wright?'

Laurel pushed the nose of her shopping cart to one side and joined me in front of it. 'Honestly? I don't know. Any original records the town had were lost when the town hall and fire department burned down.'

'And the Fargos don't have the original plans?'

Laurel tucked a strand of hair behind her ear. 'Not that they've been willing to share. From what I understand Kip's grandfather built the house and the family's stance ever since has been that it's theirs to do with as they want.'

'Then Kip just followed the family tradition?'

Laurel waggled her head. 'Not really, because his father maintained the house in its original form, except for improvements to rooms like the bathrooms and kitchens. It's only Kip who started tearing out walls and there was no way to stop him except for the liens.'

'Liens?' I'd started to set my items on the belt and stopped.

'Constructions liens – he has a habit of not paying his contractors on time.'

'And they can slap liens on the property,' I said. 'That might complicate a sale, wouldn't it?'

'Definitely. The lien follows the property, not the person. It has to be paid.'

'Sarah may be listing the house,' I told her.

'She'll do a title search and any liens will show up,' Laurel said. 'I'd have her do it sooner, rather than later. Kip was terrible about paying, as was his father before him, so who knows what's there.'

'What was it with him?' I asked her. 'Sounds like the man enjoyed stiffing people.'

'The rich,' Laurel said. 'They're differ—'

'Next!' Apparently I hadn't heard Becky the first time.

'Thank you,' I whispered to Laurel as I turned to drop my items on the belt.

'I'm here for backup if you need me,' she whispered back.

'Hi Becky!' I said brightly.

'Paper or plastic.'

'Paper.'

'We only have plastic.'

This offended me in so many ways. 'But you just gave me a choice. And you told that last gentleman to save a tree.'

She leaned forward across the belt, her face inches from mine. 'I was speaking metaphorically.'

I didn't think so, yet I took the high road. 'I don't know if you remember me, but I'm—'

'Maggy Thorsen. Amy Caprese works for you.'

'Why, yes.'

'Fifty-three thirty-two.'

'Amy told me that you were at the restaurant Wednesday . . . Fifty-three dollars? For two steaks and some salad?'

'Complain to management, if you can find him. Won't get you anywhere.'

Since management was Jacque, I didn't doubt her. The prices at Schultz's were legendary. 'Anyway, I understand you taped Kip's proposal.'

'Videoed. No more tape.'

I inserted my charge card. Hard. 'Metaphorically speaking.'

A smile played around her lips. 'Touché. And yes, I did. The sheriff's department took my phone, though, so you'll have to ask that hunky sheriff of yours if you want it.'

I would. After I made him this ridiculously expensive dinner and plied him with the cheap wine in my cabinet. 'Why did you send it to Jacque?'

She handed me my receipt and shrugged. 'He's my boss.'

'But you had to know it would upset him.'

'Which is just why I did it, don't ya know?'

No, I didn't know. 'You wanted to upset your boss? Is that a good idea?'

'Jacque Oui? Damn right. He's a jerk.' She waved at Laurel. 'Next!'

'If he's such a jerk' – which I didn't dispute – 'why work for him all these years?'

'It's a job. Have you noticed how old I am?'

I nodded.

'Right. Old as dirt, so I'm stuck here earning minimum wage. I gotta get my fun somewhere.'

'But—'

'Next!!'

'Forty-three dollars for two steaks?' Pavlik was reading the label on the butcher paper as he unwrapped the steaks. Outside the grill was pre-heating and inside Frank was pre-drooling. Mocha was hanging out by the grill.

'Schultz's.'

'Ah,' as if that explained the exorbitant price. Which it did. 'Should have gotten sirloin.'

'I thought you were worth rib-eye.'

Pavlik had transferred the steaks to a plate and was preparing to drizzle them with olive oil. He paused, oil in hand. 'What do you want?'

'Nothing,' I lied. 'But Amy said Jacque was making dinner at her place and it occurred to me that I hadn't cooked for you in a while.'

'You realize you're not cooking for me now, right?' He'd gone back to his steaks, cracking pepper and grinding sea salt onto the meat.

'Sure I am.' I hooked my finger toward the plastic box of thrice pre-washed greens and bottled salad dressing. 'Or I will be. You don't want your salad to wilt, do you?'

'That's it, steak and salad? No mushrooms? No baked

potatoes?' Setting aside the grinders, he slid his phone over to check it.

'Well, no. I didn't think to get them. But steak and salad should be plenty, don't you think?'

'Depends.' He was punching in a text. 'Is there anything in the salad but lettuce?'

'No, but it's different types of lettuce.' I picked up the box and red. 'Baby spinach, romaine, red leaf, arugula. And we have dressing.' I set down the greens and picked up the bottle. 'See? Oil and vinegar.'

'You know we can make that ourselves, right?' He had picked up the tongs and gestured toward the oil.

'Still need vinegar. And I don't think the white stuff I use to descale the coffeemaker qualifies.'

Pavlik shook his head and opened the back door before picking up the steak plate. 'Next time I shop,' he said as he disappeared onto the porch, Frank on his heels.

'Fine by me.' I picked up my wine glass and followed them out. 'I know what you're doing, by the way.'

'What's that?' He lifted the hood of the grill.

'Diverting. You know I want to talk about the case.' I offered him the wire brush to clean the stainless-steel grate.

He took it. 'You didn't clean this the last time you grilled.'

'How do you know it was me who grilled?'

'Because it wasn't cleaned.'

Fair enough. 'You're supposed to let the burned stuff build up. Better flavor.'

'Up to a point, but it's hard to get grill marks on your steak when the crud is keeping the meat hovering a half inch above the grates.'

'A mild exaggeration,' I said, as a chunk of burned stuff flew off his brush and hit me on the cheek. I wiped it onto my finger and held it up for him. 'But I surrender. I get your point.'

'Thank you.' He hung the brush on the little doo-hickey on the front of the grill and picked up the tongs.

'Back to Jacque,' I said. 'I assume you know?'

'Know what?' As he laid the steaks on the grill, both of the dogs reflexively sat in front of it. 'That his Peugeot was the second car on the street in front of the Fargo house Wednesday night?'

'Exactly. Apparently, he followed Amy and Kip from the restaurant.'

'Alerted by a helpful text message from Rebecca Ronstadt at said restaurant.' Pavlik set the now steak-less plate on the ground for the dogs.

'Ugh,' I said. 'Should they be having that blood?'

'They're dogs. Originally, nobody cooked their steaks for them.'

I felt myself flush. 'But isn't it going to give them a taste for blood?'

'Afraid you're going to be killed in your sleep?' Pavlik asked, retrieving the licked-clean plate.

'Yup.' Frank was sitting back licking his chops while Mocha balanced on her tiny back feet in front of him, cleaning the meat-leavings off his beard. 'And they'd eat the evidence.'

'Not to worry. If you're killed in your sleep, it's far more likely to be somebody from a case you've stuck your nose into.'

That was judgmental, if true. 'You're a fine one to talk. Your addition to our bed increases that risk exponentially.'

'But it's *my* job. And I might add that it's creepy that you say "our bed", like I'm the third wheel to yours and Frank's relationship.'

'You knew what you were getting into when you took us on,' I said.

Pavlik studied my face. 'You mean your stumbling over bodies or your unnatural relationship with your sheepdog?'

'Both.' I patted his cheek and went to toss my salad.

I picked up the subject of Kip's murder as we were clearing the dishes from dinner. 'Becky Ronstadt is a pretty unpleasant person. If she incited Jacque to kill Kip, I hope you can charge her with something.'

'You're really hot on Jacque Oui as a suspect.'

I straightened up from setting our plates on the floor for the dogs to lick. 'Aren't you? Jacque was there, had a motive and, according to Mary, he was not in his car when she left.'

'He wasn't? She didn't tell Fergussen that.'

'She doesn't like Fergussen. Nobody does.'

'That's not a reason to lie to him.'

'She didn't lie. She merely didn't offer more information.' Now I sounded like Mary. Or Amy. And probably Sarah. 'But my point is, if Jacque wasn't in his car, where was he?'

'Relieving himself?' Pavlik whistled for the dogs.

'Why is that the go-to answer? Do guys really just pee on a bush at the drop of a hat?'

'Bush? No?' Pavlik stepped aside to avoid being barreled over by Frank. 'But there's a gas station right around the corner on Poplar Creek. Maybe he went to get a Coke or something.'

Maybe. 'But if so, he did it because he was staking out the house. You don't think that's suspicious? When Mary left, Jacque could have been sneaking into the house.'

'Then he waited to kill Fargo in his bed a couple hours later?'

'Who knows? Do we know what time the Peugeot left?'

'Think we need to rinse these?' Pavlik had retrieved the plates.

'I suppose, to get the dog spit off them.' Dishes done, Mocha and Frank trotted into the living room for a postprandial snooze by the fireplace. 'So is that a no?'

'To rinsing the dishes?' Pavlik hesitated, mid-rinse.

'No, I'd go ahead and rinse the slimy off,' I said, taking the one he'd finished and slipping it into the dishwasher. 'I meant "no", we don't know what time the Peugeot left.'

Pavlik handed me the other plate, as his cell binged. 'No is correct. But we'll ask when we talk to Oui.'

'You haven't done that yet?' I was surprised.

'Fergussen had trouble finding him.' Pavlik held up the phone. 'But thanks to you, Oui's been taken into custody for questioning.'

Thanks to me? 'You mean, you sent Fergussen over to snag him at Amy's?'

'Yes, but I had him wait until after they finished eating.'

'But, still . . .'

'Gotta go.' He kissed me on the cheek. 'Thanks.'

'For squealing or for making – or, at least, planning – dinner?'

He grinned. 'Both.'

TWELVE

'Are you going to tell Amy you squealed?' Sarah asked me.

It was Sunday morning and our Goddard coffee rush had just vacated the premises.

The Goddard Group had originally started meeting at the lunch counter at Goddard Pharmacy, which was down the way from our original location in the strip mall, Benson Plaza. When Gloria Goddard had decided not to rebuild after her pharmacy was destroyed, the group shifted their allegiance to us, largely because we relaxed our one-refill policy for them. I knew, though, that we were just one free coffee away from them abandoning us for McDonald's.

Still, they made being open worthwhile on Sunday when there was virtually no commuter traffic.

I glanced toward the side door, making sure that Amy hadn't arrived yet for her shift. 'Not if you don't do it for me. I mean, Fergussen would have been watching her place anyway, right?'

'For all Fergussen knew, they'd broken up. Until you opened your mouth to Pavlik.'

'But I'd already told Pavlik I thought Amy still loved . . . Oh, yes. I see what you mean.'

The side door banged open. 'How *could* you, Maggy?'

As Amy rounded the corner, I held up my hands. 'I am so sorry, Amy. I just mentioned to Pavlik that I'd picked up steaks for us because I was inspired by the fact that Jacque was cooking dinner for you.' At her house. Right then.

'All perfectly innocent, right?' She was advancing on me, nose ring trembling. 'I bet you told Jason where he was, too. You *hate* Jacque!'

With that, she burst into tears.

Throwing me a withering look, Sarah led our barista to a table. 'We all hate Jacque, Amy. But we love you.'

Amy sniffled. 'I . . . um . . . I'm . . .'

'Don't listen to Sarah,' I said, sitting down next to the girl and rubbing her shoulder. 'We don't hate Jacque. We just think he's kind of . . .'

'Hard to like,' Sarah finished. 'Though at least I've tried harder than Maggy.'

'You have not,' I said.

'Will you two stop!' Amy exploded. 'The fact is, Maggy, that you passed things on to Pavlik that I'd told you in confidence.'

'I . . . well, I didn't know it was in confidence.' This was a weak argument that I'd used with Pavlik on occasion. 'You should have said—'

'For God's sake!' She was on her feet again. 'You're the one who said I shouldn't be seen with him. Then you send the sheriff's dog over there to roust us after dinner.'

'They specifically waited until you were finished,' Sarah said helpfully.

'That Fergussen ass burst in just as we were standing up from the table,' Amy said tearfully. 'He was absolutely rude, calling Jacque a Frenchie.'

Sarah cocked her head. 'Better than Pepe Le Pew.'

'Stop it!'

I ran my hand over my face. 'I'm sorry, Amy. I had no right to tell Pavlik that Jacque was at your house.'

I'd gotten fairly good at knowing what I could and couldn't share of what Pavlik told me. I really hadn't thought much about the other way around – about what I should and shouldn't be sharing with my future husband. The thought was sobering. In my first marriage, Ted and I had never kept secrets from each other – or so I thought, until his life-size secret, Rachel, landed us in divorce court. Now I imagined Pavlik and me sitting across the dinner table from each other silently, each minding our own trunk-load of secrets.

Though we'd most likely be eating at the coffee table in the living room. And we could always put on a movie.

'I'm so sorry,' I repeated. 'But you're right that I'd prefer Jacque to be Kip's killer over you, or Sarah, or Mary. Still, it was no reason to betray your trust.'

'You just can't will it to be Jacque because you don't like him,' Amy said sternly.

'Besides,' Sarah said, 'we have plenty of suspects. What about Jason? You don't like him either. And there's Jayden – isn't she just a little too nice? And what about the gardener? Or the housekeeper? Maybe a business partner?'

I was brightening. Sarah was right. There were plenty of suspects to go around. 'Business partner? I thought it was just Kip and his kids.'

'Who knows?' Sarah threw up her hands. 'I'm just saying the sky's the limit.'

She was right. But I still kind of wanted it to be Jacque.

'Creditors, too,' I said. 'Which reminds me, Sarah. Have you run a title search on the Fargo house yet?'

'Not yet. Why?'

'I had an interesting conversation with Laurel Birmingham last night at the grocery store. She suspects there are liens on the property. Maybe years of them.'

'Liens?' Amy asked.

'Mechanics or contractor's liens,' Sarah explained. 'If somebody does work on your house and you don't pay them, they can file a lien on the property for the amount they're owed.'

'And that has to be paid off before you sell?'

'Yes, because nobody is going to buy a property without clear title – they don't want to assume those debts.'

'According to Laurel, the liens could go back a full generation. Apparently, Kip's father wasn't any better at paying his bills than Kip was.'

'Let's go by the house and see what Jason can tell us,' Sarah suggested. 'I told him I'd drop off a listing contract anyway.'

'But we can't leave Amy here alone to man the shop.'

Amy held up her hands palm out, as if to fend off both me and my stoolie mojo. 'Please go. I'd prefer to be alone.'

'Amy, I . . .' But Amy was walking away.

'She'll get over it,' Sarah said. 'Either Jacque will fry, and she'll have to admit you were right or he'll be exonerated, and she'll quit.'

Reassuring. I untied my apron. 'OK, but you'd better make sure your listing contract is ironclad if you want to get paid.'

'You think the rotten apple may not have fallen far from the cheap tree?'

That's exactly what I thought. Though I probably would have put it differently.

'What did she mean about Jason?' I asked as Sarah rang the bell at the Fargo house.

'What do you mean?' She leaned on the bell again.

'Amy said she bet I told Jason where Jacque was, too. I did no such thing.'

'Sure, get all righteous about that one. You did tell the sheriff.'

'In my defense, it's not exactly rocket science. Where would you look for Jacque besides his house, Schultz's Market or Amy's house. The man doesn't have a life.'

'Where would you look for us besides our houses or Uncommon Grounds?'

Fine. As I went to punch the bell again, the door was swung open abruptly by Mrs Gilroy.

'What do you want?' she demanded.

Before I could answer, she was stalking off down the hallway.

'Are you OK?' Sarah asked, following her.

OK? The woman was nasty as ever, so far as I could see.

But then she turned, and I saw her eyes were wet, as if she'd been crying. She dabbed them with a dish towel.

'You're bleeding,' I said, pointing at the red seeping onto the towel from her hand.

'No shit, Sherlock. I cut myself.'

As we entered the kitchen, Rafael came in with a first aid kit.

'First get those disgusting things out of my kitchen,' the lovely Mrs Gilroy demanded.

Rafael sent an apologetic smile our way. 'Sorry, I was outside when I heard the cries.' He picked up a vented delivery box and his work gloves from the counter and ducked into the storeroom with them.

'This is all your fault, Miss Marple,' Mildred Gilroy wailed at me, collapsing into a kitchen chair. 'They just took my Jason away.'

Sarah and I exchanged glances and she took the chair next to Mrs Gilroy. 'The police did?'

She chin-gestured toward me. 'Her sheriff.'

'You'll have to excuse Mildred.' The gardener had returned with a variety of first aid creams and gauze bandages and set them on the table. 'She's very upset.'

It was then I saw the butcher knife on a cutting board next to a small ham. Both had blood on them, as did an open Agatha Christie paperback from whence she'd apparently gleaned my new nickname. 'What did they arrest Jason for?'

'Arrest?' Mrs Gilroy's voice was edging higher in both pitch and volume. 'They said they just wanted to talk to him.'

'Both Jason and Jacque,' Sarah said. 'That's interesting.'

Rafael unwound the towel from the housekeeper's hand. 'This doesn't look too bad, but we must clean it out.'

'Jacque Oui was taken into custody for questioning last night,' I explained. 'And you say Jason, just now?'

'Moments ago,' Rafael said, holding a multi-layer pad of gauze over the wound on Mrs Gilroy's palm to stop the bleeding. 'Mildred was so upset the knife slipped and she cut herself.'

'They're lucky I didn't use it on them,' Mrs Gilroy said, waving her hand so Rafael had to chase it to apply the bandage. 'So what if my Jason threatened that Frenchman? Who could blame him?'

Not me. 'When was this?'

Mrs Gilroy rolled her eyes. 'Moments ago. Rafael told you.'

'I meant when did Jason threaten Jacque? And why?'

'Last night, as he arrived up at that Jezebel's house. Jason knew he'd show up there eventually.'

Jezebel being Amy, obviously. 'Did Jason confront Jacque because he stole his father's girlfriend? Or because Jason thinks Jacque actually killed Kip?'

'Both, I believe,' Rafael said.

'Of course both,' Mrs Gilroy said. 'Because the first is the motive. The Frenchman had both that and opportunity. Jason was determined to get the truth out of him.'

'A little dramatic, you think?' Sarah said in a low voice to me as Rafael finished his first aid.

'Like something out of a mystery novel.' I nodded toward the bloody book.

'What are you two whispering about?' Mrs Gilroy snapped.

'We're just wondering whether Jason is accusing Jacque to divert attention from himself,' I said casually. 'After all, Jason and Jayden have the most to gain from their father's death.'

'Get out!' Mrs Gilroy thundered, rising up with Rafael still attached by adhesive tape to her hand.

And so we did.

'We might have gotten more out of her if you'd been nice,' Sarah said, as we got into my Escape.

'Role reversal. That's what I usually say to you.'

'And you're usually right.'

An amazing admission.

'And you're right in this case, too. I don't know what it is about that woman, but she irritates me.'

'Because she doesn't like you. You like people to like you.'

'Doesn't everybody?' As I started the car, my phone buzzed. 'Text message from Eric – I need to get back to him.'

'Yes,' Sarah said as I dialed. 'Everybody wants to be liked. Even people like Jacque.'

Sheesh. 'Is this supposed to be a life lesson or something, from you of all people?' I held up my finger. 'Hi, sweetie – sorry I didn't get back to you. Sure, I can hang on.'

I turned back to Sarah. 'Jacque Oui has been nothing but nasty to me. And, yes, if he went away for Kip's murder, I'd be just fine with it. I don't think he's a nice person and I don't think he's good for Amy. If—'

I held up the finger again. 'Sure,' I said into the phone. 'Of course, I'm dying to know . . . who?'

I hung up the phone a minute later and closed my eyes. 'You're not going to believe this.'

'Believe what?'

I opened them. 'I told you Eric did his DNA and found a cousin or something nearby that we didn't know about?'

'Yeah, but . . .' She stopped, and a grin spread over her face. 'Don't tell me.'

'Yup.' I turned off the key and sat back. 'Third cousin.'

'Doesn't mean you'll inherit anything, I suppose,' Sarah said. 'But that's good, since it means you won't be a suspect this time, at least. Though—'

'Inherit? What are you talking about?'

'Kip Fargo. Your cousin.' She pointed at the house where we still sat parked.

I started to laugh. 'Kip? You think I'm related to Kip?'

'Well, yeah. You said—'

'Cousin Kip? I wish.' The laughter was louder, maybe a little hysterical. 'No, it's not the victim I'm related to.'

'Then . . .' Sarah still looked bewildered.

'It's the suspect.' I started the car. 'Come on. Let's see if we can break Cousin Oui out of jail.'

'Just because Jacque's a relative now, doesn't mean you have to like him,' Sarah pointed out as we pulled into the sheriff's department parking lot. 'Or that he's not a criminal. Look at Cousin Ronny.'

'You're not actually related to Ronny by blood. Or DNA,' I said. 'And honestly, I couldn't care less about Jacque, related or not. But Eric is all excited about this and we don't have that much family on my side. A cousin – even second or third, is a big deal.'

'Even if he's French? Or faux French?'

'That's the other disturbing part,' I said, turning into a spot and switching off the engine. 'Apparently Jacque really is French. And Norwegian. As are we.'

'I'm sorry.'

I sighed. 'I promise not to get uppity with you.'

'Too late,' Sarah said, climbing out. 'But this does explain a lot of that.'

I was grinning as Pavlik emerged from the building with Jacque.

'Good timing,' Sarah said as they reached us. 'Maggy's two favorite men.'

Jacque looked over his shoulder to see who she was talking about.

'Funny,' I said to Sarah as Jacque continued on toward the

parking lot. Then I turned to Pavlik. 'Was that a bruise on his face?'

'Jason Fargo hit him.'

Physical assault was decidedly different than threats, in my book. I wondered if Mrs Gilroy just couldn't believe her boy could go there. 'Is Jacque off the hook then? I know Amy will be relieved.'

'Obviously.' He pointed.

Sarah and I turned to see Jacque getting into Amy's Jetta. She waved.

'If Amy marries Jacque, she'll be your cousin-in-law.' Sarah was enjoying this.

'That, quite honestly, would be the only good thing that could come from this,' I said.

'What are you two talking about?'

'Jacque is my cousin,' I said.

'You're just finding this out now?'

'Yes, as a matter of fact. Eric found him through one of those DNA matching things. Couldn't be worse timing.'

Pavlik grinned. 'Well, if it helps, we're not arresting him yet.'

'Yay.' It was a weak attempt. 'What about Jason Fargo? Is he in custody?'

'Fergussen brought him in. Oui isn't pressing charges, but it was a good opportunity to ask Fargo some questions without flagging him as a suspect.'

'Is he?'

'A suspect?' Pavlik shrugged. 'Aren't heirs always suspects?'

A question to answer a question. Or two questions to answer a question. I could play that game, too. 'Jason and Jayden are the sole heirs? What about Amy?'

'We've found no evidence that a new will was ever drafted, despite what Fargo told his daughter.'

'Then they killed him in the nick of time,' Sarah said.

'I thought you liked Jason and Jayden,' I said.

'I like all my new clients. Though I prefer them without strings attached, and I'm a little ticked at this lien thing. To top things off, a murder trial could throw a wrench into the sale – something about heirs not benefiting from murder?'

'When they're the ones committing it, you mean?' I asked. 'I think it's called the slayer statute.'

'Pithy,' Sarah said. 'Even if it's inconvenient in this case.'

Pavlik smiled. 'I'm going home. Anybody want to join me?'

Sarah's hand shot up.

I slapped it down before saying to Pavlik, 'I'll meet you there.'

Since we'd had rib-eye the night before, tonight's repast was peanut butter on toast. Pavlik natural chunky, me low-fat creamy.

'They took out some fat but look at all the sugar they added.' Pavlik was reading my label.

'That's why it tastes like the inside of a peanut butter cup spread on toast. Heaven.'

'If you like that sort of thing,' Pavlik said.

'Don't be a peanut butter snob,' I said, reclaiming my jar.

'I just mean each to their own. I personally prefer my peanut butter to taste like peanuts.'

I kissed him on the cheek. 'This conflict could end our relationship, you know.'

'Or we could just keep buying two kinds of peanut butter.'

'And respect each other's choices. Without judging.'

'Done.' He grabbed me around the waist and pressed his peanut-flavored mouth against my candy-coated one.

I licked my lips. 'You got peanuts in my peanut butter.'

'Funny.'

'Sometimes.' I took my toast and sat at the table, waiting for him to join me. 'Amy is really mad at me.'

'Because of me?'

'Yes. Or more specifically because I told you where Jacque was and you acted on it. Or, even worse, had Fergussen act on it. He called Jacque a derogatory name.'

I had Pavlik's attention. 'What name?'

'Frenchie.'

'Is that derogatory?'

'Sure. It's meant to be dismissive.' And as a newly minted French person, I guessed I had standing to say that. 'He also referred to Rafael Rojas as "the Mexican". When I pointed out Rafael is Colombian, he discounted it, saying "*they* all speak the same language" and something about drugs.'

Pavlik wasn't happy. 'I'll talk to him.'

'He referred to Mrs Gilroy as "the old lady". Not *an* old lady, but the old lady. I don't even like the woman and that offended me.' Which reminded me. 'She was really upset today after you picked up Jason.'

'Not me. That was Fergussen, too.'

'The man is an ass, in even Amy's estimation, and he's going to get you and the department in trouble.'

'I said I'd talk to him.'

Subject, apparently, was closed. 'K.'

There was quiet at the dinner table, such as it was.

Pavlik cleared his throat. 'Fargo's memorial service is tomorrow. Would you like to go with me?'

'I'd love to.'

THIRTEEN

'We veer toward an argument and our makeup date is an invitation to a funeral,' I said to Sarah in the narthex of the church as we waited for Pavlik to arrive.

'Kind of cool.'

'Yeah, it is.' A smile played at my mouth. 'Life with a lawman.'

'Set a date yet?'

'Uh-uh.' I was standing on my tippy toes. 'There's Jason and Jayden. And Mary. Rafael. Catherine Barry – she looks like she's been crying. There's a story there, I know it.' I craned my neck. 'I don't see Mrs Gilroy.'

'Mildred?'

I rolled my eyes. 'Yes, Mildred. Amy must be coming, right?'

'She got Tien to cover for her at the shop, so I assume so.'

'We should have brought her with us.'

Sarah glanced over. 'I don't think she's talking to you yet.'

That made me sad. 'At least it seems she's off the hook.'

'But your cousin Jacque is still snagged, which will give her no joy.' She nodded toward the door. 'There they are.'

'Amy and Jacque?' I couldn't believe it. 'Together?'

'Yup. And next in is Deputy Fergussen, the man who put the dick in dick.'

'Shh,' I said, restraining a giggle.

'What? You're the one who called him a Neanderthal.'

'I did, didn't I?' I was kind of proud of that.

'Oh shit.'

'What?' Sarah had about four inches on me, so I couldn't see what she was reacting to.

'He's going to make trouble.'

'Fergussen?' Where was Pavlik when you needed him to control his goon?

'No, Jason.'

'You've got your nerve coming here, Oui,' I heard Jason call out, as if on cue.

Leaving Sarah, I weaved my way through the crowd to the door, standing just off to the side by a pillar so they couldn't see me.

'Not now, Jason,' Jayden whispered, putting her hand on her brother's arm. 'And not here.'

'Jacque means no harm,' Amy said. 'He just came to support me.'

'Idiot. She should have come with us.' I hadn't realized Sarah was behind the pillar with me.

'Yes, she should have,' I whispered back. 'Bringing Jacque is kind of . . .'

'. . . a slap in the face to my father.' Jason had completed my thought. 'You never loved him, you just wanted his money.'

Now that, I knew, wasn't true.

'I did not,' Amy protested. 'I—'

'You two were probably in it together.' Jason shoved Jacque in the chest. He didn't move the older man, but instead staggered back himself.

'He's drunk,' I whispered to Sarah, as Jayden steadied her brother.

Fergussen, who'd been chatting up Catherine, elbowed his way in. 'Now let's not go pushing Frenchie here.'

'I can defend myself quite nicely,' Jacque said. 'And I would appreciate your using my surname, which is Oui.'

'Wee what?'

'Fergussen knows damn well what Jacque's name is,' I said. 'He brought him into the station.'

'Oui,' Amy said. 'Jacque Oui.'

'Wee-wee?'

'Oh, God – he thinks he's funny,' I whispered.

'At least when I do the "Oui, oui, oui, all the way home" it's in good fun,' Sarah said.

'I want Jacquey-boy out of here,' Jason thundered.

'Maybe it would be better if he did leave,' Jayden said to Amy.

'Let's go,' Fergussen said, hitching up his pants. 'The both of you.'

As he reached out toward Jacque, Amy slapped his hand. 'Stop harassing us. We did nothing.'

He grabbed her arm and twisted it behind her. 'Except assaulting an officer, missy.'

'She barely touched you,' Jayden protested. 'Leave her alone.'

'Unhand her,' Jacque demanded.

'Oh, geez.' I pulled out my cell phone. 'I've got to find Pavlik before this blows up.'

'Too late.'

I looked up to see Jacque's right cross connect with Fergussen's jaw.

'What was Amy thinking, bringing him?' I asked for maybe the third time.

Sarah and I were back at Uncommon Grounds with Tien. The store was closed and we'd pulled two deuce tables together, settled our chairs around them and unscrewed a bottle of white wine we kept in back for emergencies. We were using coffee cups as wine glasses.

'She was blazing mad when they left here,' Tien said, offering to top off my cup before adding to hers.

I shook my head. 'At who, besides me?'

'Mostly the situation,' Tien said. 'Look at it from Amy's side. She'd dated this guy for less than three months – a rebound relationship, really – and then all . . . this.'

'"This" being he proposes unexpectedly and then gets himself killed,' Sarah said, offering up her cup. 'It does kind of suck.'

'Sucks even more for Kip. And for Jason and Jayden,' I pointed out.

'Assuming they didn't kill their father.' A buzzer sounded somewhere in the kitchen and Tien went to seek it out.

'You know what I don't understand,' I said to Sarah. 'What exactly is the will situation? Jayden says Kip told them that he had already changed it. Jason says he was going to but didn't. Why the disconnect?'

'People hear what they want to.'

I chewed on that. 'The chicken salad lunch on Wednesday. Did Mrs Gilroy say anything about what they talked about?'

'Only that Kip told the kids he was going to propose to Amy that night.'

I sat up straighter. 'I wondered if he had. Why didn't you tell me?'

'I thought you knew. He had Jason come home so he could tell the kids together.'

'Did she say how the news was received?'

'I think "surprise" was the way she put it. The woman is the faithful family retainer. She's not going to rat on them.'

'She might to you,' I said as Tien whisked back into the room.

'Mmmmm,' Sarah said, snatching a cinnamon roll before Tien could put down the plate. 'Ouch!'

'Hot,' Tien said. 'I tell you that every time.'

'And every time she burns the roof of her mouth.'

'And complains about it for a week.'

'Mmmph.' Sarah took a mouthful of wine and swished it around, to cool the burn. 'It's worth it.'

'You're not the one who has to listen to you.' I picked up my phone. 'Nothing from Pavlik.'

The sheriff had arrived in the midst of the melee and managed to settle things down, mainly by hauling Amy and Jacque into the station and telling Fergussen to stand down.

'Do you think Jacque will be charged?' Tien asked. 'And Amy?'

'Maybe not Amy,' I said, 'though technically she did assault an officer.'

'She slapped his hand,' Sarah said. 'Fergussen completely overreacted. A dozen people will have it on their mobile phones.'

'I think she may be fine,' I said. 'As for Jacque, I don't think you can break a deputy's nose and not get charged.'

'Got to hand it to the little French' – Sarah took one look at me – 'dude. I didn't think he had it in him.'

'Me neither. And Amy, sitting on him?'

'On who?' Tien asked, taking a swipe of the frosting off the plate. Poor woman had probably made so many cinnamon rolls, she had no interest in eating them anymore.

Not the case for me. I slid one onto a napkin, trailing sticky white icing. 'Jason, after he fell down.'

'She kept him out of the fight and probably out of jail,' Sarah said. 'He should thank her.'

'Maybe he will when he sobers up.'

'Jason fell down drunk?' Tien asked. 'Yikes, what kind of funeral was this?'

'The kind that's canceled.'

'Really?' Tien asked. 'I've never heard of such a thing.'

'Son passed out, daughter hysterical, pseudo-fiancée and her lover arrested.' I shrugged. 'It seemed the right thing to do.'

'Besides,' Sarah said, 'it's not like they need to get the guy into the ground. The deceased wasn't even present.'

'The county hasn't released the body,' I explained to Tien. 'This was just to be a memorial service.'

'A memorial service no one will ever forget,' she said.

Sarah looked at me. 'I can't imagine they'll top it at the actual funeral. You?'

'Never. I wonder why Mrs Gilroy wasn't there,' I said. 'It was the middle of the afternoon, so night driving wouldn't be a problem.'

'From what you've told me about her,' Tien said, 'you'd think the two kids would have brought her. The long-time retainer. Maybe she was even their nanny.'

It hadn't occurred to me, but the woman was old enough, certainly. Maybe that's why she was so attached to Jason.

And yet, she hadn't been at the memorial service of her long-time employer. 'We should go over there, Sarah, and see if she's there. You can chat her up. Find out more about the lunch.'

'Today?' She was reaching for another cinnamon roll and twisted her wrist so she could see her watch. 'After five. She'll have headed home.'

'Do we know where that is?'

'I don't know if "we" do, but I sure don't.' Around a bite, she said. 'Besides, we mmm . . . mmm.'

'Chew and swallow.'

She did. 'I said, "besides, we've had wine". We're already going to have to call Uber to get us.' She raised her coffee cup. 'More, please.'

*　　*　　*

We did ride-share home. Pavlik arrived when I was already in bed watching television with both dogs.

'Is there room for me?' he asked, sitting down on the narrow edge of the bed still available to him.

'Always.' I sat up and muted the TV. 'What happened with Amy and Jacque?'

'Amy was released. I convinced Fergussen that a slap wasn't quite assault, though in reality it is.' He shook his head. 'What was she thinking?'

'I'm not sure she is thinking, other than that she was defending her man. But bringing Jacque in the first place? That was nuts.'

'Fergussen apparently warned her not to.'

'That would do it.'

'Do what?'

'Ensure that she would bring him.' Amy could be stubborn. Still a stupid thing to do, but at least this was some explanation. 'What about Jacque?'

'Your cousin broke my deputy's nose.' He reached over to scratch Frank.

'I thought so.' The blood and abrupt left turn were a giveaway. 'You're charging him?'

'Have to.' He got up and undid his belt.

'Sarah says Fergussen puts the dick in dick,' I said, watching him drop his pants.

'Cute.' He looked at me. 'Please tell me you're not thinking . . .'

'Oh, but I am.'

'What about them?'

I snapped my fingers. Both the sheepdog and chihuahua hopped down, albeit grumpily. 'What about them?'

I swung by the Fargo house the next morning.

I'd have preferred Sarah was with me when I talked to Mrs Gilroy, but she and, I hoped, Amy, were working at the store. I'd go in later to try to make peace with our barista and figure out how to help her help my new Cousin Jacque.

As I switched off the ignition, my phone buzzed. Eric, actually calling instead of texting. It was enough of an aberration that I picked up immediately. 'Hi, sweetie.'

'Hi, Mom! Have you told Jacque that he's our cousin yet? I was going to tag him as a relative but wanted to make sure he knew about the DNA results first.'

'Jacque's in jail.'

'Mom.'

'I'm just saying that I haven't had a chance to tell him yet.'

'Because he's in jail.'

'Not totally because of that. Partly because of the reason he's in jail.'

'Which, no doubt, kept him busy.' I guess having a step-mother doing twenty-to-life puts these things in perspective.

'It did. You know he and Amy are back together again.'

'I didn't but that's good. Maybe she'll be a relative, too, some day.'

And speak to me. 'Maybe so.'

'Will Jacque be in jail long?'

'Probably not. I assume he'll get bail.' A white truck pulled up and parked on the street behind me.

'Should we—'

'Bail him out? No. He broke the nose of one of Pavlik's deputies.'

'That's not good.'

'No, but the deputy is a bit of an ass, so I have some sympathy.'

A sigh. 'Anything else going on that I should know about?'

Rafael passed by balancing a box on his shoulder and waved.

'I don't think so.' I waved back. 'Everything good with you?'

'Yeah, good. Let me know when Jacque is out?'

'You bet. Love you, sweetie.'

'Love you, too, Mom.'

Was there a better kid on the face of the earth? I didn't think so.

I climbed out and walked up the driveway.

Rafael was crouching down at the pond.

'Are those your frogs?' I asked, pointing at the box.

'They are. Watch.' He opened the box, which I could see now had air vents. The frogs jumped out and splashed down into the pond.

'They're adorable.' I pointed. 'Look at those eyes – they're like little cartoon frogs.'

'These five are much younger than the one I showed you so they mustn't be handled,' he said. 'They're very delicate and stressed from their journey.'

The frogs were kind of cute, though I personally had no intention of touching them. 'Like puppies – they're cuter when they're little. Though don't tell my giant sheepdog and chihuahua that.'

'You have a giant chihuahua?'

'Bad sentence structure. The chihuahua is chihuahua-sized.'

'Too bad. I'd pay money to see that.' He straightened up. 'Quite the spectacle yesterday.'

'I know,' I said. 'Awful to see Kip's memorial ruined like that. Jason and Jayden must be so upset.'

'I'd say Jayden is upset. Jason is nursing a hangover. A giant one.' He grinned.

'I was surprised that Mrs Gilroy wasn't there.'

'I, as well. She went home after cutting herself on Sunday and hasn't been back. I was going to run by and check on her after this.'

'Could I go with you?'

The flash of white teeth. 'You like both frogs and housekeepers?'

'I'm tepid on the latter of the two, but I'm trying.'

'Then come along.'

'What is it you would like to know from Mildred?' Rafael asked as he pulled the white truck to the curb in front of a small yellow house.

'You don't miss anything, do you?' I said as I climbed out of the truck.

'Not very much that's in front of me. You don't either, because you're not interested in frogs or trees or even Mildred Gilroy – at least not as a person.'

'More as an information source,' I admitted, looking toward the house. 'I guess that's true.'

'And me, as well.'

'You I do find interesting. You're very smart. I understand you're a teacher.'

'Of science. Yet now I work as a gardener.'

'I understand you're working toward your credentials to teach here?' I asked, following him up the driveway.

'I am, but there's no shame in working with my hands either.'

I stopped. 'I didn't mean that there was.'

'It is a stigma here,' he said. 'Which is sad.'

It was sad. 'I serve people coffee for a living. But I believe making sure people are fully caffeinated to take on their day is a noble calling.'

He laughed. 'As do I. Shall we see if Mildred is home or playing hooky?' He rang the bell.

'You asked what I wanted to know from Mrs Gilroy,' I said as we waited. 'I heard that Kip told his kids at lunch on Wednesday that he was proposing to Amy that night. Jayden also told us that he said he had changed his will, naming Amy as his main heir.'

'As you told me.'

'But Jason says that his father intended to do that but hadn't. I don't quite understand why one heard one thing and the other another.'

Rafael rubbed his chin, thinking. 'Perhaps there was further discussion?'

'Perhaps. I'm hoping Mrs Gilroy heard exactly what Kip told them.'

'It's possible,' Rafael said, ringing the bell again. 'You said I don't miss anything, but Mildred Gilroy puts me in the shade in that respect.'

I grinned. 'Problem is will she tell me what she heard? She's not a fan.'

'Then maybe I can help. She is a fan of mine.'

'Perfect.' Now all we had to do was find the woman. 'So where is she, do you think?'

'I don't know.' He knocked. 'It's not usual for her to miss work.'

'Did she not call in?'

'Absent, you mean? No. At least not that I was told. Jayden asked me to check on her because she had missed two days in a row.'

'And the memorial service.' I stepped back from the door. 'Should we look in the windows?'

'With you along, perhaps.'

'What do you mean?'

'By my own, peeking in an elderly woman's windows would put me in jail.'

He was probably right, despite his good intentions.

I stepped off the porch and went around the side of the porch. 'This looks like the kitchen judging by the curtains. Can you see in? I'm too short.'

He kicked a box over and stood on it. 'Still not enough. Can I give you a leg up?'

'It's been a few years since I did this.' Like twenty. Or thirty.

Rafael made a sling of his hands and I stepped into it, levering myself up as he lifted. I caught the side of the window frame. 'It is the kitchen. I can see the stove. And there's coffee on the table and a chair pulled out and—'

'And?'

'Down.'

'Please?'

'Please let me down.' I was shaking.

Stepping off his hand-sling, I got out my phone. Or tried to, dropping it in the process.

Rafael seemed mystified as he picked it up for me. 'Are you all right?'

I took my phone and went to hit Pavlik on speed dial.

'Pizza delivery.'

Damn. Hanging up, I tried again, holding up a finger for Rafael to wait. 'Pavlik? Can you send a car and an ambulance to . . .' I looked to Rafael.

'254 Cedar Lane.'

I repeated it to Pavlik and rang off.

'Mildred is in the kitchen ill?' Rafael asked. 'Should we try to get in? I can break the window.'

I shook my head. 'It won't help, I'm afraid.'

'No?'

'No.' I put my hand on his arm. 'By the looks of it, Mrs Gilroy has been dead for at least a day, maybe more.'

FOURTEEN

'Mildred was wearing her uniform,' Rafael said as we watched the attendants roll the gurney past us.

'She was,' I said.

'Then if she was not dressed for yesterday's memorial, perhaps she was ill yesterday, but tried to go into work this morning?'

'Probably yesterday morning,' I said, watching them load the housekeeper into the morgue van. 'Maybe before the service.'

'Not this morning?'

'No, I . . . well, it's the flies.'

'On the body?'

'Yes, it's a little graphic, but . . .'

'I understand, but I work in nature. I understand its . . . processes.'

Still, the older woman had been his friend or, at the very least, colleague. 'The blowflies, you see, come very shortly after death. They lay their eggs and those eggs hatch into maggots at around the twenty-four-hour mark.'

'And there were,' he swallowed, 'maggots, perhaps?'

'I'm afraid so. Small ones.' Like that should make him feel any better. 'There were tea things out, so maybe she wasn't feeling well and thought a cup of tea would help.'

'A heart attack, they say?'

'That's what they think.' I nodded toward the EMTs who were packing up, though there had been nothing for them to do, really, when they arrived. I'd known that, but procedure had to be followed.

'Perhaps it's for the best. When the house is sold, she would have to find new employment. And at her age?' He shrugged.

It seemed kind of callous. But then Rafael was young – probably in his thirties – so the idea of somebody nearly eighty job hunting sounded like an impossible task. And he was probably right, unless she wanted to be a Wal-Mart greeter. An incredibly grouchy Wal-Mart greeter. 'You'll have to look for work, too, I assume.'

'Yes, but there is always work for a gardener or somebody who is good with their hands. Housekeepers are a bit of a . . .'

'Throwback?' I was thinking about her neat dress with the white collar. 'I suppose you're right.

'There may be a delay in the sale of the house,' I said. 'I understand there may be liens to be settled.'

'Tradesmen.' Rafael nodded. 'Mr Fargo did not always pay his bills in a timely manner.'

'That seems so wrong.'

'He was often unsatisfied with the work. One thing or perhaps another.'

'Or so he said.' Because he didn't want to pay.

Rafael shrugged.

'Ms Thorsen.' Pavlik had sent Fergussen. Happily, with the 'old lady' dead, the only one he could offend was 'the Mexican'. And me, of course.

'Fergussen,' I said, regarding his bruised and slightly misshapen nose. 'How are you?' Not that I cared.

His lips tightened. 'Just fine.'

'You've met Rafael Rojas?'

One curt nod. 'What were you doing here peeking in windows?'

I answered. 'Mrs Gilroy hadn't shown up to work today – or the memorial yesterday – so we came to check on her.'

'By looking in the back window?'

'More the side window,' I said.

Rafael put his hand on my shoulder. 'Mildred Gilroy was my colleague and friend. I was worried and Ms Thorsen offered to come along.'

'How kind of her.'

'It was.' Rafael met his eyes.

'Old lady's been dead for more than a day,' Fergussen said. 'Too bad you didn't get worried before this. Wouldn't have saved her from a massive heart attack but would have at least kept the insect count down.' He swiped at a passing fly.

'You're such a jerk.' The hand squeezed my shoulder in warning.

Too late. 'What?'

'I said you're a jerk. Just because the woman was old, doesn't mean her death isn't sad for her friends and relatives. Have some respect.'

'Just because you're the sheriff's petunia—'

'Fergussen.' Pavlik didn't have to raise his voice to get attention.

The deputy resettled his belt. 'Sir.'

'I'll see you in my office at two.'

'Petunia?' I repeated as the deputy turned on his heel. 'I'm your petunia?'

'The deputy has called me worse,' Rafael said.

'I'm sorry to hear that, Mr Rojas,' Pavlik said. 'Maggy told me a bit, but I'd appreciate it if you would file a formal complaint.'

'I will do that,' Rafael said with a quick nod. 'Now I must get back to work.'

'I'll ride back with you,' I said. Then to Pavlik: 'Thank you for calling everybody in.'

'Looks like a natural death, but it could have been otherwise.' He kissed me on top of the head. 'I'll see you tonight.'

'He's a good man,' Rafael said, as we walked down the front steps to the sidewalk. 'I've been worried about something – a thing that I feared might get me into trouble.'

'Connected to Kip's murder?' I'd stopped by the truck. 'Something you did? Or saw?'

'Neither,' he said, opening my door for me so I could climb in. 'Not really, at least. It's just something that didn't quite fit. Something I've wondered about but was loathe to investigate on my own.'

He got into the other side and started the truck.

'Then let's investigate it together,' I said.

Rafael pulled around the back of the Fargo house and up the service drive and stopped the truck. 'It's here.'

'But I thought you were in the front of the house on Thursday when Jayden came running out after finding Kip's body.'

'I was,' he said. 'But it was the day before I was thinking of.'

'You weren't here.'

'No, but I told you the trees were delivered. It was what you were saying. About tradesmen not being paid that made me think of it.'

'Because Kip hasn't paid the nursery.'

'No, but as I said, that's not unusual. And as I told you, I believe he did not pay to have the trees planted or even placed.'

'Right,' I said, opening the door and climbing out. 'You said the nursery left them here by the service drive.'

'Correct, except this one here.' He pointed at the nearest tree. 'It was in the hole.'

'And that strikes you as odd?' I examined the tree.

'It's the way it was there. Toppled, like it had been shoved to the edge and dropped.'

'Seems fine now.'

'I straightened and staked it. Filled in the hole.'

'You said something didn't quite fit?'

'Exactly that. This nursery is very good and meticulous in their work. So much so that I didn't think they'd have left the tree like that. The other three were lined up like soldiers.'

'Did you call and ask the nursery?'

He hesitated and then nodded. 'At first I didn't want to. I worried that if one of the workers dumped the tree in the hole to do me a favor, I would get them in trouble.'

'But then you did? Call, I mean.'

'I ran into the foreman at another job. He said they left all four there, like I said.'

'In a line like soldiers,' I repeated, staring up at the tree.

It took the two of us nearly an hour to take out the stakes supporting the tree and clear enough soil from around the root ball for Rafael to get down in the hole next to it.

'Do you see anything?'

'Uh-uh,' he said. 'Can you help me tip it?'

I reached out over the open hole and got hold of the trunk. 'Toward me?'

'Yes, please.'

He pushed and I pulled. Finally, the thing shifted.

'Timber,' I cried, jumping out of the way. It was a bit of

an overreaction, given the tree was still in the hole and could at best reach a forty-five-degree angle. 'Still nothing?'

'No, I . . . wait. Can you hand me that spade?'

I snagged the little red-handled shovel and passed it down to him.

'A bit more,' he said, wedging the blade of the spade under the burlap of the root ball while pushing at the tree.

I gave another pull and he levered the spade up.

'Yes!'

'Careful,' I warned. 'Is it . . .?'

'A gun,' he said, brushing the dirt off and passing it up to me.

'Semi-automatic pistol.' I took the gun gingerly. 'Nine millimeter?'

'I think so,' he said. 'If it is the murder weapon then the killer took the gun with him and dropped it in the open hole that night.'

'The trees were already here, so he could have dragged one over and toppled it into the hole to cover the gun,' I said.

'That's why it didn't appear to me to meet the nursery's standards. They weren't the ones to place the tree.'

'The killer could just have kicked some dirt over the gun,' I said, nodding toward the adjacent pile. 'Why bother with the tree?'

'If it had been just soil covering it, I probably would have discovered the gun on Thursday.'

'Not just dropped the tree in and filled the hole?'

'No, I dug the holes before I left for my holiday home. So, when I came back, I loosened the soil before I planted the other trees.'

'How did you move them yourself?' I asked, surveying the three-foot-wide root ball. 'They had to weigh a ton.'

'You don't lift the tree – you roll it by the root ball into position and then let it drop into the hole before you right it.'

I surveyed the relative positions of the tree we'd just disinterred and the three planted nearer to the house. 'That explains why they chose this hole to hide the gun. Anybody, probably even me, could have rolled one a short distance.'

'I don't mean to make it sound overly easy,' Rafael said.

'They can get away from you. In fact, Jason came out to give me a hand when he saw what I was doing.'

'Jason did?' I frowned. 'When was that?'

'That would have been late Thursday afternoon. With the discovery of Mr Fargo's body, I didn't get to work on it as early as I'd have liked.'

'Obviously it was after Jason came home from Madison.' Kid gets the call his father was murdered, drives an hour home from school and then helps plant trees, one of which was covering the murder weapon. 'I'm surprised the police let you bury anything, quite honestly.'

Rafael cocked his head. 'That's true. Perhaps the deputy checked the holes earlier, before I filled them?'

Perhaps. 'Which deputy?'

'The one that neither of us likes very much,' Rafael said with a grin. 'Fergussen.'

I'd have paid money to see Fergussen poking around in a four-foot-deep hole. Or better, six. 'You said you loosened up the dirt in the other holes before dropping in the trees. Did you do anything to this one?'

He shook his head. 'I couldn't get beneath the tree effectively once it was in the hole, so I spaded around the perimeter to loosen the soil, filled in the hole and watered.'

'Somebody thought this through,' I said, getting to my feet and setting down the gun so I could offer him a hand.

He took it.

'That is very true,' he said as he put one foot up on the burlap ball to lever himself out of the hole.

'But who?'

'That is a good question.' He inserted his finger into the trigger guard to pick up the gun.

'Drop it,' a voice ordered.

Rafael did.

Both of us raised our hands over our heads before we had to be told. It was sad we knew the drill for two entirely different reasons.

'We just dug it up, Fergussen,' I told the man, who had his own nine millimeter trained on us.

'Tampering with evidence?'

'More finding it for you.' I knew my tone was sarcastic. Probably not smart, since the man had a gun on us. He just rubbed me the wrong way. And I couldn't help but wonder what the deputy would have done if he'd found Rafael here alone with the gun. 'Did you think to check the holes for the murder weapon?'

'I poked around. This one was filled already.'

'Uh-uh. The tree was in it, but the dirt hadn't been filled in.' I looked to Rafael for confirmation. 'Right?'

'Right.' His hands lowered and then shot back up.

'Will you grab the gun so we can put our hands down, already,' I said irritably.

'Push it over with your foot.'

I obliged and Fergussen snagged it and then holstered his own to slip it into an evidence bag. 'Where'd you find it? This hole, you say?'

I nodded.

'Under the root ball,' Rafael said.

'Now that's interesting,' Fergussen said. 'We just saw you being a good "colleague" and all over at the old lady's house and now you're digging up evidence.'

'That's right,' I said.

'I meant him.' Fergussen gestured with the evidence bag. 'You come home and dig up a random tree and there happens to be a gun under it. You expect me to believe that?'

'Of course,' I said. 'It's a coincidence. Eeny, meeny, miney, murder weapon.'

'Exactly my point,' Fergussen snapped. 'He had to know where to look.'

He had his hand on his holster.

'Cease and desist,' I said, holding up my hands. 'Rafael told me that one of the trees had been dropped into its hole and the nursery denied doing it. We decided to investigate.'

'How about deciding to call the department?'

'And have you inform us that you'd already checked the holes?'

Fergussen took a step toward me.

'You interrupted the chain of evidence,' Pavlik said. 'Fergussen had a right to be angry.'

The deputy transported us to the station in the back of the squad. The only thing missing was the handcuffs. I had a hunch he'd been dressed down enough by Pavlik and figured it was our turn.

As it was. We were in an interrogation room. Rafael and me on one side of the table, Pavlik on the other.

'In retrospect we should have called the authorities immediately,' Rafael was saying. 'I apologize.'

'But we were acting on a hunch,' I protested. 'We might have found nothing. What was Fergussen doing there anyway?'

'His job.'

That was all I was going to get. Probably all I deserved. 'I'm sorry, but we really didn't want to waste your time.'

'Next time, waste our time.'

'I sincerely hope there is not a next time,' Rafael said.

With that, Rafael was excused, but I was recipient of both barrels in Pavlik's office a few minutes later.

'You took the gun out of the hole.' Pavlik was pacing, while I was sitting in the guest chair in his office. 'And then both of you handled it. You know better than that, Maggy.'

'We had to get it out from under the tree in order to see that it was a gun.' It was a weak excuse and I knew it.

'Or you could have called us and we could have lifted the tree out, preserving the scene.' My fiancé was none too pleased with me.

'Don't I have enough problems with Fergussen already?' Pavlik continued. 'The last thing I need is for you to bait him.'

'*Bait* him? Fergussen is a small-minded jerk. He doesn't need any help from me.'

'Then do me a favor and stop helping him.' Pavlik stopped pacing. 'And, while you're at it, stop helping me, too. Just stay out of this.'

FIFTEEN

Ouch.

'Pavlik is as angry as I've ever seen him,' I told Sarah as we waited for the last commuter train from the city to arrive so we could clean up and close down. 'At least as mad as he's ever been at me.'

'Have you talked since you left his office?'

'What am I going to say? I'm sorry your deputy is a small-minded jerk? I'm sorry I found the murder weapon for him? Pavlik wants me to butt out, but it seems like I'm the only one doing anything.'

'You sound mad at him, too.'

I thought about that. 'I guess I am. He's never talked to me like that before and I don't like it.'

'Do you think he had a point about the gun?'

'Probably. And to be fair, I did send him a text apologizing.'

'The damage had been done, though.'

'Stop being reasonable,' I said. 'Just take my side.'

'Fine. It was very smart of you to find the gun. And touch it.'

'So, OK. I should have told Rafael to just leave it in place, that's on me. But we had to tip the tree to reach it, so before it tipped back . . .'

'He snagged the gun.'

'Exactly.'

'And handed it to you.'

'Yes, but I dangled it by the trigger guard.'

'Points for you,' Sarah said, as my phone buzzed once.

I checked. Eric, not Pavlik. 'Eric is asking if Jacque is out of jail yet.'

'Is he?'

'Damned if I know. And damned if I'm going to ask Pavlik.'

Sarah closed one eye and thought. 'Amy. She'll know.'

'She's not talking to me either.' I was running out of sources. And friends. And I was plumb out of lovers.

'I think she's softening,' Sarah said. 'Give her a try.'

'OK, I'll text her.' I did and set down the phone. 'That way she doesn't have to get back to me if she doesn't want to.'

'About the gun: nine-millimeter Glock, you said? Registered?'

'Maybe.'

'But you've had a fight with our main source of information, so we can't find out.'

'Unfortunately. Hopefully we'll be back on good terms before the ballistics results come in.'

'Make crow for dinner tonight and eat it,' was Sarah's advice.

'The gun has to match the bullet that killed Kip,' I said. 'Why else would it be there?'

'You said it was a hollow point. Don't suppose you happened to check the magazine for the type of bullets.'

'I got chewed out for picking up the gun. You seriously think I removed the magazine?'

'No, but figured it was worth the question. Problem with a hollow point in the skull, of course, is that once it ricochets around inside the skull there might not be much left to match.'

'True,' I said, and then brightened. 'Pavlik said there was a single shot, but what if he's wrong? The dresser mirror was broken. If there *was* an errant shot, there might be a second shell somewhere in better shape.'

'And that Pavlik will tell you about.' Sarah thought for a second. 'Eat crow, then make him a nice dinner and have sex. Preferably in a sexy negligee and high heels.'

'For dinner or sex?'

'Both.'

'I work in a coffeehouse and sleep with a man, a sheepdog and a chihuahua,' I said as my telephone pinged. 'Unless your definition of negligee is an extra-large T-shirt and "high" is two inches, I don't have the wardrobe.'

'It's Amy,' I said, punching up the message. 'What the hell? My screen is locked. I can't get the message.'

'Hello?' the phone said.

'She's calling,' Sarah said.

I punched speaker. 'Sorry, Amy. I thought you were texting. You never call.'

'I know, but I decided we should talk.'

'Thank you. And I'm sorry.'

'You're welcome. And I forgive you.'

Well that was easy. If a little . . . coolish. But we'd work through it. 'What's the word on Jacque?'

'He's being released on bail. I have to go down there in about an hour.' She sounded nervous.

I glanced at Sarah and she mouthed, 'Go.'

'Want company?' I said into the phone.

If I haven't mentioned it before, Cousin Jacque Oui is about five feet, eight inches tall and French. That's the best I can describe him.

Coming out of lock-up with Amy, he looked a tad shorter and less French. 'What eez Maggy doing here?'

Still Jacque, though.

'I'm your cousin, so shut up.' And I was still me.

'Zee cousin?' He seemed astonished.

'Not *the* cousin, *your* cousin. And, yes. Eric did his DNA as, I assume, did you. Surprise! Instant relatives you don't want.'

'I had no idea,' he said, rubbing the stubble on his chin. 'Yet, I see no reason for you to be here.'

'Be nice,' Amy told him. 'Maggy is here to help.'

Jacque looked skeptical.

'And Eric made me come.'

That Oui seemed to believe. 'Tell zee boy I am out of zee prison and am about to embark on the road to prove my innocence.'

'By finding the one-armed man?'

'Zee what??'

'Never mind.' No use explaining classic American television to—

'Oh, yes,' Jacque said. 'That would make me Zee Richard Kimble.'

'Played by David Janssen,' I said, 'but I'm surprised you—'

'No, Harrison Ford,' Amy corrected us. 'But why are we talking about old movies at a time like this?'

'*The Fugitive* was a television series before it was a movie.'

'It must be really old then,' Amy said. 'That movie was more than twenty-five years ago. Harrison Ford was young.'

'Impossible,' Jacque said. 'It was . . .'

'1993,' I told him, proving Amy's math. 'This is what you get by associating with a younger woman, Jacque. Our recent memories are their "olden days".'

'No, this is what I get for dating this woman,' Jacque said, looping his arm around Amy's waist. 'Thank you for standing by me, my dear.'

Amy pinked up. 'You're welcome.'

'Sweet.' I would have added 'in a sickening, candy corn kind of way', except I was trying to turn over a new leaf where Jacque was concerned. 'So what happened, Jacque? Were you charged with punching Fergussen?'

'That was zee trumped-up charge,' he said indignantly, moving toward Amy's car. 'Designed to allow the authorities to question me about zee murder, itself.'

'Actually, it's not,' I said, checking my phone and then sliding it into my pocket to follow them. 'I saw you punch the guy.' Not that I hadn't wanted to do it myself at various times.

'Barely a graze.' He stopped by the passenger seat and waited for Amy to unlock the door.

'You broke his nose.'

'Perhaps he has zee glass nose?' He laughed, sliding into the seat.

I reached past him to snag the purse I'd left on the floor of the passenger seat and climbed into the back. 'You two probably haven't heard the latest: the gun was found.'

Amy had just gotten into the driver seat and now she twisted around to face me. 'The gun that killed Kip? Why didn't you tell me?'

'I wasn't sure Pavlik would want the word out.' But since he wasn't getting back to me, it seemed fair game. Besides, I wanted to see Jacque's reaction.

'Good,' he said.

'Good?'

'Yes.' The Frenchman swiveled in his seat, too. 'It is not my gun, so why would its discovery bother me?'

'Where did they find it, Maggy?' Amy asked.

'Under a newly planted tree in the backyard.'

Amy frowned. 'How did it get there?'

'We assume whoever shot Kip dumped it in the hole as they ran out the back door and then dragged the tree on top of it. Rafael filled in the hole, never knowing it was there.'

'Is that how the killer got in?' Amy asked. 'The kitchen door?'

'There's a broken pane of glass. Somebody could have reached through and turned the deadbolt to get in. Went out the same way.'

'That seems suspicious,' Jacque said.

'What?'

'The gardener finding the murder weapon.'

'He wasn't in the country when Kip died.'

'No doubt about that?' Amy asked. 'Not that I want it to be Rafael. He's nice. But anybody else—'

'Besides you and Jacque?' I said. 'I get it.'

When nobody said anything, I continued. 'Did Kip own a gun, Amy?'

'Honestly, I have no idea. What kind was it?'

That specific information was likely something that wouldn't be released to the public just yet. And angry though I might be at Pavlik – and vice versa – I wasn't about to overstep that. 'Not sure.'

'I didn't see anything about the bullet in the autopsy.'

'You saw Kip's autopsy?'

'Jayden showed me. Very creepy. Did you know Kip was a drinker?'

'Like an alcoholic kind of drinker?'

She nodded. 'Enough to cause liver damage, can you believe it? Jayden was shocked. I think she's worried about Jason now, with all his partying.'

'Poor kid.' I meant Jayden. She'd lost her dad and now she had to worry about her older brother Jason. 'How much do you think Jayden knows about Kip's business dealings?'

Amy started the car. 'She worked in his office, so I assume she knows something. You're thinking about the missing money?'

'There is money missing?' That perked Jacque right up. He'd turned to face front and I thought he might have been snoozing up there. 'Whose money? They must be suspects, as well.'

'They must,' I said. 'Unfortunately, the only ones I know about are Mary Callahan, who invested with Kip at your recommendation, I understand, and Sarah.'

'And why is that unfortunate?'

'Because they're my friends, and I prefer they not be suspected of murder.'

'Even if that takes zee pressure off your own flesh and blood?'

Playing the cousin card so soon. 'Yes.'

'Maggy,' Amy warned, backing out of the parking spot. 'You said you would be nice.'

'I'm being nice and honest.'

'It is not anything I do not expect. One family member turning against another. It is a story told over the ages.'

'Where in the world does this penchant for drama come from, Jacque?' I asked. 'It's not in *my* blood line.'

Jacque huffed.

And Amy changed the subject back to an earlier one – one that seemed to be bothering her. 'Speaking of blood lines, don't you wonder if we know anybody? I had no idea Kip was a problem drinker, but neither did his children. They said usually he drank iced tea. How can you drink that much alcohol and hide it?'

Put it in your iced tea. 'I remember my mother telling me once that alcoholics are liars. It's part of the disease.' She had been talking about my father.

'Maybe, but do they lie about everything? He had cancer, too, and didn't tell anybody.'

Poor Amy. I wondered whether she was considering taking Jacque in for a full work-up before she committed. Buy 'em used and that's what you get.

'The autopsy showed Kip had cancer, too?' I asked.

'That he'd had surgery to remove a squamous cell carcinoma.'

'Skin cancer,' I said.

'In zee man's defense,' Jacque said, 'he probably thought it was no big deal to have a mole or small imperfection removed.'

I wondered what Jacque had had removed.

'Thing is,' Amy continued, 'the autopsy opened a whole Pandora's box of information about Kip for Jayden and Jason.'

'Things that you were never aware of either, my dear,' Jacque said. 'And you were going to marry the man.'

She pulled up to the curb and swiveled in her seat. 'Never. I . . . well, I never would have gotten over you.'

As they made moon-y sounds and leaned in for a smooch, I climbed out of the back seat, only to find I was in front of my house. Pavlik's Harley was parked in the driveway.

Time to patch up my own relationship.

Ready or not.

Pavlik was sitting on the back stoop, throwing the ball for the dogs.

'I still don't know how she does that,' I said, nodding at the chihuahua who had managed to wrangle a tennis ball.

'Tiny sharp teeth.' He slid to make room. 'Fuzzy ball.'

I sat down. 'Are we talking again?'

'I didn't know we'd stopped.' He took the ball from Mocha and threw it for Frank.

The sheepdog jogged up to it and, apparently spent, laid down.

'I texted. You didn't text back.'

'I thought actually talking, like face-to-face, would be better.'

That sounded suspiciously like 'we have to talk' – the death knell for any relationship.

But then he surprised me. 'I'm sorry I snapped at you.'

I laid my head against his shoulder. 'And I'm sorry I didn't call when Rafael told me he had an idea where the gun might be. It just seemed like a long shot.'

'And an adventure.' Pavlik watched as Mocha trotted up to where the ball and sheepdog both lay, gave Frank a dark look and picked up the ball.

'She's thinking, "Do I have to do *everything*?",' I said. 'But you're right. It did seem like a fun thing to check out.' I frowned. 'What does that say about me?'

'That digging up murder weapons is "fun"?' Pavlik asked. 'Welcome to my life. I don't blame you for being curious and, to be honest, it's Rojas who should have called us.'

'He was afraid, I think,' I said. 'He doesn't entirely trust Fergussen and I don't blame him.'

'I guess that's the other reason I was so angry.'

'You think Fergussen is a good guy? A good cop?'

'I think he's brusque and small-minded.' Pavlik tilted his head to look me in the eye. 'I believed at one point that we could make a good cop of him. Al Taylor started out very much the same way.'

'Al Taylor was a pain in the butt, but I don't think he was a bad guy.' Deputy Taylor had died a few months earlier.

'No. With Al I think it was more that he enjoyed playing "bad cop".' Pavlik's grin was weak. Losing Taylor had been a blow.

'You saw something of Taylor in Fergussen.'

Pavlik lifted his shoulders and let them drop. 'Or just wanted to. The jury is still out.'

'If this case ever gets to jury.' I held out my hand for the ball and Mocha dropped it in. 'Anything back from ballistics?'

'It's still too early, but I'm pretty certain it's the gun that killed Fargo. Wiped clean. Semi-automatic pistol loaded with nine-millimeter, hollow point bullets buried in the yard of somebody killed by a—'

'Semi-automatic pistol loaded with nine-millimeter hollow points.' I threw the ball. 'The killer must have gone out the back and saw his or her opportunity to get rid of the gun. But why not take it with them?'

'It's not as easy to get rid of a gun as you imagine.'

'I do imagine those things,' I said, smiling.

'I know you do. Just be aware that it's not like the movies. Hiding things is tough these days.'

With CC cameras and mobile phones and people everywhere. None of which was true in this case. 'Was the gun registered?'

'To Fargo.'

'Shot with his own gun.' As I said it, I realized it was a little too much on the mark if Pavlik had Al Taylor on his mind.

'Which means the killer knew it was in the house.'

I chewed on that. 'It can't be anybody he struggled with – anybody who took the gun. Kip was shot in bed . . . asleep?'

'He was on his back with his eyes closed. Shot in the temple.'

'Close range?'

A nod.

'It's like a hit. Or assassination.' I shivered. 'Who could do that?'

'I don't know. But probably somebody who knew where the gun was.'

'Unless he had it out on the nightstand or something for self-protection,' I said. 'Maybe he was worried that one of the people he swindled was coming after him. That person showed up, saw the gun and blam!'

'Blam?'

'Blam! Kip was apparently a real piece of work. Embezzling, not paying for work, even stiffing waiters. Apparently his father was like that before him. Laurel thinks there are probably liens on the house. Do you know—'

He held up his hand. 'The Feds are looking into Fargo's finances – the money part of this case.'

'Which is why you told me to stay out of it.'

'Which is what they told me as well.'

Pavlik wouldn't have liked that any more than I had. 'How do you separate the two? The "money part" could well be the motive.'

'If it appears that way, I'm to let them know. At this point, they're just crunching numbers.'

Which is the way I'm sure Pavlik wanted to keep it.

'Then people like Sarah or Mary, who Kip may have cheated. They're not suspects?'

'They're not suspects I can question, at least effectively, because I don't have any of the information on their possible losses. Or even if there are losses.'

'Well, that's frustrating.'

'Tell me about it. For now, though, it looks like the killer had access to the house and knew about the gun.'

'Meaning Jason and Jayden.'

'And the housekeeper and gardener.'

'Rafael didn't know about the gun.'

'So he says,' Pavlik said. 'Not that it matters. He was out of the country when Fargo was killed.'

'No doubt then?'

'Nope. And the housekeeper is dead of natural causes.'

'You're sure about that, too.'

'Heart failure. Apparently after she got home on Sunday night.'

'Sunday night.' My maggots lined up with that, but I'd thought perhaps the woman had died the next morning – the day of the funeral. 'She was in her uniform.'

'Probably didn't have a chance to change out of it.' Pavlik was trying to pry the ball from Mocha's tiny little teeth.

'She was making tea,' I said. 'Maybe she felt ill and didn't realize what was happening. A lot of women don't recognize the symptoms because they're different than the symptoms that men usually get.'

'They think it's indigestion or heartburn, like my mom did.' Pavlik's mother had taken ill when having dinner with us at a restaurant in Chicago. She died a few hours later.

'That leaves us with Jayden and Jason. Jason is my favorite.'

'Mine, too, but turns out he was in Madison all night.'

Damn. I opened my mouth. 'You're—'

'Sure? Yes.' He held up two fingers. 'Two girls.'

'Aww, that's just wrong.' Two men, sure! 'All night?'

'Close enough.'

'And then there was one.'

'Nope. Jayden has an alibi, too.'

'Two guys?'

'Just one, but she has roommates, too.'

'Damn.' I brightened. 'I still like Jacque for this.'

'Your cousin?'

Apparently, blood isn't all that much thicker than water, in my case. 'Yes.'

'Still a possibility.' Pavlik set down the ball. 'But I just don't see him walking up to a sleeping man and putting a gun to his temple. Do you?'

'Sure, I . . .' I sighed. 'No.'

'Which brings us back to Amy.'

I sat back. 'You're telling me you honestly think she snuck into Kip's house and . . .' A thought struck me. 'How did the killer get in? That broken kitchen window?'

'Yes. Somebody just had to reach in to turn the deadbolt and get in.'

'The rest of the doors and windows were locked?'

He nodded.

Which jibed with what Jayden had told me. She'd had to unlock the front door when she arrived.

'Well, enough,' Pavlik said, standing. 'We've arrived at the same brick wall that I've been knocking my head against all day.'

I stood, too. 'You want something to drink while I get dinner?'

Pavlik smiled. 'While you order dinner? Sure. Got a lemonade or maybe iced tea?'

Lemonade or iced tea – it jogged the memory of Jason in the kitchen, asking Mrs Gilroy for the same drinks. The way the woman doted on bad-boy Jason.

And she hadn't been the only one.

SIXTEEN

Wednesday was my day off this week. Good, because I had the time to do what I needed. Bad because with both Amy and Sarah working, I didn't have a sidekick and every Nick needs a Nora, every Nero Wolfe needs an Archie Goodwin.

'You think you're up to it Frankie-boy?'

The sheepdog raised his mug from his dish and shook, sending water in all directions.

'Good,' I said, getting the leash.

At the sound of the jangle, Mocha looked up from where she was doing her morning ablutions. 'Frank is going detecting with me. You need to stay here, OK?'

If I'd expected an argument, I was disappointed. The chihuahua loved her baths and then, I knew, she'd spend an hour lounging in the puddle of sun streaming in through the front window.

Frank trotted over and I snapped his leash on. As we went down the porch steps to the driveway, he licked my hand. 'It *is* nice to spend some quality time together, isn't it?'

While I didn't regret the addition of Pavlik – and more recently Mocha – to our household, Frank and I had made a series of adjustments, not least of which was sharing both our bed and our pizza.

At one time it had seemed pathetic that Frank was the one I told my troubles to and who always had my back no matter what. Now I kind of missed that closeness and imagined he did the same.

'Loving others just increases our capacity to love,' I told him, as I opened the passenger door for him.

He sat down on the sidewalk and refused to move.

'Yeah, I think it's kind of bullshit, too. But you'll like riding shotgun today, right?'

Non-existent tail wagging, he galumphed up onto the seat.

I went around and got into the driver's side. 'You're going to have to duck your head so I can see the mirror, OK?'

He circled and managed to lay on the seat, his butt just hanging off.

'That'll work.'

I'd told Jayden I'd meet her at the house at ten and she was out front as I pulled up. She waved for me to turn into the circle driveway and park behind a bright, yellow-green Porsche. As I did, I saw a Kingston Realty sign had sprouted on the lawn.

'Sarah re-started her company?' I asked Jayden, as I climbed out.

'I think she just had an old sign left over. If you look closely, she's turned the "o" in Kingston into an "a" with a marker and down below written "not to be confused with Kingston Realty".'

Kingstan Realty. 'That makes no sense.'

'I didn't think so either, but she seems to think it'll keep the woman she sold the realty to from suing her.'

Good luck with that. I wondered if Sarah had even bothered to do a title search and make sure there was a clear title. 'I'm sure Sarah couldn't resist coming out of retirement for this one. It is gorgeous.' Or it would be, if they just left it alone.

'Well, I think this one is gorgeous,' Jayden said. 'Yes, you are. Yes, you are.'

She was talking to Frank, of course, who had stuffed the entire front of his gorgeousness out the window to lick her face.

Jayden giggled. 'Oh, what a sweetie. What's his name?'

'Frank. You can let him out if you want.'

She swung the door open and Frank jumped out.

The girl was immediately on the ground with the sheepdog, scratching him behind the ears. 'You are such a lover. I should get a dog.'

'Are you going to move out of your apartment?'

'I think so,' she said, straightening. 'It'll probably depend on how much is left after the estate is settled. I'll have college to pay for on my own, too.'

'But surely you don't have to worry. I mean, look at this place.' Even as I said it, I felt disingenuous, knowing what I did.

Jayden shrugged, like somebody who had lived on 'this place' all her life. 'Daddy had lots of stuff, but he also had lots of debt. Jason is the executor, so he has to sort it out, thank God. I'm just glad it wasn't me.'

Actually, given Jason's reputation for partying, I was surprised her father hadn't chosen her as executor. But she had given me my opening. 'Jason is the executor and you and he are the beneficiaries? No Amy?'

'No, I guess I was wrong about that.' As she said it, a blush rose. 'Daddy must have said he was going to do it, not that he had.'

An odd thing to get wrong, especially when Jason had gotten it right. Jason had called her attitude 'wishful thinking', said that Jayden had always wanted a sister.

But had she wished for one she'd have to split her inheritance with, at best?

Who was that generous? Certainly not me. 'When did you all talk about it? When you had lunch the day before your dad died?'

'Yes,' she said, looking surprised. 'You know about that?'

'She probably even knows what we ate for lunch.' Jason was coming down the porch steps.

'Chicken salad,' I said, turning with my most pleasant smile. 'Curried. With grapes.'

'Very good,' he said, passing the three of us to get to the Porsche. 'But red or green?'

I raised my hands in surrender. 'I'm good, but not that good.'

'Apparently not.' He touched the door handle to unlock the door and then opened it. Leather seats, leather-covered steering wheel, pretty much leather everything.

The lettering on the side said GTS not GT2, which was the model Amy said Kip drove. Was this Jason's car? If so, I couldn't help but wonder how much it cost. And if it was paid for.

Not that it was any of my business, of course.

Sure was pretty though.

'Why can't we have nice things?' I whispered to Frank as Jason waved his sister over to talk to him.

'Was he telling you to be careful what you said to me?' I asked her as we watched the Porsche roar out of the driveway.

'Actually, he was asking why you were here at all.' She'd been scratching Frank again and looked up. 'I had to tell him I didn't know. Why are you here?'

'Because I think you're the one who hid the gun under the tree.'

Her eyes went a little buggy. 'You think I killed my father?'

'I didn't say that.' I sat on the porch step and motioned for her to join me.

She stayed where she was. 'Then what are you saying?'

'Exactly what I told you. You put the gun in the hole Rafael had dug and then pushed the tree in to hide it.'

'I'm all of a hundred and five pounds. Sure, I could drop a pistol in a hole. But how would I move a tree? And when? And also why? You said you don't believe I killed my father.'

I took one question at a time. 'First' – I raised my index finger – 'the nursery placed the trees in a row. The first one was fairly close to this particular hole.'

'You know how much those things weigh?'

'You'd roll it,' I said, watching her face. 'I'm sure you've seen it done.'

She didn't deny it. She didn't say anything.

'Second question' – the middle finger joined the index – 'when?'

'I wasn't here on Wednesday night. My roommates already told the sheriff.'

'You didn't do it Wednesday night. You did it Thursday morning when you found your father's body.'

'Rafael saw me go in the front and then come running out that same door. I didn't go into the backyard.'

'Somebody did,' I said.

'The killer, of course.' She was still petting Frank, but a little frenetically. Frank had his head cocked, like what's with this broad? Not that he talks like that. 'The glass was broken in the kitchen door.'

'Right. The sheriff thinks that's how the killer got in.'

'It makes sense.' She seemed to be settling down a bit, thinking I was buying the narrative. 'And it explains why the gun was stashed in back.'

'Of course,' I said, patting the step next to me. 'The killer left the same way they came in.'

She came over to sit. Frank stayed where he was, turning to lick the place she'd been petting, probably hoping there was still fur there.

'Where did your dad keep his gun?'

Her head swiveled toward me and then away, like she'd caught herself. 'His gun? You're saying it was my dad's?'

'The sheriff didn't tell you that?' I wondered whether I'd get in trouble for dropping this nugget of information. Probably so, which made it important for me to get the truth out of the girl right here and now.

'No.'

I studied her face. 'Then how did you know?'

'Know?' She shifted a little away from me. 'I just told you that I didn't know it was my dad's pistol.'

'But you knew it was a pistol.'

'You said it was.'

'I said it was a gun. I didn't say it was a pistol, which is by definition a semi-automatic.'

'I don't know gun terms.' Her face had gone white. 'Besides, this isn't the Wild West.'

She did know at least a little about guns if she knew the alternative to a pistol would be a revolver. 'So where *did* your dad keep his pistol?'

'I . . . well, I'm not sure. He used to keep it in his nightstand when I was little, but—'

I held up my hand. 'Wait. Your father kept a loaded gun in his nightstand when you were a little girl?'

'I assume it was loaded.' She shrugged. 'Why else have it there?'

So your kids could accidentally shoot themselves? 'That's really dangerous. He—' I broke it off. Not exactly the time to be talking about gun safety. 'Was your father afraid of somebody?'

'Who, somebody?' She didn't seem to understand.

'I just mean, he kept a gun in his nightstand. I wondered whether there was somebody in particular that he was afraid might want to do him harm.'

'Oh.' Her face cleared. 'Not that I know of, but there have been times like when the stock market went down and stuff that I think customers might have gotten mad at him.' She wrinkled her nose. 'He said it was just the business.'

I wondered what part of 'the business' the Feds were looking into right now, but I moved back to my main line of inquiry. 'Whoever shot your dad would have to have known the gun was in the drawer.'

'Frank, come here,' she called, presumably buying time.

My sheepdog looked at me, and I chin-gestured for him to acquiesce.

I think he sighed.

'Anyway,' she said, when she had Frank sitting next to her. Animal therapy. 'That was where he kept the gun when we were here. Maybe with no kids in the house he didn't bother to put it in the drawer.'

And left it out on the nightstand for the housekeeper to clean around. 'I'm sorry about Mrs Gilroy.'

Jayden's hand on Frank's back stopped. She seemed surprised and not just a little relieved at the apparent change of topic. 'It's so sad, but she was getting up there, I suppose. She'd been with us all my life.'

The faithful retainer. 'She probably could have answered our question easily. Or at least could have when she was younger.'

'What question?'

'Where your dad kept his gun. If it was out in the open, she – or whoever cleans nowadays – would have seen it.' And I wouldn't mind talking to whoever that was.

'Oh, Mrs Gilroy still cleaned. Until she died, of course. Now we'll bring in a cleaning service to get the place ready to sell, do a deep clean.'

I frowned and glanced behind me at the sprawling house. 'Mrs Gilroy must have been eighty. She cleaned the whole house?'

'The whole thing?' Jayden said. 'Don't be silly.'

'Oh, good. Then who—'

'She'd just do a room or two a day. Eventually the whole thing would get done, but not all at the same time, of course. Sometimes it drove Daddy crazy.'

Poor Daddy. Poor elderly woman couldn't clean his 4500 square feet house in one day. Even spread out over a week, it seemed a lot, especially when you threw in the cooking, too. I hoped they had paid her well. Though given what I'd heard about Kip stiffing servers, contractors and CPAs, I feared not.

'We can't ask her now, unfortunately,' I said. 'Both you and Jason must miss her a lot. She seemed to dote on him.'

'He was definitely her favorite,' Jayden said, relaxing again. 'But then it's hard not to love Jason, even when he gets himself into scrapes.'

'Scrapes?'

She glanced over at me. 'At school and stuff. He's smart, but always preferred having fun to studying. He'd be off at a party and we'd be doing his special credit project at the end of the semester just to keep him from getting booted.'

'Special credit projects?'

'Oh, things like papier-mâché topical maps and science experiments in grade school. Mrs Gilroy and I would do them together. Then we wrote papers in high school and college. He had no time for that sort of thing.'

'I'm surprised he graduated.'

'Like I said, Jason is smart and must be a good exam taker. But I always told him that our projects were the only reason he graduated.' She grinned. 'He owes me big time.'

'I bet he does.'

Something in my tone made the hand that was stroking Frank pause for a moment. 'I should really go in. I have things to do in the house.'

She stood up and brushed imaginary dog hair off her jeans. Frank doesn't shed.

At least, not much. 'You do know why he told you not to talk to me.'

'Who?' She was standing on the porch above me.

I twisted to face her. 'Your brother.' Duh.

'He doesn't know . . .' She swallowed. 'I mean, he didn't know what you wanted. That's what he asked me. Not anything else.'

'He didn't ask you to keep protecting him, like you did in school? If your brother is so smart, he should have thought about disposing of the gun, not left it there for you to hide.'

'He just didn't think—' She put her hand to her mouth.

'He never did, did he? You had to do that for him. And when you found your father dead, you realized immediately what had happened. After all, Kip had told the two of you not twenty-four hours earlier that he was getting married and changing his will. If Jason wanted the good times to keep on rolling, he had to kill your dad.'

'That's just not true.' She was backed against the brick wall that hid the front door.

'No?' I stood up. 'Then why did you lie about the will?'

'What do you mean?' Frank had nosed up to her, sensing something was wrong. She tangled her hand in his fur, seemingly for support.

'The night of your father's death when you came by Amy's place, you told us your father had already changed his will in favor of her. That meant that it was Amy who had the motive to kill Kip, not Jason.'

'But I came to help Amy.' Tears were filling her eyes and Frank gave me a reproachful look.

'Because you're not a bad person, Jayden,' I told the girl, gently. 'You wanted to save Jason, but not at the expense of Amy.'

She didn't answer so I kept going, admittedly making up parts as I went. 'You knew it had to be Jason because the doors were all locked when you arrived.'

'But the window in the kitchen door—'

'You broke it. You realized that if there was no sign of forced entry it would be clear to the police – as it was to you – that the killer had a key.'

'But what about the damage? The lamp? The broken mirror?'

'Also your work and, frankly, a little clumsy compared to the broken window. Your father was in bed, wouldn't he have heard the lamp fall? And only one shot was fired and that was still in your father's head. How was the mirror broken?'

She didn't answer, just kept petting my sheepdog.

'But then you didn't have much time to think. You'd already had to wipe the gun of what you supposed were Jason's fingerprints and go out the back door and hide it. If you didn't "find your father"' – air quotes – 'and run outside screaming while Rafael was still working out front, you wouldn't have a witness. Luckily for you, he was busy and not looking at the clock. He didn't realize you'd been in the house just a little longer than necessary if you'd simply done what you said.'

'What I'd said?' She seemed to be sliding down the wall.

'Gone into the house to find your dad. And, sadly, found him.'

'It, it . . . Oh, God. I'm so sorry.' Fully collapsing onto the porch floor, she sobbed into my surprised sheepdog's back.

SEVENTEEN

'You would make an excellent emotional support animal,' I told Frank, as we watched Pavlik talking to Jayden.

I'd called him when Jayden had broken down and, happily, her brother Jason – aka the killer – hadn't returned before the sheriff's department arrived.

'What is happening?' A voice at my elbow asked.

I turned to see Rafael, his work gloves in one hand and a bucket in the other.

'Is Jayden being arrested?' As he asked it, he reached down to give Frank a scratch.

'Not sure,' I said. 'At worst it probably would be for accessory to a crime or tampering with evidence. She's the one who hid the gun.'

Genuine astonishment crossed his face and then understanding. 'Before she came to me out front.'

'Exactly.'

He shook his head. 'But then she is a very good actress. She was exceedingly shaken up.'

'Wouldn't you be if you found your dad dead, killed by your brother, and then hid the gun?'

'It is a point. So it was Jason then.' This time he didn't sound so surprised.

'Yes. Kip told him he was changing the will. Jason didn't want that to happen.'

'Or couldn't afford it,' Rafael, said, watching the girl with Pavlik.

'He had debts?'

'I assume so. Fancy car, when he's still in school. Nice clothes.'

'How fancy?'

'What?'

'That pretty car. How much does one of those go for?' OK, so I was curious.

'The Targa that looks like a caution sign? I'm told maybe two hundred thousand?'

'For a car for a kid?' Though I supposed that was dirt cheap compared to Kip's own GT2. The Fargo men had expensive taste in cars. And what else? 'You didn't seem surprised when I said that Jason killed his father.'

'I am surprised, but more so because I thought he was at school, with witnesses.'

'Two girls he was having sex with,' I said. 'I'm not sure that counts.'

Rafael's head snapped back. 'But one would certainly remember it.'

The roar of an engine made us turn our heads and down-shifted to a gurgling rumble as the 'caution sign Targa' pulled into the driveway.

Three grown men and a woman – that would be Pavlik, his two deputies and me – turned to look. Rafael, who had seen it a million times, was less impressed.

Jason got out of the car. 'What's going on?'

I didn't know how to answer that, so I was glad when Pavlik strode up. 'We need to talk to both your sister and you at the station.'

'Why?' he asked. 'What did she do?'

What did *she* do? Nice guy.

'We'll talk at the station.' Pavlik seemed at his calmest, but his eyes were dark gray, belying that.

'Hey, get that dog away from my car.'

That dog being Frank, who was sniffing the tires. He looked up, startled at the tone.

'Frank,' I said warningly. My sheepdog had been known to vengeance pee. 'Don't even think of it.'

He stalked away.

'Unless you're going to charge us, we don't have to go anywhere with you,' Jason said. 'I'm calling my lawyer.'

'You do that,' Pavlik said, signaling his deputies. 'Tell him or her to meet you at the station.'

'What are we being charged with?' Jason yelled as the deputy cuffed him.

'Your sister, tampering with evidence. You, we'll see about.'

Jason was still swearing as they closed the squad door.

'Honest to God,' I told Sarah and Amy at the shop after I dropped Frank off at home, 'I almost asked if I could park his car for him. That thing is beautiful. Kind of yellow.'

'Since when do you like cars so much? You've never cared a whit about my Firebird.'

'Your Firebird doesn't smell new.' Just the opposite, in fact. You could still smell the cigarettes smoked in it over forty-some years, despite Sarah's best attempts to fumigate.

'It's yellow.'

'It's not this yellow. Here I took a picture.'

'Wow,' Sarah said. 'That *is* yellow.'

'Or green,' Amy said, looking over her shoulder. 'It's like a highlighter.'

She was right. It was practically the color of the frogs in the front pond.

'Paint to sample, most likely.' Sarah was grudgingly impressed, I could tell. Key word, grudgingly. 'Couldn't get away with anything in that car.'

'Not even murder, apparently,' Amy said, getting us back on subject.

I put my phone away.

'So the case is solved,' Sarah said. 'Is Pavlik pleased?'

'He'd have been more pleased if I'd simply presented my thesis to him, I'm sure, but he's pretty much given up on that happening.'

'It's not very exciting that way,' Amy said.

No, it's not. So not going to happen. But I had kept my cell phone recording in my pocket when I conducted my ad hoc interview with Jayden. Can't say I don't learn from experience.

'Pavlik still has to build a case against Jason,' I told them. 'Hopefully his alibis will fall apart under questioning. They're young.'

'His alibis are young?' Amy asked.

'Yes. Like two eighteen-year-old girls. They were both with Jason—'

Amy held up her hand. 'Never mind. I don't want to know.'

'Maggy, please,' Sarah said, 'that's Amy's nearly ex-stepson you're talking about.'

'Stop it.' Amy turned to me. 'How did you know it was Jayden who had hidden the gun, Maggy?'

'The discrepancy between Jayden's understanding and Jason's understanding of what Kip told them about the will over lunch bothered me all along. It seemed too important a thing for one of them to get so badly wrong. As time went by, it was clear that Jason was right, and Kip had intended to change his will but hadn't had the chance.'

'Luckily for Jason and Jayden,' Sarah said.

'Exactly. It gives one or both of them a motive to kill their father. Then Pavlik asked if we had any lemonade or iced tea.'

'Say what?' from Sarah.

'I know it's stupid, but it reminded me of Jason asking Mrs Gilroy about those same two drinks and how cloyingly sweet she was to him.' Versus to me. 'More than one person has told me how devoted both she – and, more importantly, Jayden – were to Jason.'

'It's true,' Amy said. 'Do you think Mrs Gilroy was involved?'

'I don't know,' I said. 'Maybe she helped after the fact in some way, but she wasn't there on Thursday when Jayden found Kip and hid the gun. It's her day off.'

'How did it go down with Jayden?' Sarah asked. 'You mentioned iced tea and she folded?'

'Sadly, no. But she made a mistake. She referred to the weapon that was found as a pistol, even though I'd repeatedly just called it a gun.'

'Pistol, gun – what's the difference?' Amy asked.

'A pistol is a semi-automatic,' Sarah told her. 'You'd never call a revolver a pistol.'

Well I had, once, and been corrected. 'Jayden supposedly had never seen the weapon. How did she know it was a semi-automatic?'

Amy looked doubtful. 'Maybe she just assumed. I mean, do people even use revolvers anymore?'

'Yes, in fact they do,' Sarah said, a little miffed. 'But the point is that anybody who knows enough about guns to use the word pistol knows there's a difference and wouldn't just "assume".'

'For all she knew, it could have been an assault rifle,' I pointed out. 'Like I said, I just referred to it as a gun.'

'But it was under a tree,' Amy said. 'Wouldn't an assault rifle be too big?'

'*Anyway*,' I said, 'it really doesn't matter, because when I called her on it, Jayden freaked.'

'She confessed?' Sarah said disgustedly. 'What a wuss.'

'It took a little more work than that,' I said. 'I accused her of breaking the window to make it look like an outside job and tipping over the lamp. Pointed out that breaking the mirror was overkill, since only one shot was fired.'

'And it stayed in her father's head.'

'Yeah,' I said ruefully, 'I actually said that to her. Kind of regret it now.'

'I would think so,' Amy said. 'Don't you feel at all sorry for Jayden? She's just eighteen years old.'

'Of course. I feel awful for her,' I said. 'Saddest thing is that she did it out of love for her brother.'

'Who killed her father,' Sarah said. 'Which is kind of messed up.'

Kind of.

'But other than that, you must be pretty damn proud of yourself,' Sarah continued. 'Solved the case and it turns out to be your favorite suspect. Or your favorite suspect after Jacque.'

Amy faced me. 'You genuinely thought Jacque did it?'

'More like she wanted Jacque to have done it,' Sarah said. 'Then she found out he's her cousin and became all sunshine and charity. It was disgusting.'

'Knowing that I loved Jacque wasn't enough for you?' Amy demanded.

'No, actually, I wasn't too keen on your loving him,' I told her. 'Wasn't sure it was a good thing.'

'And now?'

'Still not sure,' Sarah supplied.

Amy looked at me and I shrugged.

'But I am glad this is over,' I said. 'And I really want you to be happ—'

My phone rang. Pavlik.

I held up a finger and said, 'Hi there. Have you booked our suspects?'

I listened and listened. 'But they're probably— You have it? And it's . . . Yeah, I understand. But where?'

Amy and Sarah were signaling wildly that they wanted the scoop. I hung up.

'Well?' Sarah asked.

'Well, Jason's alibi is holding up.'

'Up?' Sarah crooked her index finger. 'Like his weenie with those two girls?'

'Please,' I said. 'A little maturity?'

'Aww, who's all sad now? You were patting yourself on the back a minute ago.'

'You really were, Maggy,' Amy said. 'I'm surprised you didn't dislocate your shoulder.'

'Wait a second.' I was punching up something on my cell phone.

'Well, not to worry,' Sarah said. 'He probably convinced the girls to lie and they're sticking to it.'

'Tell the sheriff to send Fergussen in to question them,' Amy suggested. 'That'll scare them into telling the truth.'

'They swear they *are* telling the truth,' I said.

'They'll have to prove it.' Sarah said. 'It's Jason and the two girls' word against the evidence. If the fingerpri—'

'Oh, no.' I was staring at my phone.

'What?' Sarah asked, craning her neck to see over my shoulder.

'Oh, no, this.' I held up my phone.

EIGHTEEN

'They taped themselves,' I said for the third time. The first two had been to Sarah and Amy at the shop and now I was home with Pavlik, grilling hot dogs.

'That surprises you?' Pavlik got up from the porch steps to check the dogs on the grill. 'These done enough for you?'

'If they're not black, they're not ready,' I said. 'And yes, it does surprise me. At least from the side of the girls. For Jason I suppose it was like he was posting a trophy. Two girls, on the hood of a Porsche. Look at me!' I was sad for the poor car.

'And the girls couldn't have been doing the same thing?' Pavlik closed the grill lid and came back to sit. 'That's a bit of a double standard, isn't it?'

'I'm doing a girl and a guy, look at me?' I groaned. 'I suppose so. But where does this leave us?'

'Looking like idiots.'

'Thanks to me.'

He put his arm around me and squeezed. 'Yes.'

I started to pull away and then relaxed. 'Jayden did hide the gun. I was right about that.'

'You were. She jumped to the same conclusion that we did. She thought her brother killed her father.'

'So, she wiped off the prints, disposed of the gun and made it appear to be a break-in,' I said.

'Not a bad cover-up,' Pavlik said.

'Especially for a kid,' I said. 'Maybe Mrs Gilroy read classic mysteries to her when she was a baby.'

Pavlik got up again and flipped up the lid of the grill. 'Black as charcoal.'

'Perfect,' I said, picking up the plate and going to join him. 'Is it possible Jayden was protecting herself, not Jason? That she killed her father.'

'She too has a rock-solid alibi,' Pavlik said, tonging the dogs into buns. 'Nearly as solid as these hotdogs.'

'Don't be silly. They're perfect,' I said, waving the aroma from the grilled sausage toward my nose. 'Don't you love the smell?'

'Carcinogens?'

Spoilsport. 'Jayden's alibi. Do we have that on video, too?'

'No, but she and her roommates were watching a show and texting and tweeting about it simultaneously.'

Multi-tasking like her brother.

'And the texts came through the right towers and all?'

'"And all",' Pavlik said with a grin. 'Do you want me to explain how it works again?'

'I prefer not.' I took a bite.

'Do we have anything healthy to go with these?' Pavlik asked. 'Maybe a salad?'

'Potato chips. Which are vegetables.'

'Only in Maggy-land.' He tried a bite. 'These are beyond burned.'

'Yeah, they kind of are,' I admitted, setting mine down, too. 'I think I had you keep them on a little too long.' Can't say I don't take responsibility for my failings.

'I'll put on a couple more,' Pavlik said, picking up the pack and sliding two sausages out. 'And this time I'll decide when they're done.'

Control freak. 'Have you released Kip's body yet?'

Pavlik lifted his head. 'Let's see if I can follow your train of thought. Hot dogs. Burnt. Incinerated . . .'

'Cremated, exactly.' I settled back on the porch step, the plate of burned hot dogs next to me.

'Not yet, and it's a good thing, considering we're back at square one.'

'The killer wasn't Jason or Jayden, who stood to gain the most from their father's death. What does that leave us with?'

'Suspect-wise, Amy, of course, and Jacque. Sarah. Mary. Anybody else who Fargo may have bilked.' Pavlik said it bleakly.

'Any "bilking" connection takes the case back to the Feds?'

'I'm afraid so.' He settled the hot dogs on the grill and left the lid up this time.

'Pretty much every suspect is a friend of mine,' I said as Frank and Mocha zoomed around the corner.

'You say that like it's unusual.' He rotated the wieners.

It did happen with some frequency. 'What about Mrs Gilroy?'

Pavlik turned, tong in hand. 'Killing Fargo? Why?'

I stood up. 'Same reason that Jayden hid the gun. To protect Jason. Or in Mrs Gilroy's case, to protect the fortunes of both Jason and Jayden.'

'Killing her long-time employer to keep him from changing the will?' He turned the dogs again. 'Can you hand me another plate?'

I pulled a plate out from under the one holding the burned wieners. 'Maybe the night-vision thing is fiction. Something she made up early on so she wouldn't have to stay late and now it worked to her advantage.'

'When she returned to the house in the dead of night to kill Fargo?'

'With his own gun, which she'd certainly know was there,' I reminded him.

'Do we have more buns?'

I pulled them out of the plastic bag and opened them so he could place the sausages in them. 'You sure those are done?'

'They're pre-cooked. You just have to heat them.'

There was heating and then there was heating. But I'd already had my shot. 'Anyway, back to Mrs Gilroy. She's the perfect perp.'

'Because she's dead?'

'And I don't like her. Or *didn't* like her.'

'And she didn't like you and spill her guts to you?' Pavlik had taken Sarah's theory of 'like' and added an investigative component.

'Hey, I tried everything. Sympathizing with her loss, bonding over her reading material—' I stopped.

'Here, try one.' He offered me a bun with a perfectly grilled hot dog in it.

I didn't take it.

'You're honestly going to make me burn yours?' he asked, looking a little hurt.

'What?' I took the dog. 'No, I just had a thought and now . . .'

'Gone.'

'Exactly,' I said. 'I was thinking about talking to Mrs Gilroy and her book and all and—'

'No, I mean the burned hot dogs.'

Sure enough, the plate was empty, and the dogs were licking their chops.

'I Googled it and apparently charcoal can't kill a dog,' I said to Sarah from behind the counter.

We were in the sweet spot between the commuters going and the lunch crowd arriving.

'You're hilarious,' she said, checking the cream container. 'You were prepared to eat "incinerated" wieners yourself, but your dogs eat them and you're all worried.'

Well, yes.

'Did you ever remember what you were thinking of when the dogs ate the dogs?' She dropped the lid back onto the creamer. Apparently, it was either already full or she just didn't feel like filling it.

'No. It had something to do with talking to Mrs Gilroy in the kitchen. And maybe something you told me, too.' I stuck out my hand. 'Does that creamer need filling?'

She ignored me. 'Something I told you about Mrs Gilroy?'

'I think so.'

The bell jangled on the door and Catherine Barry stuck her head in. 'Good morning, ladies. Just stopped to see if you'd made a decision.'

'About what?' I asked, as she came up to the counter.

'Why, becoming the JavaDo representative in Brookhills, of course. You've forgotten.'

'She's having a pretty forgetful day today,' Sarah said, pulling out another stack of napkins for the condiment cart.

I'd have said I remembered the important things, but even that didn't seem to be true. 'I'm sorry, Catherine, with Kip's death and Amy and Sarah's involvement—'

'Oh, Sarah was involved with Kip as well?' She put both elbows on the counter and rested her chin on her linked hands. 'That makes three – or three hundred – of us. Do tell.'

'I wasn't "involved" the way I think you mean,' Sarah said, coming up behind her. 'But interesting to know you were.'

'A long time ago,' I told her.

'Years,' Catherine said. 'But if you weren't Kip's lover, Sarah, you must have been a client. Did that not go well? It usually didn't with him, at least ultimately.'

I cocked my head. 'You sound a little bitter. Or at least more bitter than you did the last time we spoke about Kip. I thought he was a friend – you know, helping you find outlets like ours for your espresso machines?'

'For a healthy finder's fee and an ongoing cut, thank you very much.'

I exchanged glances with Sarah. 'I have to admit I'm not astonished at the "finder's fee", but the ongoing cut seems unusual.'

'It was,' she said. 'But with either scenario or both, he had a responsibility to his personal clients to disclose his financial arrangement with JavaDo.'

It sounded like she was parroting something she'd been told. Maybe by the Feds?

'A breach of ethics,' Sarah was saying. 'Not surprising, since Kip didn't have any. But you didn't appear to have a problem with it either.'

Catherine shrugged. 'It was a symbiotic relationship. But when he started screwing me—'

'Literally or figuratively?' I interrupted, wanting to stay on the same page of the playbook. Or maybe just being curious.

'Figuratively, this time.' She tossed her hair. 'He was managing the receivables and investing a portion for us—'

'Let me guess. Poof, it's gone,' Sarah said. 'Boo hoo for you.'

Catherine's eyes narrowed. 'Damn right. Boo hoo for me.'

'Only because it happened to you this time,' I said. 'You were just fine with Kip cheating everybody else.'

'No, I wasn't . . . OK, maybe I was.' She'd apparently run out of indignant steam and turned around a chair at the nearest table to sink into. 'He'd just changed so much lately. It was like he was running away from something.'

'His creditors?' Sarah offered.

'Yes, but more himself. It's like suddenly he was feeling his age. Here he was, maybe mid-forties and freaked because he thought he might have an ulcer and his hairline was receding. It was all he talked about.'

'Mid-life crisis,' Sarah said. 'What's so unusual about that?'

'And it sounds like he did have health problems,' I told them. 'Liver damage, for one. A bout with skin cancer for another.'

'Really?' Catherine said, pausing in her commentary. 'I didn't realize Kip was a drinker, though maybe he was just trying to drown his sorrows.'

'At getting old?' I asked. 'Kip was my age – that's not exactly dead.'

'In his case it is,' Sarah reminded me. 'But what Catherine is talking about, his fear of getting older, explains the bum's rush on Amy.'

Like I'd told Pavlik, 'Bag the younger woman before it's too late.'

'Exactly,' Sarah said.

Catherine stood. 'Well, if you're a no-go on JavaDo, I'm going to blow this popcorn stand.'

'Have you reported your losses to the sheriff?' I asked as she picked up her purse.

'My losses?'

'The money you say Kip stole?'

She grimaced. 'It would open a bit of a can of worms, I'm afraid. Internal Revenue has already paid me a call.'

As I'd suspected.

'Catherine's right about the risk of reporting Kip,' I said as the door closed behind the woman.

'Because the arrangement was probably illegal.'

'But also because it makes her a suspect in Kip's murder.' I was watching the JavaDo rep hurry down the sidewalk, digging her car keys out of her purse. 'And I think she's just realized that.'

NINETEEN

Amy came in at noon. 'Are you going to tell the sheriff?'

'Are you kidding?' Sarah said, as she untied her apron. 'Maggy was on the phone with him before Catherine Barry started the car.'

I shrugged. 'Hey, I wanted Pavlik to talk to her before she "blows this popcorn stand".'

'That's what she said?' Amy asked. 'Suspicious, don't you think?'

'Yes, and the more suspects the merrier at this point,' Sarah said. 'What did Pavlik say?'

'He was interested, but he has to pass it on to the Feds since it involves Kip's financial dealings. It's all very awkward.'

'I got a call this morning,' Sarah said.

'About what?'

'Taking the Fargo house off the market, for one. I guess it's impounded or whatever they call it. And they also want to talk to me. I assume about my missing money.'

'I'm sure,' I said as the front door jangled, 'some bean counter somewhere is trying to unravel all this.'

'Bean counter.' Fergussen had entered. 'Funny. That's right where I'm standing, isn't it? The bean counter.'

I stepped to the other side of said counter. 'It is. Can I help you?'

'I'm actually here to talk to this little gal.' He pointed to Amy. Even when the man didn't seem to be trying to be offensive, he just . . . was.

'Yes, Detective?' Amy said.

'I'm just trying to nail down some things. Mind if we sit?' He swept his hand toward the tables.

'I just started my shift.'

'Go ahead, Amy,' Sarah said. 'I'll stay for a bit.'

'Why did you do that?' I whispered to Sarah as the other

two took seats at a nearby deuce table. 'She shouldn't talk to him without her lawyer.'

'Gilbert is useless,' she said, and added before I could, 'just like you said. He's drinking again.'

'And Rhonda isn't picking up the slack?'

'Shh,' she said, moving closer to Fergussen and Amy. 'I want to listen.'

The deputy had out his notebook. 'Now I just wanted to confirm your whereabouts at the time of Kip Fargo's death.'

'Shouldn't you tell her when that was?' I piped in before Amy could answer. I'd found that best policy when talking to the police was to give them exactly the information they asked and no more.

Fergussen threw an irritated look over his shoulder but answered. 'Between eleven and two a.m. last Wednesday night.'

'I was sleeping,' Amy said. 'I told you.'

'Yes, you did,' Fergussen said, tapping his pen. 'But we have reason to believe that you weren't entirely honest. Got me wondering if we have us one of those *Body Heat* situations.'

Say what? 'I think Amy should have her lawyer—'

Amy held up a hand. Her chin was quivering. 'No, it's all right. It's true that I was sleeping. I just . . . well, I just never said where.'

Uh-oh. Please God, don't tell me . . .

'It's just that . . . I was at Jacque's.'

Yup. There it was.

'I don't understand why you're so upset,' Amy said to me after Sarah and a smug Fergussen had gone. 'I have an alibi. Jacque. And he has me.'

'Exactly the problem. You're giving each other an alibi, but you could both be lying.'

'Well, we're not.'

So there. I was surprised she didn't stamp her little foot. 'Jacque's car was still in front of Kip's house when Mary left. Jacque wasn't in it. Do you know where he was?'

'No,' she said, 'and I was telling you the truth when I said I didn't see his car there.'

I wasn't sure I could believe her anymore. 'How did you connect with him, then?'

'I just . . . well, I was so upset when I left that I drove right to his house.'

'He wasn't there.'

She shook her head. 'No, the house was dark, but I texted him and waited until he got there.'

'When was that?'

'Maybe a half hour later?'

'Then ten o'clock?'

She frowned. 'Maybe a little later, since I hadn't left Kip's until after nine thirty. By the time I got to Jacque's it was probably going on ten. So maybe ten thirty.'

Still before the eleven to two a.m. window when Kip was killed. But not by much and time of death was an inexact science. 'You need to check your text messages, so you have your times correct before you talk to the sheriff.'

Fergussen had 'requested' her presence at the sheriff's office the next morning. 'And maybe take Gilbert, for what use he is. Or get another lawyer.'

I must have sounded like I was washing my hands of her situation, because Amy touched my arm. 'You have to believe me, Maggy. I was embarrassed to say I'd gone running to Jacque after Kip proposed, but that's exactly what I did.'

'Unfortunately.'

Amy frowned. 'It was about comfort, not sex. And I didn't like Fergussen calling me hot.'

'Hot?' I hadn't heard him say that.

'Hot body?' Amy said. 'You didn't hear that?'

Ohhh. 'Actually, he said *Body Heat*, which is even worse.'

'Worse than being a sexist?'

'In this case yes. You've never heard of the movie *Body Heat*? Kathleen Turner and William Hurt?'

'No, what is it?'

'Steamy movie, in a couple of different ways, but the reason it pertains here is—' I stopped.

'What?'

'I don't want to ruin it for you, if you haven't seen it.'

'I haven't seen it and probably never will. So spill.'

'It's so good. You really should.'

'I'm busy being accused of murder right now. If I have time tomorrow before they put me in prison, maybe I'll stream it.'

Amy, in desperation, sounded a lot like Sarah every day.

'Fine. Kathleen Turner and William Hurt plot to kill her husband.'

'Together?' Amy could see where I was going with this.

'Yes, though she does most of the plotting and he does all of the killing.'

'Fergussen is suggesting that Jacque killed Kip for me. Or we did it together.'

'Which is exactly why your alibi-ing each other is not a good thing.'

'But why would we want to kill Kip? I can see Jacque doing it—' She broke off. 'I don't mean that.'

'Yes, you do, and I agree. Jacque's motive would be jealousy. But your being with him that night shows he had no reason to be jealous.'

Amy visibly relaxes. 'So, we're good.'

I ducked my head. 'Unless Jacque had already killed Kip when he got the text from you saying you were at his house. Or—'

'No way, Maggy. It was before eleven.'

But, like I said, not by much. '*Or* Fergussen can come up with a way you'd benefit from Kip's death.'

'We know there's no will in my favor,' Amy said.

'That's true,' I said. 'Kip planned to make the change, but never did. Jayden confirmed that he'd told her and her brother that – and that he planned to propose to you – during their lunch on Wednesday at the house. All very proper and ceremonial, like the proposal. Inviting the children to lunch, white linen tablecloth, Mrs Gilroy making the curried chicken salad—' I stopped.

'Like I told you,' Amy said. 'Kip was very old-timey. I know you say he was your age, but he looked and acted so much older.'

'That's it,' I said.

'That's what?'

'I'm not sure I can explain,' I said, untying my apron. 'At least not yet. Can you close by yourself?'

'I can, but where are you going?'

I checked the clocks above the service counter. 'The library. I should be able to get there just before they close.'

On the way home from the library, I took a run past the Fargo house. Rafael was taking down the For Sale sign so I parked the car.

'Hello,' he called out when he saw me.

'Sarah told me the house was off the market. I suppose Jason and Jayden are bummed.'

'There are a lot of bills to pay and no money coming in.'

'Welcome to my life,' I said.

He laughed. 'And mine. Even more so going forward.'

'Won't they be able to pay you?'

'Paychecks were a hit-and-miss thing with Mr Fargo, always,' Rafael said, leaning the sign against the house. 'But now . . .'

'It's more miss.'

'Exactly.'

I gestured toward the length of PVC pipe next to the frog pond. 'New frog refuge didn't work out?'

'The new frogs, more so.' He nodded toward the empty ventilated boxes sitting at the ready, along with a net. 'They are from my country and not doing well. I think it's best that we both go home.'

'You're returning to Colombia?'

'I am,' he said, walking me to my car.

'I'm sorry to hear that.'

He shrugged and opened my door for me. 'The country is a much better place than it was when I left.'

'What will you do?' I ducked in to toss my purse onto the passenger seat, knocking the stack of Agatha Christie novels onto the floor. I'd gotten a little carried away at the library.

'I think I will teach,' Rafael was saying as I emerged.

'I think you will like that.'

We shook hands.

'*What Mrs McGillicuddy Saw*?' Pavlik read over my shoulder.

'The American version,' I said. 'Mrs Gilroy had the UK release, which is called *4.50 From Paddington*. It's about a woman who thinks she saw a murder on a passing train.'

'And you're reading it why?'

'Because there's something in it that pertains to Kip's death. I'm sure of it.'

'It didn't happen on a train. Of that I'm certain.'

'I know, but . . . here. The arsenic poisoning. That's the part I was trying to remember.'

'How does it pertain?'

'It doesn't literally, but . . .'

'Maybe literarily?'

'Excellent,' I said. 'And, yes. There's a suggestion in the book that Lucy Eyelesbarrow is poisoning the family by putting arsenic in their curry.'

'And our Mrs Gilroy is Miss Eyelesbarrow? You think she fed the family arsenic?'

'No, only Kip.' I set aside the book. 'Would the autopsy have turned up arsenic?'

'Arsenic dissipates quickly and since the cause of death was obviously a gunshot wound, I don't know that they'd immediately test for it. Why?'

Now I had out my phone. 'Let's see, the World Health Organization says the symptoms of long-term exposure include skin and pigmentation changes, skin cancer. This one says hair loss and liver disease, whitish lines on fingernails. Amy talked about Kip having her father's fingers. I wonder if that's what she meant. And . . . oh, look at this, garlicky breath.'

'Seems like a minor discomfort given the rest of it.'

I smiled. 'It is, but it's also one of those things Amy complained about.'

'Kip had garlic breath?'

'Constant, apparently, which would be a turn-off.'

Pavlik blew into his hand and sniffed it. 'No garlic.'

'Unless we order a pizza.' I set down the phone. 'Don't you see? Kip had squamous cell skin cancer, which is linked to arsenic exposure. Hair loss, liver disease, stomach problems—'

'And garlic breath.'

'I rest my case.'

'So you're thinking Mrs Gilroy was gradually poisoning Fargo with arsenic? Why?'

'Got me. She doted on Jason – maybe she wanted him to inherit.'

'Along with Jayden? Or did Mildred Gilroy plan on killing her, too?'

'I don't think she was that crazy, but it probably wouldn't hurt to test Jayden for exposure.'

Pavlik gestured toward the book. 'Not that crazy. Just crazy enough to copycat an old mystery where the curry is laced with arsenic.'

'Chicken curry, I think. And also the tea. It is an English mystery, after all, and both tea and curry would be strong enough tasting to cover the arsenic.'

'It would.'

'And here, in the modern version, Kip drinks iced tea. He wouldn't have been able to taste arsenic in that either and it would fit nicely into Mrs Gilroy's sense of order.' I would say I was warming to my idea, but I'd downright fallen in love with it. 'She also served curried chicken salad for lunch the day Kip announced the proposal and the changing of the will. A homage to the book?'

'Then the chicken salad was poisoned, too?' Homage aside, Pavlik seemed more concerned now that the living might have been poisoned, rather than just the guy whose head was subsequently blown off.

'Never. She'd never have hurt Jason. But that lunch might have sealed Kip's fate.'

'But there's the problem,' Pavlik said. 'A woman who poisons somebody for years suddenly turns around and shoots him in the head?'

'Ran out of time?'

'Maybe.' Pavlik's tone was skeptical.

As for me, I again had the perfect murder suspect. Dead. 'Can you at least see if any traces of arsenic turned up? Or if they can run tests for it, if they didn't.'

Pavlik hesitated and then nodded. 'Until then, let's just keep this to ourselves. And Sarah, because I know you'll tell her.'

I held up the book. 'My theory is a little out there for you?'

'A little.'

'What about Catherine Barry as suspect?' I asked, setting aside the book. 'Is she more to your liking?'

'Ms JavaDo? Definitely, though until Fargo's financial affairs can be unraveled, it's difficult to know how much of a motive she really has.'

'Have they told you anything?'

'The Feds?'

I nodded.

'Enough to know that despite his show of wealth, Kip Fargo was incredibly cheap about some things.'

'Amy said he'd stiff the waiter and she'd have to make up the tip. And the night Kip proposed, he left the restaurant without paying.'

'There's a pattern of that with him. Paying late. Stiffing workers and contractors. Open tabs at practically every restaurant in town. I'm surprised anybody dealt with him.'

'How did he get away with it?'

'Oh, he'd eventually pay, but it was nearly always with somebody else's money.'

What a sleaze. But even sleazes deserve justice.

Right?

'Wrong,' Sarah said at Uncommon Grounds the next morning.

'I thought you liked Kip.' I was making myself a latte.

'Liked. Past tense. When he was making me money.'

'Rafael was taking down the For Sale sign when I went by.'

'I know.' Sarah sighed, yearning for the one that got away. 'Kip's assets have been frozen until his estate is closed. And that can't be done until the financial audits are finished, and creditors are paid.'

'And the embezzled money returned, I assume.'

'I damn well hope so. I can't imagine there'll be much left for Jason and Jayden after all this is over.'

'Well, if they find arsenic in Kip's body, maybe Pavlik can prove Mrs Gilroy is the killer and that part of the investigation can be closed at least.'

'Pavlik's right, though,' Sarah said. 'Two very different methods. Poisoning somebody's iced tea is kind of a passive-aggressive way of doing things. Maybe he'll get sick, maybe he'll die, but I won't be there. Shooting somebody in the head? That takes balls.'

If it did, only men would be killers. 'But she did it for Jason. Maybe that was impetus enough.'

'Or Fargo had tipped to the arsenic,' Sarah suggested. 'Self-preservation can be a big motivator.'

My phone buzzed. 'Pavlik,' I said, setting aside my drink to pick it up.

'Well, answer it.'

I swiped.

'You were right,' the sheriff's voice said.

'I was right?' I repeated for Sarah's benefit.

'Put me on speaker, it'll save time,' Pavlik said.

'OK. You were saying?'

'I was saying that hair and urine samples showed arsenic levels that could have led to the symptoms Fargo was having. But it didn't kill him, obviously.'

'No, that was lead poisoning,' Sarah said.

'Funny,' from Pavlik's side.

'I guess you've heard it before.'

'Once or twice,' Pavlik said dryly. 'Anyway, we're looking into Mrs Gilroy's movements on Wednesday night. Making sure she actually did get home and stay there.'

'Didn't you already do that?'

'Fergussen checked, but since he just considered her "an old lady", he may not have been as thorough as he should have been.' Pavlik didn't sound happy. 'He's also the reason a full tox screen wasn't run on Fargo. Told the coroner we already knew the cause of death.'

'Which was true, so far as it went.'

'Which wasn't far enough. An effective investigator has to have an open mind, not set out to prove his or her own set of facts.'

Seemed the very opposite of Fergussen, in my opinion.

'Anything I can do?' I asked.

'No, you've already been more helpful than most of my department. I'll be late tonight. Don't wait up.' He rang off.

'He's really ticked,' Sarah said.

'And for once, it's not at me.'

*   *   *

It was Friday night, but no date night for Pavlik and me. Not that it usually was, at least since we'd been living together. Friday was mostly pizza night, a tradition that Frank, Mocha and I carried on bravely in the sheriff's absence.

When the pizza came this time, I made sure I tipped the guy extra generously. 'Somebody has to make up for the Fargos of the world,' I told the dogs.

As I cut up their slices, I thought about Rafael. Paid 'hit-and-miss' by Kip Fargo. Did he know what Mrs Gilroy was doing? If he had, would he have stopped her?

'I don't know,' I told Frank as I put his bowl on the floor. 'I'm not even sure I'd have stopped her.'

Mocha whined.

'OK, I probably would have,' I said as I set her bowl down, too. Both dogs dug in for about three seconds, which is all it took for the pizza to disappear.

'Best part of the day, over,' I told them as I picked up their dishes. 'Depressing, huh?'

Then again, life was so simple for them. Eat, sleep, repeat.

I paused with both dishes in my hand. Everything in this case had gotten so complicated. The proposal, the will, the missing money, the gun, the arsenic. What if the simplest theory was the right one?

Could Kip Fargo – feeling old and sick, thanks to the arsenic – have shot himself?

The only thing that had countered that theory at the beginning was the absence of the gun. You can't kill yourself and hide the gun. But now we knew it was Jayden who took the gun and hid it, thinking she was protecting her brother.

I set the dishes in the sink and returned to the living room to pour myself a glass of Pinot Noir. Leaving the bottle on the coffee table, I sat down at the computer.

And if hadn't been suicide, what was the alternative?

Suspect-wise, we were down to an old woman who had more loyalty to her employer's son than to her employer. And probably for good reason, given what Rafael had said. Had the pleasure of knowing she was gradually poisoning her employer to death made up for years of missed or late paychecks? Of cooking and cleaning for an ingrate?

Might have helped. And as a plus, the housekeeper was clearing the way for Jason.

But . . . had she actually cleared the way? Had she actually come back to the house that Wednesday night and shot Kip in the head? Or could somebody have done it for her? Was there an accomplice?

The obvious person, though I hated to think it, was Rafael. As a Fargo employee he'd have the same beefs with Kip as Mrs Gilroy had, if for not as long. But when Kip was shot, Rafael was out of the country. In Colombia, where he and his frogs would soon return.

I was thinking of Fergussen's allusion to *Body Heat.*

Could we have some whacked-out, fun-house mirror version of *Body Heat*, featuring Rafael Rojas and Mildred Gilroy instead of Amy and Jacque?

Might Rafael and Mrs Gilroy have hatched the plan to poison Kip and – when it looked like he was about to change his will – accelerated it?

Mrs Gilroy would have had to shoot Kip since Rafael was out of the country, and that would leave her, like William Hurt's Ned Racine, as the fall guy.

And now Mrs Gilroy – also like fall guy Ned Racine – was dead, leaving Maddy/Rafael free to take off for 'an exotic land'.

Firing up the computer, I punched in 'Colombia'. Then, because I had nothing else to go on, I added 'frog'.

What came up was the small, greenish-gold frog with the cartoon eyes, the one that matched the Porsche and that I had held in my very own hand. Golden poison frog . . . *Phyllobates terribilis.*

I scrolled down the Wikipedia listing:

> The golden poison frog's skin is densely coated in an alkaloid toxin, one of a number of poisons common to dart frogs (batrachotoxins). This poison prevents its victim's nerves from transmitting impulses, leaving the muscles in an inactive state of contraction, which can lead to heart failure or fibrillation.

'Holy shit,' I said out loud, rubbing my hand on my pants.

And then the doorbell rang.

TWENTY

'**Y**ou know.'

It wasn't a question. Yet Rafael Rojas still looked like the nice man I'd befriended over frogs and information in the Fargos' front yard.

Since I didn't want to open up a can of poison frogs in this case, I went with the theory I could pin on Mrs Gilroy. 'That Kip was being poisoned with arsenic? Yes. But how did you know that I was on to it?'

'I saw the books in your car,' he said, moving into the living room. 'Mrs Gilroy was entertained by Dame Agatha Christie.'

'And influenced?' I stepped back. 'Arsenic is undoubtedly a classic.'

'Just as Christie was.' He shrugged. 'I think it amused Mildred – or perhaps kept her sane – to be dropping a bit in Mr Fargo's iced tea every day.'

'You consider that sane?'

Mocha skittered in, followed by Frank. They both stopped when they saw we had a visitor. Not exactly attack dogs, but somehow it comforted me to have them there, as did the fact that the front door was still open.

Rafael smiled at the dogs before answering my question. 'She said a little arsenic was good for the complexion.'

'That's in the book, too,' I said, stepping over Frank to get to the coffee table where I'd left the book. As I picked it up, I slid my phone, which was next to the stack of books, between the pages before I turned back to Rafael. 'But over time it causes the problems Kip was experiencing. He must have thought he was falling apart.'

'Aging prematurely. And then a young woman turned down his proposal.'

'You think Kip shot himself.'

'Don't you?'

I shrugged. 'It's the most likely conclusion – and would

have been from the beginning if Jayden hadn't removed the gun from the scene to protect Jason.'

'The boy isn't worth it.' Mocha was sniffing around Rafael's ankles, and he leaned down to scratch behind one of her tiny ears.

I didn't have time to set the phone to record, but I did manage to hit '1' on speed dial and close the book again before Rafael straightened. 'You said your brother teaches at the university in Madison. Is Jason one of his students there?'

'Jason studying Herpetology? I think not. He's more interested in money than living things.'

'Do you think that was part of it?'

Rafael cocked his head, not understanding.

'I meant did Mrs Gilroy want Kip out of the way for Jason's sake?'

'You mean to inherit?' He frowned. 'I think not. I don't think she actually meant to kill Mr Fargo, just inconvenience him.'

'Otherwise you wouldn't have given her the arsenic.' I shrugged. 'Or rat poison or whatever it was. Much easier for a gardener to have access, I would think, than a housekeeper.'

'You'd be surprised. Arsenic is in many things.'

I didn't say anything.

'For what it's worth,' he said finally, 'Mrs Gilroy was a bitter woman.'

No kidding.

'She had spent her life working for the family and Fargo treated her like an indentured servant.'

'But indentured servants can't leave,' I said. 'She could have.'

'How many people are advertising for an elderly cook and housekeeper these days?'

'And change is hard,' I admitted. 'You did know about the poisoning then.'

Mine hadn't been a question either.

He hesitated before nodding. 'As someone versed in the sciences, the signs were unmistakable.'

'Yet you didn't stop her.'

He shrugged. 'Mr Fargo was not a nice man. He was

arrogant and cheap. He didn't pay what he owed me for my work and demeaned me, despite the fact I was better educated than he was. It was hard to feel sorry for him.'

'What did you think when he died?'

He raised his shoulders and let them fall. 'I didn't know what to think. But it seemed unlikely he had been murdered.'

'Despite all his faults?'

'We – Mrs Gilroy and I – were more aware of his faults than most.'

Not anymore. 'Did you know Jayden had put the gun in the hole? Did she tell you? Ask you for help?'

He ducked his head. 'No, but I saw the gun when I went to finish planting the tree.'

'But you didn't say anything.'

'Not at the time. I assumed the arsenic would be found at the autopsy and I needed a chance to think about the ramifications.'

'But it wasn't found.' Thanks to Fergussen.

'No, though you figured it out anyway.'

'But only after Mrs Gilroy was dead and couldn't implicate anybody else.'

'You mean me.'

'Yes.' I felt a vibration from the phone inside the book. Probably Pavlik texting back, meaning he'd gotten my call and was listening to what was going on. The thought made me brave. 'Tell me about the frogs.'

Rafael regarded me with . . . I'd say more appreciation than surprise. 'The frogs.'

'You stocked Kip's pond with Colombian poison dart frogs. Was that another passive-aggressive way of getting back at him?'

He rolled his head side to side, considering, before he answered. 'Perhaps.'

'You handed one to me that day. There's no antidote for the poison. Were you trying to kill me?'

'Didn't your research tell you the frog produces the poison when it's threatened or in pain?'

I hadn't scrolled down far enough, evidently. 'So I'm lucky I didn't squeeze it?'

A flash of a white-tooth grin. 'Actually, while one small

Phyllobates terribilis has enough poison to kill ten men where they stand, the frog loses its toxicity away from its environment in Colombia. Scientists believe the poison is a result of the diet they eat in their natural habitat – probably certain beetles and insects.'

'Then the frog you gave me wasn't poisonous?' No wonder Rafael was smiling. My theory had just gone down the PVC pipe drain.

'Not anymore.' He seemed hurt I'd had to ask the question. 'Nor are the ones you can order online.'

'You can order poisonous frogs online?'

'You can. Though I prefer to eliminate the retailer and get them directly from Colombia through my brother.'

'The professor.'

'Yes.' Rafael ducked out the still open door to the porch and returned with a box.

One of the ventilated frog boxes I'd seen by the pond. 'These were just shipped from Colombia, which is why I didn't let you touch them on Tuesday.' He closed the door.

A shiver went up my spine. 'They're still poisonous.'

'Hard to say.' He was holding up the box to peer through a hole.

'That was the day you thought of it,' I said, remembering back. 'Not this Tuesday, but the day after Kip died, when you gave me the frog to hold. You stopped talking suddenly and waved distractedly as I left, because that's when it occurred to you: somebody here in the U.S. could die from frog toxin and nobody would ever suspect.'

'It's possible, I suppose.' He was still frog-gazing.

I pressed the point. 'You're having second thoughts now, I suppose – worried the poison will be traced to you. That's why you took those new frogs out of the pond.'

'Traced to me?' He looked up now.

'Batrachotoxin causes heart failure. Mrs Gilroy's cause of death.'

'Mrs Gilroy was an old woman.'

'And you were in a tough spot. Came back from a nice vacation in Colombia and found that Kip was dead and Mrs Gilroy was panicking.'

It was a shot in the dark, but a logical one.

It landed. 'As I said to you, Mildred and I feared the arsenic would be found in the autopsy. Then when it appeared Jason had killed his father, she wanted to make the dramatic gesture and confess to the crime, like in a book.'

'Confess to shooting Kip or poisoning him?'

'Both. Mildred thought that if she admitted to the arsenic, the police would readily believe she'd taken it a step further and returned to shoot him.'

'What about the night blindness?'

'That was true and one of the flaws in her plan. I told you she was old. She wasn't thinking straight.'

'So, you decided to stop her. How? Hand her a frog?' As I said it, I gestured with the book in my hand and my mobile slipped out, hitting the floor at Rafael's feet.

His expression shifted. Still affable but with an emptiness, or maybe it was desperation, behind it. 'I'd be happy to hand you one right now, if you're curious.' He set the box on the ground to open it.

'Leave it!' I commanded Mocha, who had come up to sniff. Frank was still laying on the floor in front of us.

'Oh, let them play,' Rafael said. 'The toxin probably won't kill them at this point unless they ingest a whole frog or perhaps have an open wound.' He shrugged. 'But then who knows, really.'

An open wound. And the vented frog box had been in the kitchen the day Mrs Gilroy cut herself. In fact, she'd ordered Rafael to move 'those disgusting things'.

'Mrs Gilroy was so upset when Jason was brought in for questioning that she cut herself.' I wanted to distract him, keep him from removing the lid of the box. 'You dressed the wound. Is that how you did it?'

'Apparently so.' Another shrug. 'I honestly didn't think it would work.'

'If the poison is so toxic, why didn't she die immediately, right there in the kitchen?'

'It's hard to say what the toxicity level was at that point. The new frogs had been out of their natural habitat and away from their usual poisonous diet for a few days. Besides, I didn't use a lot – to do that, you'd have to stress the frog, even torture it to make it release the poison as a defense mechanism. I would never do that.'

But he'd kill a human. 'Then what *did* you do?'

'Very little, really. Gave the frog just a little squeeze, as you said, and wiped it on the gauze before I came out of the storeroom. I didn't even put that layer closest to the wound.'

Kudos. 'You preferred that Mrs Gilroy be home when it took effect. Work its way into the wound from the gauze?'

'Or the other way – the blood works its way to the toxin. Mildred was apparently washing dishes after she got home, so maybe the water flooded the toxin into the wound.' He straightened and toed the box on the floor. 'I'd honestly love to do some research to see, but I don't have time.'

'When is your flight?' I asked it casually like I was taking him to the airport.

'Two hours.' He sighed. 'I wish I knew what to do with you. I'm not a killer, really.'

I heard a car door slam out front. Pavlik.

I took a deep breath. 'You are, really. You just do it the coward's way.'

'You believe shooting somebody is brave?'

'No, but I think dosing them with toxin and then pretending you don't know what will happen is chicken shit.'

The doorbell rang.

What the hell? The cavalry was ringing the doorbell?

Rafael twisted to glance toward the door, too, and I did the only thing I could think of: smack him in the head with the book. 'Help!'

Surprised, Rafael took a step toward me but managed to step hard on Mocha. A bit of a street fighter, she gave it right back to him.

She sunk her sharp little teeth into his ankle and hung on for dear life.

'Shit!' As he danced around on one leg, I gave a shove and toppled him over a still-prone Frank.

Harrumph, was all Frank had to say.

'Help! Help!' I screamed.

On the floor, Rafael was swearing in Spanish.

The doorbell rang again.

As I started toward the door, Rafael grabbed my leg and swung me back around. That's when I saw the bottle of wine on the coffee table. As I stumbled past, I made a grab for it and, continuing my circular trajectory, brought the thing down on my assailant's head.

The Pinot worked infinitely better than the book. Rafael let go of my leg. Not stopping to see if I'd killed him or merely stunned the man, I made for the door and swung it wide open for my rescuers. 'Pavlik—'

'You order a pizza?'

TWENTY-ONE

'Wait a second,' Sarah said. 'Number one on your speed dial is Mr Pizza Pie?'

'I asked the same thing,' Pavlik said. 'It was kind of hurtful, to be truthful.'

As he said it, he helped himself to a second slice.

'I thought I'd changed it,' I said sheepishly. 'I honestly couldn't figure out why you were ringing the bell in your own house. Especially when I assumed you were on the line and hearing what was going on.'

'So what does Mr Pie bring you when you just dial them up like that?' Amy asked.

'Pepperoni is my go-to and I'd already ordered one,' I said. 'They texted back to confirm – which I mistook for Pavlik letting me know the cavalry was on its way – and sent out a second pizza assuming one wasn't enough.'

'It never is,' Sarah said, finishing her piece. 'Good thing the delivery kid was big enough to hold Rojas down while you dialed "number two".'

'Which is what I'll be known as forever after,' Pavlik said.

'The kid was pretty freaked out,' I said. 'The bottle I hit Rafael over the head with was still half full of red wine, so it looked like he was covered with blood.'

'Hey, any kid who doesn't know the difference between blood and Pinot Noir shouldn't be let out of the house,' was my partner's pronouncement. She pointed at the stain on the area rug. 'Going to be a bitch getting that out.'

'Better than blood, though,' I said from experience.

'What happened to the frogs?' Amy was looking around like *Phyllobates terribilis*es were going to hop out at us from under the couch at any moment.

'Animal control took them away,' Pavlik told her.

'I have to tell you I was never more afraid than when he

put that box down and threatened to open it for the dogs.'
Nobody messes with my kids. Canine or human.

I gave a tiny piece of peperoni to the smaller of the two
heroes of the hour. 'I commanded, "leave it!" and Mocha did.'

'And then bit Rojas' ankle when he stepped on her,' Pavlik
said, pulling the little dog onto his lap. 'You saved the day,
didn't you?'

Mocha kissed him.

'Don't undervalue Frank's contribution either,' I said. 'He
laid on the floor nobly.'

Frank lifted his head high enough to take the piece of
peperoni I was offering and then harrumphed back down.

Amy tucked her legs under her. She looked very small in
my big easy chair. 'After all this, it comes down to suicide.
Kip killed himself because of me.'

I got up and went to sit next to her. 'He killed himself
because he'd been poisoned for months and months. He felt
sick and old and the creditors were closing in on him.'

'Not to mention the FBI,' Pavlik said. 'He'd been under
investigation for months.'

'See?' I told Amy. 'You were not the cause.'

'I was supposed to be the antidote,' she said. 'Except I
said no.'

'And if you'd said yes, God knows what Mrs Gilroy would
have done to you.' I pointed at the stack of mystery classics.
'She had plenty of reference material.'

'She – and murder by arsenic – are classic,' Pavlik said.
'Don't see it much anymore.'

'Probably don't see a lot of death-by-frog either,' Sarah
said. 'What was that all about? The guy seemed normal.'

'I think he was – or is – normal,' I said. 'In fact, I really feel
sorry for him. Other than threatening to frog-poison my puppies.'

'It must have been hard being so highly educated, so smart,
and having to do yardwork,' Amy said.

'I don't think it was the work,' I said. 'Rafael said he enjoyed
that, and I believe him. I think it was working for somebody
like Kip, who saw him as lesser because of it.'

'And took advantage of him,' Pavlik said. 'The guy owed
tens of thousands of dollars to people who did work for him.'

'What an ass.' Amy put her hand over her mouth. 'I can't believe I said that.'

'Dead or not, Kip was an ass,' I said. 'Which was why Mrs Gilroy took such joy in secretly taking him down.'

'And Rafael didn't rat on her,' Sarah said and then grinned. 'Arsenic joke.'

'Nice,' I said.

'Neither of them were bad people,' Amy said. 'At least they didn't start out that way.'

'Slippery slope,' I said. 'You do something that's a little wrong—'

'Poisoning somebody is a "little" wrong?' Pavlik asked, checking his phone.

'Arsenic is good for the complexion,' I reminded him, and then grinned. 'I just think she dropped a little in his tea that first time and then . . . it got out of hand.'

'Like Rafael putting frog poison on the gauze?' Sarah demanded.

'Maybe not exactly like that. But not so different either. He gave Mrs Gilroy the arsenic in the first place, but then looked the other way as she dosed Kip with it. Rubbed frog sweat on gauze in the heat of the moment' – words I thought I'd never say – 'and taped it on an open wound. Then he's surprised the woman died.'

'Probably pleasantly surprised,' Pavlik said. 'He nearly got away with it.' Pavlik held up his phone. 'The passive-aggressiveness started in Colombia, apparently. Rafael is not quite the man he portrayed himself to be.'

'What do you mean? Wasn't he a science teacher?'

'He was that and a good one. But at the same time, he turned a blind eye to drugs being sold on campus. In fact, there were rumors that his classroom equipment might have been financed by the drug traffickers.'

'Because he kept quiet?' Sarah asked.

'That was the rumor, like I said. I can't prove it and it's likely nobody can.'

'I imagine that getting in the way of the drug trade was dangerous in Colombia.'

'It was especially back then, but others in his school did

stand up and worked together to make things better. He just left.'

'I hate it,' I said to Pavlik that night as we lay together in bed. Frank was next to me and Mocha, the other side of the sheriff. Pavlik may have more room, but I would never be cold.

'You hate what?'

'That Fergussen probably thinks he was right. He insinuated that if Rafael was Colombian, he had to be involved in drugs. And the thing is, even though Rafael wasn't really, it was happening in his own backyard and he did nothing. Maybe even profited from it.' Though the teacher would probably argue his students were the ones who profited, by way of lab equipment and supplies.

Pavlik took my hand. 'I'm reminded of the quote: "The only thing necessary for the triumph of evil is for good men to do nothing".'

'Edmund Burke, though there's some doubt about that attribution.'

'Even so, Ms Know-it-all, it's true. Whoever said it, whenever.'

'That slippery slope again? Like after you ignore evil, you're one step closer to committing it yourself.'

'Because you're desensitized somehow?'

'Maybe.' I sat up. 'First Rafael turned a blind eye to the drug trafficking on campus, then he gave Mrs Gilroy the rat poison, but ignored that she was poisoning Kip with it.'

'At best. I think the DA will argue that he was an accomplice, rather than just an accessory.'

'But that's probably not how Rafael saw it.'

'And how would he see rubbing a poison frog on a bandage over an open wound to see what would happen? A science experiment?'

'Visions of mad scientists in bad sci-fi movies.' I laid back down. 'Building monsters from body parts and turning people into flies.'

'You love those movies.'

'I do, but I'm also willing to admit that most scientists aren't mad.'

'Look at you,' Pavlik said, propping himself on one elbow. 'Busting all those stereotypes. The next will be that not all Norwegian-rooted coffeehouse owners eat only pizza and Chinese take-out for dinner.'

'The alternative would be cooking.' I brightened. 'But now I'm part French.'

'Lavish meals every night?' Pavlik asked, pulling me near. 'Heavy sauces?'

'Yet another stereotype. But I do love me a nice baguette. And maybe we'll add French wine to the rotation.' I snuggled my butt back against him.

'Oooh, la-la,' he said as he pulled me closer to him again.